Soutine's Last Journey

THE
SEAGULL
LIBRARY OF
GERMAN
LITERATURE

RALPH DUTLI

Soutine's Last Journey

A NOVEL

TRANSLATED BY KATHARINA ROUT

LONDON NEW YORK CALCUTTA

This publication was supported by a grant from
the Goethe-Institut, India.

Excerpts from Lautréamont's *Songs of Maldoror* in the chapter 'Modi
and the Flying Woman' have been drawn from Comte de Lautréamont,
Maldoror and Poems (Paul Knight trans. and introd.) (Harmondsworth,
New York: Penguin Books, 1978), pp. 87–8, 90.

The excerpt from César Vallejo's poem 'The Nine Monsters' on the final
pages of the novel are drawn from César Vallejo, *The Complete Posthumous
Poetry* (Clayton Eshleman and José Rubia Barcia trans) (Berkley:
University of California Press, 1978), pp. 173–5.

Both excerpts printed here with kind permission from respective
publishers.

Seagull Books, 2022

Originally published in German as *Soutines letzte Fahrt*
© Wallstein Verlag, Göttingen, 2013

First published in English translation by Seagull Books, 2020
English translation © Katharina Rout, 2020

ISBN 978 1 8030 9 216 4

British Library Cataloguing-in-Publication Data
A catalogue record for this book is available from the British Library

Typeset by Seagull Books, Calcutta, India
Printed and bound by WordsWorth India, New Delhi, India

For Catherine

Chartres 1989

We look almost happy out in the sun,
while we bleed to death from wounds
we know nothing about.

Tomas Tranströmer, *For the Living and the Dead*

They slam the backdoor's two black wings shut. A sharp click as if from a weapon, a dry snap from the waiting lock. The vehicle judders and, startled, panicky pigeons take off for the blue beyond the hospital roof. Brief laughter bursts into the black monster. It must come from the older one; the boy, who just like occupied France had caught a chill in August and wears a woollen scarf around his neck, would not have dared to laugh. No, the painter must have got it wrong. It can't have been laughter. The boss drills it into his employees on their first day that this job is no place for jokes, only for quiet dignity and simple piety. They owe it to the bereaved, and to the company's reputation.

But everything is different on this glorious August day. Today, it is a living corpse they have to take to Paris in their hearse, a black Citroën Corbillard. The car has accompanied many corpses old and young to their final rest. It is a large, quiet beast that they guard and take care of. After each deployment it has to be washed with the sponge and polished with the chamois. The boss checks, and he is merciless. A filthy hearse is inconceivable; his company treasures golden cleanliness, even in times of war. But never have his drivers transported a living corpse.

He is supposed to be some painter, the doctor had casually mentioned in the hallway. They must take him to Paris for operation; there is no other way, it is what the angels want. But how can they thumb their noses at the Occupier, the armoured giant eye that wants to control every single act? A short metallic sound, like a door's clenched, pained laugh. Like a weapon's click. The air is intoxicating with the fragrance of linden trees. Are there any next to the clinic? It may be the carbolic acid the painter carries in his crumpled hospital gown, the aroma of operation.

The painter mumbles to himself; again and again he seems to address someone, an imploring murmur on his lips, but the two undertakers do not understand; he speaks too softly, and the sounds of his language are unknown to them.

Are you from the Sacred Fellowship . . . have you brought the *sargenes* with you . . . *Chevra Kadisha* . . . break an egg into the water . . . the new corpse must be cleansed with life . . . if it isn't too late . . . he will come himself . . . don't forget the egg . . . it has to be dropped into the water . . . the egg blooms in the water . . .

The two undertakers give each other a questioning look and push him on his metal gurney into the belly of the hearse. It is 6 August 1943. It is summer, and war. Their country is occupied. They know what will happen if they end up in front of the black barrels of the Occupiers' guns. The two undertakers, the chubby older one and the coughing boy, could be camouflaged resistance fighters and saboteurs who transport their tools in a hearse. Off to the railway embankments, up the tracks, a few well-practised moves and the tracks explode skyward.

They are to stay clear of the checkpoints on the main arteries. As they were heading for the exit, a gaunt, nameless doctor had suddenly stepped into the hallway, lowered his eyes and sheepishly handed them the yellow roadmap with the blue laughing, running Michelin Man—*Bibendum*, as they call him—whose torso, arms and legs are made of tyres. Sometimes the little man had run through the painter's dreams and threatened him with angry looks. Were anyone to detect their live freight, the undertakers themselves would be corpses. Passengers in a hearse must be dead, and nothing but. No one would believe the excuse that the painter had seemed deceased and, to their amazement, had just risen from the dead. Certain spots are inconspicuously doubled in pencil.

And the black guys with the gamma sign, have they already fanned out north of the demarcation line? Since January 1943, Darnand's militias have been on the prowl. Searching for the resistance and anyone refusing to enlist for *le service du travail obligatoire*, the compulsory work service. STO means STO. Also, no vehicle is sacrosanct to black marketeers, not even a black raven. Their tricks show shameless ingenuity. But where are those rich sides of bacon, the cognac, the wine-dark pickled and potted rabbit ragout?

Pigeons ascending in slow motion, whispers, carbolic linden trees, a fluttering fragrance both soothing and sharp.

On 31 July, an ambulance had taken him to the hospital. The last days of the month had been terrible, painting out of the question, and the nagging pain in his upper belly had ceased to give him the merciful breaks that it had previously granted with unpredictable casualness. I am here, I will go away for a moment, but will be back. Just be patient, I'll be back shortly, trust me. Don't imagine I'll be gone for long. Don't think I'll disappear. I will never again leave you.

Ma-Be, can you hear me? Are you still here? I can't see you.

The painter has closed his eyes; he is aware of the effort it takes to look through his lids. He cannot open them.

That morning, he lay on his mattress with a fever, tossing about like an injured animal, his stammer incomprehensible; no longer speaking the French he had picked up, which seemed erased, but snippets that Marie-Berthe could not understand. She took it as a bad sign and paced restlessly like a tigress in a cage.

The painter groans and rolls over on his mattress, changing sides. Neither side brings relief. The landlord, Monsieur Gérard, comes upstairs with a warm mustard poultice that he carries with the dignity of a priest and offers to the painter as if imitating their village pastor on Sundays: *Prenez ce cataplasme*. His wife knows all about poultices, has one for every need. To the painter, whose ears since his arrival in Paris thirty years ago had to tentatively and tenaciously get accustomed to the twangy language so entirely different from the singing language of his Smilovichi childhood or the bite-size fragments of the Tatars' Russian, *cataplasme* sounds like an unmitigated catastrophe. Marie-Berthe accepts the landlord's poultice without a word and places it on the painter's belly.

He writhes on his hospital bed, wearing the small pious cross that Ma-Be has draped around his neck. All through July she has prayed doggedly, having long returned to her fine Catholic faith, driven by her fury at the whole rabble of Montparnasse painters. Christ dangles from his neck, the Messiah has come, may he stop the fierce pain.

Christ will help you, Chaim, have faith, Marie-Berthe had stammered from time to time. He died on the cross for you. You are saved.

The painter no longer understands; his pain is all he knows.

Stay in bed and let the poultice do its job; it will do you good.

No, I have to . . . to my studio . . . have to . . . no choice . . . before they come . . . as you know . . .

No one can stop him. Ma-Be and her bickering, her threats, are futile; he has to go. He wants no company, brusquely waves her off. He always does it alone. He drags himself to his studio, the small house near the entrance to the Grand Parc on the road to Pouant. And he should drop by the tiny room at Monsieur Crochard's, carpenter and mayor of Champigny; there should still be some canvasses. Half-paralysed with pain, he jerks himself up with that dog-like yelp he has long become familiar with, his hand pressed flat against his belly. He has one more job to do, more important than anything else.

Grab the matchsticks, quickly crumple some newspaper and off with it into the fireplace, which in this hot July still holds the ashes from the last time his old destructive frenzy overcame him. Hastily drag out the canvasses, cast a last furious glance at them and off to hell they go. As if it were their fault, this affliction that had never relented through the past months. Not once, since the beginning of the war, that 3 September 1939, still beyond belief though they clearly saw it coming, when they lived in the small Burgundy village of Civry, he and Mademoiselle Garde, and learnt about France's entry into the war, and when the mayor banned them—the two conspicuous foreigners with their suspicious German and Slav accents—from leaving town 'until further orders'. They were stuck. Magdeburg, Smilovichi: suspicious birthplaces.

The old ritual, the frenzy of dragging out the canvasses, of blindly setting them ablaze, sometimes brought a small smug relief; even the pain in the belly seemed to deceptively pause, or allow itself to be numbed by the fire. The summer fire stank of turpentine, this execution of an immutable act, practised since his years in the Pyrenees.

And each time he heard the voice of art dealer Zborowski, dead for more than ten years, horrified, piercing his ears: Don't! Stop doing that! You are killing yourself!

He always responded with a scornful grimace no one could see. The painter cannot remember when exactly he first blurted out the sentence: I am the murderer of my paintings, don't you understand? I'll show you. I am . . . the murderer . . . of my paintings.

It didn't always have to be fire that brought the solution. More often, knife attacks did it, a blind slashing so as to no longer have to see the livid ulcers on the canvas. To do away with them. The knife or scissors ritual was shorter, less controlled. Dive deep into the right bottom corner and blindly pull the blade across to the left top edge, repeat until nothing remains discernible. Until strips hang like bloody shreds of lacerated bellies. No satisfaction, though, never. Nothing but numb sadness and emptiness. The fire ritual was a more furious triumph: drag forth the canvasses with fists clenching frames, fling everything into the smoke-spilling fireplace and watch the flare-up when the flames lick the oil. No one has destroyed more paintings than he has. No one.

Ma-Be, can you hear me? Has the car arrived from Chinon? Tell it to wait.

He whispers. He curses.

The orgy of destruction on this last July day, like countless ones before, is part of the ongoing blind annihilation of his earlier life. Its effects couldn't be relied upon. He wants to sweep away, rid himself of these images from his life, including the part of himself imprisoned in them. Self-obliterator, self-slasher, self-immolator: Soutine, Chaim.

No one understood the ritual. No painter, not Zborowski, not the two women of the last years, neither Mademoiselle Garde nor Marie-Berthe. And no one could stop him. He himself did not understand, either. The whole park is ablaze in front of his eyes, his pupils reflecting the flames. He knows it has to be, that's all. On 31 July 1943, it gives no relief. And the pain returns right after the ritual.

A few paintings remain that Madame Moulin had discreetly rolled up and taken to Paris to offer to gallery owners, acts that provided for bread and eggs after the Paris account had been blocked. There had been a few carefully chosen visitors who had made it from Paris to Champigny. The paintings of the past years. Two wallowing pigs, one pink, the other one so field-grey, soiled with mud and dirt so uniform-green, that a few know-it-alls claimed he had represented soldiers of the Wehrmacht. What people come up with! Twice, a mother with a child, darksome-blue injured childhoods, bitter women, icons of the Occupation. Schoolchildren lashed by the wind on their way home, small and tossed about in the stormy dusk, holding hands in a panic. Children on a felled tree trunk. Who has saved these images from the painter and his Occupiers, quietly taken them aside and put them into inconspicuous shadow when the park was aflame?

Paintings he wrenched from himself and his ulcer in the past months—off into the fire. He has little time left. And does not know whether this is his last burning. Cremation, a simple, blind routine. The fire was excellent. Only ashes are left and a few wooden embers, fragments of a frame. His last chance to extinguish what never had a chance. The only paintings left are those pledged to the butcher, Monsieur Avril, after they kept having to postpone paying their debts, which have grown over the past weeks. May they remain hostages. The debt cannot be settled. Nothing can ever be settled, anywhere.

Ma-Be, run to the farmer and try again, just this one more time.

The time for barter is over; things no longer work this July when everything has gone wrong with the farmers now unwilling, in exchange for eggs and butter, to look at canvasses on which they cannot recognize the world for all those crooked paths, staggering, bending trees, brown and blue smudges, scratches and streaks. On which nothing seems to look like the world, not even like the world at war, unless the world has already gone to ruin with torment, a blind tussle, a last twitch. As a single, raging stomach ulcer. Eggs and butter and milk were gold.

You understand, don't you, it's war. We need the food ourselves.

Later Ma-Be goes downstairs and from the landlord's living room calls Doctor Ranvoisé in Chinon, who, to make matters worse, has gone on holiday in this July's emptiness, or is off to visit relatives farther down the Loire to rustle up some food, now that there is no more talk of holidays. The lives of bag men. Bag booty. His locum arrives, a Doctor Borri, who takes a brief look at

the painter, lightly palpates his belly and orders hospital-
ization. No time to lose. You need to go to Chinon, to the
Saint-Michel Clinic. The painter knows his diagnosis well
enough; for years, he has existed as a twin: Soutine and
his ulcer. For years, he has had a doppelganger who has
taunted and tormented him.

A black, painful shadow that time and again has assaulted
him.

By the time the ambulance arrived late in the afternoon, the painter had hobbled back to Monsieur Gérard's
house and the poultice lay crumpled next to his mattress.
He cannot remember the ride to Chinon; his pain has
reclaimed the driver's seat, swaddles his body too tightly
and obliterates all that is not him.

The driver had introduced himself: Foucaul, Achille.
But names no longer meant a thing. He had barely seen
his face before Monsieur Foucaul tactfully slammed the
door shut and drove him to Chinon, his confident hands
on the hot steering wheel of one of those ancient Peugeots
that crawl around like exhausted July beetles.

Arrival at the Saint-Michel Clinic. At the admission,
'Soutine Charles' was entered in the box because his real
first name had so often caused trouble and led to questions, annoying requests to repeat or spell it, and to
misunderstandings. 'Charles' was good, sounded incon-
trovertibly and unquestionably French; the name itself
was an identity document. Also, one could resort to the

disguise of its abbreviation, which made everybody assume the more common first name.

Ch. Ch. Ch.

Admission: Soutine Charles, 50 years of age. Profession: Painter, *artiste-peintre*. Severe pain across upper abdomen, radiating beyond sternum to the back. Feverish. Urgent! *Urgence*. Serious!

They have their forged papers on them that Fernand Moulin, veterinarian and mayor of Richelieu, got stamped for them at the Tours Prefecture. A clerk had owed him a favour. Besides, the mayor hated the occupying forces and was happy for anyone he could wrest from them. So that's what it says, immutably on the yellow paper that constitutes his identity: Soutine Charles.

The way he lies there with his eyes pressed shut, his facial expressions clenched, could make one mistake him for an Egyptian mummy.

He is in critical condition. The doctor wants to lose no time and operate immediately. Right away, not wait until the next day. Possibly it is already way too late. Perforation of the stomach wall is likely. Internal bleeding is only part of it. The bigger risk is gastric acid spilling into the abdominal cavity, leading to inflammation of the membrane lining the inside of the abdomen—peritonitis, are you following me, madam?—which, untreated, is bound to be fatal. The internal bleeding is not the main problem. But we must act immediately. Billroth I gastric resection, removal of two-thirds of the stomach, with vagotomy. Cut the section of the vagus nerve that innervates the stomach.

The word 'cut' makes her cry out. Soutine's black, screaming angel decides that he is to have his operation in Paris, not in this small-town hospital. In the city where they have real doctors, not these quacks in their tiny clinical kingdoms whom the Occupiers left with barely any dressings. She rails, she threatens, she stomps her feet.

The doctor politely tries to convince her that they have no choice. He wants to appease her and asks respectfully: Marie-Berthe Aurenche? That's the name of the wife of that German painter Max Ernst, isn't it? You see, I studied in Paris and at the time was very impressed with the Surrealists. Actually, I was mad about them. I raved about Nadja, ran through the streets clutching Breton's book, fantasized about the revolver with white hair . . . Medicine was one thing; I owed it to my father. But at night I roamed the cafes of Montparnasse to catch glimpses of those crazy cats. As for Ernst, I loved his *Approaching Puberty, The Wavering Woman* . . .

He said the wrong thing. She instantly assumed the wavering woman was about her. At least he had the good taste not to call her the ex-wife. All her acquaintances knew not to mention Max Ernst's name in her presence lest she turn into a fury.

The madness of saying one wrong word, one wrong name: wavering . . . woman . . . Max . . . Ernst. One single word, or two, and fate flips.

Yes, Ma-Be was around him, her voice everywhere, always ready to abruptly turn shrill and argumentative, he knew all too well. Hectoring, blaming, insisting on something he could not hear through the wall of his pain. Her palm banging the table, with exhausted but implacable severity. She was at her wit's end. The quick succession of rooms and hiding places, the haggling with farmers over half a dozen eggs, the wrangling over bread. Six times they changed their lodgings in Champigny. The frozen money in Paris, the illegal trips to the capital, the painter at her side ground down by pain. She wanted to put an end to it all, fast, or see defeated whatever had not already been lost long ago. He hears her screech and threaten on the other side of the door, as he lies in the hallway and watches white ghosts wordlessly scurry past him. A rustling, then suddenly whispers he cannot make out. An outline approaching him, taking his arm. A brief flash.

In the hallway, where he lies on a wheeled hospital bed, covered to his shoulders by a sheet, there is no one to be seen any longer. But in his ear a single voice rings out.

Here, take this white sheet. Cover yourself. Play dead. If only you could paint it.

Where did he first hear these sentences? In Minsk? Vilna? Certainly not in Paris. Who said them? Kiko or Krem? The memory is more ancient than this provincial town on the Loire. Where is he now? Certainly not in Chinon.

Pretend you are dead. It will make it easier. It will make everything easier. You are dead already, can no longer lose your life. Always lost already, we are already half-free. There is nothing you can lose. Hence you leave with lightness. If only you could paint it.

Suddenly, silence. He opens his eyes, immediately squeezes them shut. Opens them again as if to make sure he is not dreaming. At the end of the hallway stands a large white billy goat. No doubt about it. Clearly a billy goat, his large, rising horns thrown back, his astonishingly long beard reaching towards the floor, the thick tufts on his throat hanging down. How on earth did that buck get in here?

The painter remembers how he saw the image in a magazine of a markhor with its monstrous horns spiralling from its head in an upward V-shape. The buck stared out of the picture with the stern and intelligent look of a god among his faithful. It was Sunday, and he had been ambling along the Seine when he opened the magazine at one of the *bouquinistes* and was given a fright by the buck, who looked straight out at him. He had quickly shut the magazine and tossed it back on the pile.

But it is not him. No, here at the end of the deserted hallway in the Saint-Michel Hospital it is a big white domestic billy goat who curiously and with brightly clicking hooves is slowly approaching the painter on his wheeled bed, at first hesitantly, then with increasingly faster steps. The astonishment erases all memory. What is he doing here?

Already he has reached the painter, whose left hand hangs over the edge of his wheeled bed. The white buck softly sniffs the air, his head now level with the painter's. His slit pupils look straight into the patient's eyes. Without reproach. Without anger. And with his rough, cold tongue he licks the drooping, salty hand that Soutine dares not pull away. Once more he opens his right eye and looks into the buck's eyes. He is here. He has arrived. He is white. That was enough. It was no dream.

Then a door is jerked open; alarmed, the painter opens his eyes wide, and the white billy goat is gone. The hallway springs back to life; through the wall, broken sentences can be heard pleading, sentences aborted in a fury, menacingly emphasized syllables.

Excess stomach acid, chronic inflammation, severely damaged stomach lining. He thinks he hears the word 'perforation' and is terrified by the word 'resection'. The old ulcer has burnt through the stomach wall, gastric juice is leaking into his abdominal cavity. The surgeon pleads to operate, immediately, now, without another moment's delay. Straight to anaesthesia. Madam, this is an emergency. They can't do much more for your painter in Paris, either.

The patient wants it, too: right away, anything. Anything to cut out the pain, no more delays, right now and right here.

But not here, with these country quacks, these horse butchers, says Ma-Be; you need to be operated on by a specialist, not here, but in Paris. Gosset, Guttmann, Abramy, one of the doctors that know you will know who can save you.

She is the harping, hissing angel of death, who wants the best and demands the worst, who will accompany the painter's stomach on its endless odyssey towards its last possible operation.

Suddenly the decision is made; he is no longer asked. Marie-Berthe has made calls to some voices. That such spirits were still around in this war-month of August. In a clinic in the Sixteenth Arrondissement he will be operated on by real doctors. Its name is long: *Maison de Santé Lyautey*.

In Chinon, a doctor gives him a morphine injection as a merciful provision for the journey; she knows the dosage is risky but intends it to have the longest possible effect. Lannegrace is the doctor's name; she has introduced herself in a soft voice and all he hears in her name is the echo of *grâce*, grace. It makes him think of *coup de grâce* and his ears take it to be a good sign. The generous, pain-numbing morphine promises fast relaxation, disperses quickly through his bloodstream and swaddles him in a cottony calm.

In the early morning of 6 August the black Corbillard pulls up to take the pain to Paris. Let's move, off to the capital of pain, wasn't that what it was called by one of those crazy Surrealists he wanted nothing to do with? A combative angel with a nasal voice urges the wavering fate simultaneously to make haste and take diversions. To avoid the checkpoints, but also to gather up paintings, scattered possessions, to cover traces that need to disappear. Haste and diversions—each necessary, both impossible.

The gravel in Chinon's hospital yard crunches beneath the tyres and continues to screech in his ears when the hearse starts to move that morning. And so do all those other sounds of the last while. He had noticed that his eyes had become less hungry; they had seen enough, had tired themselves out on the narrow paths in Champigny-sur-Veude, while sounds had suddenly become more distinct, even shriller. Sound likes to join forces with pain.

The crunching cuts into his ear as into his stomach, as if the operation is about to begin that he desires more than anything else in this world, because the pain—a pain first fluttering and dizzily spiralling, then throbbing, and soon jabbing, piercing and burrowing—has for years been part of his body like an additional organ and is now so unbearable that an incision into his belly, any incision, appears to him like salvation itself. If only you could destroy yourself like a painting.

In the end it was an idea born from her despair that gave the wrong advice. As she was leaving, Lannegrace pressed a snow-white nurse's uniform into her trembling hand. The Surrealists' muse as a bewildered nurse. If worse came to worst, she would claim that, as a nurse, she had to accompany the deathly white and visibly weakened patient to Paris, where a surgeon was expecting him. Not to the Salpêtrière of course, the former gunpowder factory behind the Gare d'Austerlitz having been turned into a German hospital. No, to an inconspicuous clinic in the bourgeois Sixteenth Arrondissement, where the Occupiers have their administrative offices. Under their very eyes, so to speak: the best hiding place. No ambulance had been available, she would have to say; there was a serious fire at a nearby farmhouse, in this glowing August heat, and all vehicles were needed. She would wave her forged papers like tickets to salvation.

If all goes well, you will pass unnoticed through the villages and suburbs and straight into Paris. Avoid the main arterial roads at all costs. The shy doctor with the Michelin map and the blue, laughing, running little Michelin Man. They mix, and blend with the poplar *allées*.

An egg must be broken into the water for washing the body. The Chevra Kadisha knows the way. The Sacred

Fellowship is already on the road before daybreak. The eggshell hits the rim of the dented tin bowl, hesitates and breaks. The protective film tears, the slime of life plops into the water and the yellow disperses as an opaque blessing.

MA-BE

Opening his eyes is difficult. When he tries and squints, he sees Marie-Berthe in the shadow against the light, hunched over on a stool, muttering, occasionally sighing, pressing a handkerchief to her lips. She seems to be elsewhere, but the misery has lodged itself deep inside her. Is she asleep, or quietly talking to herself? How much she has changed. The search for new hiding places, quarrels with landlords, constant fear when military vehicles roar through town on their way to Tours, and the increasing difficulty of chasing down even the most basic food—all has engraved itself on her body, in the wrinkles of her skin and the blue darkness around her eyes.

It happened at the Café de Flore. Was it October, or November '40? He had been on his own for the past six months. On 15 May that year, Mademoiselle Garde had gone to the prescribed collection point, the Vélodrome d'Hiver, and had not returned. In Montparnasse it was rumoured that thousands of German immigrants, even hapless refugees, were being shipped off as enemy aliens to the Pyrenees, to the Gurs camp in south-western

France. Swept up by a rough broom, like drifting leaves. Five days earlier, German troops had started to push through the Ardennes. Doctor Tennenbaum turned out to have been right when he implored them in a whisper at the Hôtel de la Paix on the Boulevard Raspail, Escape while you can. Listen to me: Go!

The painter can no longer think of Garde without feeling a burden of guilt. He keeps seeing her leave with her tiny leather case, turn around one last time and smile at him over her shoulder. Mademoiselle Garde! In an often recurring dream he sees her sit on the edge of his bed, mute, without reproach, but with large, questioning eyes. The painter is left behind alone, wandering the streets of Montparnasse like a lost flounder. Delambre, Grande Chaumière, Champagne Première, Passage d'Enfer. He winces whenever he turns into the Passageway to Hell. Many have left.

He is to meet the Castaings at the cafe to discuss the delivery of a painting. Maurice Sachs sits next to a dark-haired beauty the painter has seen somewhere before. Flashing eyes. What was her name? Madelaine Castaing introduces her: Marie-Berthe Aurenche. And the American painter next to her whispers into his ear, As you know, the ex of Max Ernst.

Later he will learn that Maurice Sachs leant over to Madelaine Castaing and rebuked her with cynical irony, How careless of you to introduce Marie-Berthe to him! You have just signed his death warrant.

Marie-Berthe is known as one of those half-crazed muses the Surrealists lusted after. Now thirty-four, she has that beautifully sad, milky face and looks infinitely unhappy . . . He is aware that she had been married for nine years to that German painter; in Montparnasse, everyone knows everyone else, and whatever people don't know about one another, they can piece together from the ever-present rumours. From a girls' boarding school run by strict nuns she is said to have come to Paris full of a zest for life and a spirit of adventure. Rosary and raging desire. There is gossip that Man Ray took nude photos of the eighteen-year-old. And Max does indeed abduct her—a warrant is issued for his arrest—but the shocked Aurenche parents eventually relent and consent to their marriage, which takes place in November '27. Nine years later, all that is left to connect her with Max is her insane, incurable rage.

She was his wife until the autumn of '36 when he met Leonora in London, a pretty little minx Max fell in love with instantly. Ma-Be hated her even before laying eyes on her. She wasn't going to be casual about relinquishing her place to a young, painting *bourgeoise* called Carrington, who happened to appear just when Max was casting about for a fresh muse. He needed muses, and used them up faster than he could paint them.

The bastard, *le salaud!* Ma-Be later hissed at Le Dôme, when she told him the whole story and Soutine was spooked by the rage with which she cursed Max. She trembled and looked as if she were about to fling the cups against the wall. She talked rapidly, without regard for Soutine, as if she needed to vomit out her deep, rage-fuelled misery. Max had eloped with his English conquest to the Ardèche where the humiliated Marie-Berthe ferreted out the lovers in their love nest in Saint-Martin d'Ardèche. She knew the area well because her family was from there, and turned up at innkeeper Fanfan's, drank in her boisterous pub, barked, begged and blubbered. This time Max went back to Ma-Be, stayed with her in Paris through the winter of '37/38, leaving his *Anglaise* on her own down in the Ardèche. Half out of her senses and to expunge the torments of jealousy and abandonment from her mind, Leonora wrote her *Little Francis* with Ma-Be as Amelia, who grabs a hammer and smashes her—the beauty's—horse head. Ma-Be lured her to Paris under false pretences, where the rivals brawled, and whacked and scratched each other like cats gone crazy. He's mine, what is it you aren't getting? Max graciously tolerated their fighting and then, in the spring of '38, went back to his beautiful Englishwoman in the Ardèche. Ma-Be had lost the battle for good.

The stool slides. Wisps of greasy hair fall over her eyes, which are occasionally closing; her lips move without sound. Soutine sees it through the veil of his lashes, cannot do anything for her, drowses on, cradled by cottony morphine. Opening his eyes is difficult.

Now she was sitting in front of him looking so lost he would have liked to paint her. Miserable women and children startled him, he recognized himself in them; something about them leapt across to him, and as soon as the ball of his thumb had rubbed their misery onto his canvas, it had intangibly become his. But Ma-Be. The Surreals used their muses and cast them off like dirty socks. Unpredictable, half-crazy these women had to be, spreading chaos and making themselves available in exchange for a few cocktails. Cheap, raving muses. He remembers what people whispered about in the cafes. Breton's novel about a madwoman fired up everybody's fantasies, his Nadja, his beautiful lunatic. He held forth about her purity: a child-woman simultaneously innocent and depraved, a Bride of the Wind who electrified the pope of the Surrealists. Ma-Be was just one of the flock and enjoyed playing her part, the fluttering closeness to madness, the hysterical outbursts, garish costumes, malicious hoaxes. She read their palms, mumbled gibberish, clouded the minds of Max's Dada cronies. That she sometimes despaired and felt at the end of her tether, that she was haunted by moments of infinite sadness, was of no interest to anyone.

Look pretty and shut up, *sois belle et tais-toi!*

But Breton dumped his Nadja before the doors to the lunatic asylum closed again. Colourful butterflies of Montparnasse, ringed with madness.

And now here she was, sitting across from him in the cafe, her face twitching nervously, lying that she was twenty-five, and knowing he knew she was lying. But her lie was beautiful and full of despair. The pale wreckage of a shattered, ruined muse. Max, she later confessed, had forced her to abort her child. What the backstreet abortionist had wreaked for a few francs with knitting needles on her kitchen table had been sheer butchery, *une boucherie*; it had taken her months to recover. Once she threw herself into the Seine, but the water was bitterly cold and she swam to the bank and, with chattering teeth, was hauled from the water by bystanders. Again she dressed up, in outrageous, pathetic clown costumes, tried to rehash the old routines of the prattling fairy. Wide girly eyes and ridiculous bangs.

The painter liked her sobbing hatred of all who had betrayed her, for in her rage he recognized his own. He had never liked the Surreals, their disciples in the cafes endlessly chattering about liberation, magic dictation, magnetic fields, the straitjacket they had to blow up. What nonsense La Rotonde and Le Dôme had to listen to! If the red felt had ears, could remember it all . . . All they wanted was the dream and their grim little games.

He had hated dreams since childhood. They never offered consolation, only left him warped and battered. His dreams were never beautiful, and he distrusted those hypocritical harbingers of bad luck, the Cossack boots that goose-stepped through his studio, smooth black-leather gloves that ripped lacerated canvasses from his easel, loud fanfares from which sudden shots rang out. Spanish was spoken, Mussolinish, or *Gitlerdaytsh*. A night without dreams was a good night. The Surreals loved chaos but had never witnessed a pogrom; names such as Berdichev, Zhitomir, Nikolaev meant nothing to them. They relished being despised by *les bourgeois* but had never been forced to flee into the forests to save their skins. Pampered sons of the bourgeoisie, who treated themselves to a few titbits of anarchy. In Germany, dark masses were now throwing their arms up in the air and cheering a bellowing, choking Guignol buffoon. When he heard that he'd once been a painter, he wanted to spit.

He had to punish the canvas for his unwanted dreams. It was his skin that he smudged down, slashed, tormented. Rough and scabby. He slept poorly, tossed like a bear all night, sometimes fell into a grim deep sleep from which he never seemed to resurface. He had seen Breton from afar, a man who had struck him as arrogant and snobbish, and he turned his back on him so he wouldn't have to look at him, and stared into the ashtray instead. They did not understand him. How were they to deal with a Belorussian Yid who was mute as a fish and doggedly painted his warped landscapes? Still lifes! Portraits! All that outdated stuff. Their god was called Max, with his insects, trees and monsters, the ribbed rocks and bony ferns. Dadamax, Schnabelmax, Loplop: frivolous self-portraits of a windbag, a charmer, a philanderer, whom he couldn't even envy. He wanted nothing to do with them.

Then he took Marie-Berthe to his place; she went along with him, saying she wanted to see his paintings. Her rage and his despondency, her distress and his despair over the war and the Occupiers meshed. The two hung on to each other by the wrist. Were Mademoiselle Garde ever to return from his guilt-ridden dreams, he would try to explain it to her. For now, Ma-Be was suddenly with him, a lost, crazy fairy, a Catholic with all the ardour common to the world of her childhood. Dangling from her neck she wore the little golden crosses she had been given for her first communion, as if she needed to punish the unfaithful Surreals by returning to the faith of her roots, which they all disdained. Max had painted the Virgin Mary with the Baby Jesus across her lap, her hand raised to spank his reddened buttocks. Breton, Éluard and Max are watching through the window. And Ma-Be's father was a respectable French civil servant—a retired tax collector, it was rumoured—and, who's to know, maybe one day one might expect some support from him. For now, let's wait and see.

Out of her own sheer misery Ma-Be wanted to exorcize his, and keep him as her sad painter-pet. She wanted to hang crosses around his neck, too, and babbled on about salvation just as she had earlier read the Surrealists' palms. She also wanted to banish the memory of his guardian angel, of his Mademoiselle Garde with her unhelpful German accent. Let go of your guilt. You no longer owe her.

What do you want? Such are the times.

Your guardian angel has been interned, Ma-Be said; she will not come back. Your guardian angel wears a yellow star, she said a few months later; she couldn't help you anyway. This is Paris, and you need someone without a star. The Pyrenees are a long way away, but I am here, and I can hide you.

She persuaded him that in these accursed times one needed a guardian angel and that that angel's face could change, as could her language. Ma-Be's fury over Max, Soutine's own despair about the Occupiers and about the pain burning through his stomach wall: two unhappy people who shackle each other, yet who together feel united against a world that has conspired against them. The misery of the abandoned Marie-Berthe quickly allies itself with Soutine's fear and feelings of guilt, and their combined unhappiness binds them together more intensely than happiness could. Happiness is no solution, and for a long time has not existed in this city occupied by a roar. What still exists is a simple bed, and the catastrophe of the whole damn world. He takes Ma-Be, as he calls her for simplicity's sake, back home to the Villa Seurat, where it is cold; his studio cannot be heated. They never again speak of Max.

They crawl into a cave and burrow into each other; their tongues tangle, as do their trembling legs; her sad sex flogs his. As if that could chase away the unhappiness that is spreading through the world and nests in their bodies and sneers at them. They made love furiously and tearfully. A clay pot fell from the shelf above them during their first evening when they panted and thrust into each other on rumpled sheets, into the infinite country of hellish misery.

The pot crashed to the floor beside them, and they took fright but continued to make love. It was as if the pot had tried to slay them before they reached their climax. When they later got up and wordlessly gathered up the cheap clay shards, they both sensed clearly what it meant. Montparnasse lay shattered and crushed behind their backs, the capital of art was no longer but had been erased from the map, and where Le Dôme and La Rotonde and La Coupole had once stood like smoke-filled cathedrals was now a desert where a bomb had exploded and driven away the painters. Sand was trickling into the craters, filling them with its musty thousand-year infinity. They felt as though they were the last survivors of the bombing.

And how she could fight. She nagged and hissed, hit him, argued about money, called him cheap. She was unpredictable; any moment a swift reptile could burst from her. He opened his eyes wide and, terrified, stared at the suddenly unleashed beast.

No, he did not paint her. But he did paint her! Marc Laloë saw the painting, Christmas '42, when he and Olga visited the couple, who were then hiding in Champigny. Stunned, Laloë stood before it and could only stammer: A masterpiece. A composition of green and purple, dark reptilian colours, chameleon skin, on her dress the sparkling brilliance of jewels never seen before. But Ma-Be vigorously disputed any resemblance. She thought herself far too aged in the painting, her features monstrously distorted. What had Soutine done to her beautiful mouth, her delicate nose? Pure mockery of faded beauty. When he went outside, she took a paintbrush and improved her face.

Soutine let out a cry when he discovered the damage, complained bitterly to Laloë: Look at what she's done. Sheer madness!

Without hesitation he shredded the canvas in front of Laloë's shocked eyes with several knife strokes, and no one could have stopped him. The dark, beautiful reptile was not to be saved. Marie-Berthe would later try in vain to glue together the strips of canvas . . . An execution cannot be undone.

And to this hissing angel he owed the hiding places in Paris, in the Rue Littré at her father's, in the Rue des Plantes at the Laloës', and the six different lodgings in Champigny. A broken muse protected him. And destroyed him.

She sat on the seat in the travelling hearse and occasionally slid slightly, her hair dishevelled; a shudder made her body quiver when the undertakers on their quest turned off the road. She started, pulled back, sobbed, sighed and mumbled things to herself that he no longer understood.

MORPHINE

Like a heavy black sleigh the hearse glides into the summery French countryside, from Chinon northward over the most inconspicuous bridge that crosses the capricious Loire upriver from Saumur, and on into the sparse mown wheat that lies pale as snow. The reeds won't remember, and neither will the tiny bays or the shrieking waterfowl. On along lonely poplar-lined country roads, through sleepy villages and the narrowest of streets that cling to the wheels as if trying to brake the hearse's forward thrust, the Corbillard presses northward, albeit in a cautious zigzag, creeping around the cities and larger towns as if they harboured the plague and could be infectious. Avoiding the main axes and Occupiers' checkpoints, using side roads that normally see only hay carts and lumbering horse-drawn manure carts. Northward, moving rhythmically back and forth, keeping its distance from Tours and Orléans or Chartres, desperately and quietly dodging them like a rabbit with a paralysed leg, northward through Sarthe and Orne and Eure and utterly unexpectedly into Normandie, and only then striking an eastward course towards its secret destination, Paris. How vast France has suddenly become. Going north, going east, in frighteningly slow motion, time running out like sand trickling from a bulging pierced sack, like blood trickling into the stomach.

He is the pain at the centre of his belly, from its root near the top pushing through the stomach lining with acidic force and radiating into areas it had never been before. For years he has been his pain, now he is draining away. His gastric juices empty into his abdominal cavity. He empties himself out; his peritonitis pulses and the fiercest pains burn through his belly. It may still take hours, but what are hours? No one knows their true length. They have no measure.

As if they had vowed to take the most impossible diversions in order to trick fate, as if the black hearse sensed where they were waiting, death's checkpoints, the red-and-white barriers that yelled 'Stop' with a hissing 'sh'. Where the Cyclopes carrying machine guns were sitting on motorcycles with sidecars, rubber-latex goggles on their helmets, metal sheaths on their chests, waiting to deploy.

A torn poster at the small pumping station at the village entrance, calling for voluntary labour service in Germany: They Give Their Blood. Give Them Your Labour. Save Europe from Bolshevism. No one wants to enlist, so Vichy establishes compulsory labour service west of the

Rhine. Suddenly young people vanish, go off to the Maquis, disperse into forests and stables, haylofts and remote barns. Voluntary? What a joke. A farmer's quick hand rips down the poster in passing.

A painter rolls through villages that have never heard of him. The journey takes a full day. Twenty-four hours. An eternity. Forever they sacrifice to the god of diversions until the god can take it no longer. They must reach the heart of the capital through the most delicate capillaries, dirt roads almost. What's a hearse doing travelling between wheat and fruit trees, avoiding all arteries where they might be stationed?

No one knows the path. No one will ever know. And what good would it do to list all the villages and hamlets, the narrow lanes, the bends and wrong turns? The painter does not see the path. He lies in semi-darkness inside the Citroën, protected by grey, pleated curtains. From flickering memories his life calls out one more time into his numbed pain, his tattered old desires, into the fear his dreams continue to weave. It had been his last burning. No one knows the path. No one will ever know. No one can know who the man is who rolls past in the hearse. There are only the paintings, those few he has not slashed or burnt. No one knows him.

Lannegrace had warned Ma-Be when she explained how to administer the morphine. The effects can't always be foreseen. He often won't know where he is, what he is, what time it is. He will have inaccurate memories, will experience clouding of consciousness, disorganization of sensations, deregulated hallucinations. Peritonitis usually causes a high fever; his morphine delirium may be compounded by a fever delirium. His state of consciousness will alternate; he will lie awake but also seem drowsy and drift into a deep sleep. Because of his fever his face will be reddened, he will glow, beads of sweat will appear on his forehead. Racing pulse, faster breathing, initially rather high blood pressure due to the pain and the fever. At other times he'll seem comatose and lie there like a living corpse.

Speechless and horrified, Marie-Berthe stares at the doctor's mouth. She hears the words that pour from it, comprehends none, and only starts when she hears 'living corpse', which seems to wake her up.

Time seeps away like the gastric acid that trickles through his perforated stomach wall into his abdominal cavity and flows around his organs. The painter enters into his own milky-red bowels, into the red of tissue, the red of the gladioli he painted in Céret. Where exactly those checkpoints of pain were located was impossible to determine. The morphine with which the gracious Lannegrace has injected him creates a different time in his body, nests here and there and distends the pathways, cushions the sensations, and facilitates his sleep like a Greek brother.

A glorious discovery, an unalloyed gift for pained humanity. Divine plant. *Papaver somniferum*. From the opium poppy's dried milk the gentle substance rises that blocks the transmission of pain signals to the higher places. Blessed opium, praise be to the tinkering German pharmacist Sertürner in the provincial backwater of Paderborn, who released the alkaloid of opium from eternities of dreaming. In Paderborn! It sounds like a faraway paradise. Praise be to Séguin and Courtois, to all the German and French discoverers who waged war against pain. And now their countries, which had given morphine to tormented humankind, wage war against each other. What an infinite potential for pain without the magic opiate, what an imperfect, unredeemed humankind without this messiah!

The painter struggles to remember who told him the story of morphine's discovery. Oh yes, Tennenbaum. The Austrian doctor, who was passing through Paris before making the break for America. Doctor Tennenbaum, who left Vienna when he saw the mob screaming with excitement. He immediately understood, went home, told his wife to pack their suitcases. Just a little trip to Paris. Just a few days. Just the essentials.

Mademoiselle Garde was determined to ask his advice for the pain-stricken painter. She went to the Austrian family at the Hôtel de la Paix on the Boulevard Raspail, where she herself had stayed. Theirs was the room next to hers. From the hallway she had overheard them speak German. And she would learn about their plans.

Tennenbaum, who no longer expected anything good until the day he would set foot on American soil, had spoken of the coming age of pain and of the discoverer of morphine. They had a long conversation in German, Gerda Groth, the shy woman from Magdeburg, and the doctor of utter despair.

The world makes sure the prophet of doom is sooner or later proven right, you understand?

He implored her so intensely that Gerda returned to her painter on the Villa Seurat in a daze. Tennenbaum had cried out to her: Escape with him while there is time! Now, right away. If you don't, you'll always be sorry. Nothing good will come from it, you understand: There will be war. They will occupy France, all of Europe, Russia, all the way to Asia. Everywhere they will plant their hacked-up crosses; everywhere they will fly those oversize red-white flags. They want to set up the thousand-year Reich of pain. Leave before it's too late!

And he had jotted down the names of possible medications. Papaverine, histidine, bismuth salts. She memorized them all. A few days later she took her painter to see him. It was supposed to be a friendly conversation, casual, so as to not scare away Soutine. He would need to get an X-ray. The painter agreed, to please Mademoiselle Garde. She went back, this time without him. Tennenbaum held in his hands the result that the blurry image had revealed.

A very deep-seated gastric ulcer, you understand? Too far progressed to be cured. His organism is weak and worn out.

Can you speak louder, more clearly, Doctor Tennenbaum? I can't hear you properly with the motor running.

Doctor Tennenbaum and his litany of the great pain to come, which now reaches him again in fragments and in Gerda's voice, in this slow-moving hearse as it inches towards the capital of pain. Imploring, unhopeful. It was like a great, terrifying credo. She had memorized everything.

Whoever does not give man ultimate painlessness is no god. No, not an absence of pain. Freedom from pain.

Whoever doubles over with pain, writhes in spasms, bows and scrapes instead of standing up straight, who squirms on the floor under the boot, can recognize no god but the morphine messiah. Sertürner is his god. The makers of painkillers are the true apostles.

The least credible religion of all is the one that makes up a crucified god in order to reconcile people with their pain. There is no reconciliation! Doctor Tennenbaum was almost shouting. The permanent exhibition of his martyrdom is heaping scorn on humanity. Don't you see what pain does to you? Your god has invented pain. What an ingenious tinkerer!

You think you can temporarily forget him, but the millions of representations of the crucifixion almost summon the pain back into your body. Grünewald, his Isenheim altarpiece, the bulging veins, the tormented green flesh. Every image of torture evokes another torture, the unimaginable possibilities of pain. The Roman nails that a heavy hammer bangs through tendons and muscle and nerves do not make only the Son of God howl and whimper with pain. The Anointed One nailed to the cross is a gigantic card sharp's trick. Jesus Christ is the son of pain, the embodied *reconciliation* with pain. Behold, He died of pain for you. For your salvation. Salvation from what? What freedom can there be but the freedom from pain? Absolutely no reconciliation with pain! No quiet resignation, no meek acceptance!

Whoever for years doubles over with pain becomes irreconcilable. The meaning of pain, like god, will be lost on him. To ease that pain, to numb it, physically, of course physically, not mentally or spiritually—that would be a divine task. To finally abolish pain would be the foremost task for any god worth that name. Or not worth it.

Tennenbaum was visibly agitated by his credo. It was his gospel, the glad tidings of freedom from pain according to Sertürner. He kept his eyes fixed on Gerda's, as if he were speaking only to those eyes.

Because he installs pain in the body, this god promotes the occupation of countries, an occupation that exports pain, carries it across borders. Across the world's threshold of pain. The thousand-year Reich is the world empire of the body in pain. The Gestapo would be impotent without it, just imagine! Pliers that pull out fingernails in basements, useless tools; blows at the testes, a waste of time. Without the empire of pain, there would be no dictatorship by the grace of god. The countless methods of inflicting pain attest to the torturers' power, you understand?

The God of creation condemned himself when out of deep thoughtlessness he invented pain along with the body. A creation without pain—that would be a benevolent, righteous invention, Doctor Tennenbaum said bitterly. But God didn't deliver. He failed. Pain exists. And cannot be eliminated from a world whose creator has made off with the potential painkillers.

The only one who keeps getting resurrected is the pain. Pain is the permanently risen god who awaits his eradication. There is no saviour but in the shape of effective painkillers. O holy morphine, blessed art thou among the gifts of the poppy!

And with that Doctor Tennenbaum had a frenzied, mad look in his eyes that suddenly terrified Gerda.

Lurching in his hearse towards Paris, the painter could no longer understand the slurring Doctor Tennenbaum. But his stomach wall wanted to keep on listening. Soon he only saw the doctor's lips move but no longer heard the sounds. His voice had vanished into a faraway America.

Soutine's ulcer curses God. Only his art will survive the agonies of this journey. Sertürner, the morphine messiah, has invented the right thing. How to block pain.

41

How to prevent transmission to the key pain centres and to the monitoring sites. A tender, shrewd quieting of pain. An index finger placed on a pair of lips. Don't tell, don't pass it on. But its power is limited, lasts two, perhaps three, at most four hours, then the messiah must return. Lannegrace had slipped Marie-Berthe the dark-brown vial with the tincture. They did not have much in Chinon. The Occupiers had confiscated the painkillers.

You realize we are short of everything. They loot even hospitals, strip them of dressings, surgical instruments, anaesthetics. No matter how much we plead, we barely get the basics. They probably need the medical plunder in the east. Did you not listen to the radio last winter? Radio Londres kept talking about that city on the Volga, about an encirclement, even capitulation. They got stopped in Russia, you understand? We cheered under our seven blankets when we heard it.

The morphine messiah rides along in the hearse, closes the painter's eyes, flickers with a dim light in his consciousness. He sends dreams and causes the painter to lose his sense of time. He neither knows where he is, nor what he is. The painter does not see the landscapes gliding past the black Citroën. Flat landscapes north of the Loire—he needed others, always others, to paint. To never paint again.

Ma-Be, where are we going? To Raspberrytown. To the Pyrenees? Where is Paris? North is south in the east. So it's the Pyrenees then. To the Vélodrome d'Hiver? To the Passageway to Hell, where he lived in 1929 when the stock market crashed? He can never think of that address without wincing. *Passage d'Enfer*. Where will he arrive? How often has he already arrived, in Minsk, Vilna, Paris. It no longer matters. Everyone eventually arrives. He has to reach Paris for his operation, but in his head he clearly travels to the Pyrenees.

The hills of Céret. The little town is famous for its cherries, its cork industry, the production of barrels and sandals. Art dealer Zborowski sent him to Céret in 1919. Off you go! Down to the Cubists' mecca near the Spanish border, where Picasso and Braque had left their footprints a few years earlier. Soutine hates their paintings, but his brush strokes suddenly sense the attraction and steer him where he does not want to go; later he can free himself of this energy only by burning his paintings. He hates Céret, suffers the torments of hell on those hills that his paintings need to capture.

Zbo pays five francs per day, which is barely enough for the tubes of paint at the haberdasher Sageloly's. Sometimes a loaf of bread, Roquefort cheese for five sous. They speak Catalan, he doesn't understand the locals, is an alien again just like six years earlier when he first arrived in Paris. And the nickname, whispered behind his back, would soon stick: *el pintre brut*. The grubby painter.

The hills of Céret.

His canvasses are tortured sisters of the landscapes. Paints like lava, green-orange-red, applied with panic and rage. Wavering houses in a frightened landscape, windows the eyes of ghosts. Twisted trees like the tentacles of octopuses. Roads rearing up. Sinkholes. Windswept, bucking, bursting paths.

For him, the earth shook in the Pyrenees. There is a danger no one can name. Landscape as landslide; a raging, epileptic landscape, licking earthquake air. The crust we live on is thin. The flow of magma pushes upward; lava wants to burst through. The images he paints in Céret are his decorations for the Day of Judgment. He is a screaming Jeremiah who spits his paint into the landscape. Whiplash. In the stillest landscape of all.

He needs this landscape to push against. But how he mangles, mutilates it. Landscape viscera, intestines, unexpected convolutions. Is there a way back? Of course not. No amends can be made. Not for anything that happened to him. Everything is still there. His childhood, cursed forever. His hatred of the Pyrenees. His fury at the paintings from Céret, inciting his orgies of destruction. Reports of fights, hacks by his paintbrush, a pulsating convulsion that shakes him. Fingertips scour through the flow from the paint tube.

The hills of Céret.

How late is it outside, Marie-Berthe? He wants to ask but can't. Paris alone counts, and the operation. At four in the morning he sets out again, runs through the hills, twenty kilometres and more. He is looking for his place, a particular spot from which to look at his life. And to argue with the landscape. He is unapproachable, remains mute, wary, shy. Lives in an abandoned pigsty or some tool shed among the vineyards, without light, has nailed up the shutters, throws himself on the dirty straw that was left lying around, covers himself with his canvasses, rolls himself into them as if he were lying in the hearse already. He returns utterly exhausted, forgets to eat, doesn't wash, doesn't change his ribbed trousers, everything stained with streaks of green and splats of red. The pile of canvasses grows and still he has not found any truth. He must continue to burrow into the landscape. Three years of punishment. No sufferance, no salvation.

The hills of Céret.

And so he carries the hurricane from hill to hill. No one has been here before. No one has ever seen anything like it. Nothing can be recognized. But all is still there. His worst enemies are the prying ramblers. Everyone is an expert about the holy similitude. As soon as he sees one of them emerge, he folds up his easel and disappears under the trees until the danger has passed. Alone with himself and the landscape, a long way from galleries, trends, Montparnasse. Soutine runs across the hills by himself. A lonesome runner with colourful baggage. And the hills bear it. He can see himself run, even now. He is in a hurry. He has to get to his operation. No one has been here before.

But no, there is an observer. A petty, envious man from Montparnasse. Emile Bourrachon, aka Justin Francœur, aka what's-his-name, who passes around his discovery. He stalks the painter like a rare, filthy beast. He approaches the sty, looks around a few times. Everyone knows that Soutine can't be found there during daytime. And that he dashes through the hills, paints, abruptly stops, then rushes on.

The farther I entered the dark and moist blackness, which smelt sour from sweat and animal effluvium, and the farther I got away from the trapezium of light that the sun cut through the entrance and projected onto the dusty floor, the less I doubted my first impression: Soutine was an animal! I lit a match and looked for some lamp or candle that would make the evil darkness back off . . .

In the flickering light I saw two piles protrude from the straw that covered the compacted mud floor. One was an orderly pile of stretched canvasses in different sizes whose turned-down fronts were apparently painted, the other a chaotic mess of scraped or virginal canvasses that the brute probably rolled up in to sleep. I turned over one canvas after another from the first pile to visit in this nightmarish museum the twists and turns of a brain whose procreative drive subverted all rules of art. What words could I use to describe this outpouring of violence, thick as the blood streaming from the sacrificial bull's carotid artery that will anoint Mithras's brothers-in-arms?

And the canvasses that I lifted to carry into the daylight that never penetrated beyond the door step were heavy with the furiously smeared stuff . . .

Soutine could return any moment and I wanted to avoid at all costs being surprised by him; still, I continued my sinister excavation, simultaneously appalled by the brutality of his art and fascinated with its sheer violence, a violence that briefly whispered into my ear that it was a violence I might appreciate . . .

I left this obscene cave, not without casting a last glance at a green something: green cypresses warped by wind, green globes of shrubs whirling towards a stormy green sky filled with clouds that were illuminated by slashes of lightning. With relief I found the world again, those same cypresses, now calm on both sides of the country road. On my way back home, his frightening vision kept pushing itself in front of the quiet afternoon landscape that Soutine had subjected to the unleashed elements . . . Visions of hell were superimposed over the charming reality of this enchanting little town in the south . . .

I turned around a hedge and suddenly saw, about thirty metres away, Soutine with his back to me, pissing against a tree. Without a sound I stepped back towards the hedge . . . Soutine was whistling, buttoned up his fly and began to walk in my direction. He was about to notice me when he suddenly stopped, put both hands on his belly and doubled over as if about to break in half . . . and groaned with pain. I was gripped with terror and ran away without looking back.

What madman has painted these images, Leopold Zborowski's clients cry out in his living room on the Rue Joseph-Bara. And the chief tin god, Paul Guillaume, who hoards African statues, fares no better on the Rue de Miromesnil. Potential clients flee into the streets so as not to be crushed by a falling, now invisible sky. Modigliani calls out, drunk: Everything dances in front of my eyes like a landscape by Soutine.

The painter still hears him. And is no longer frightened.

Black smoke rises from the small yard of the Garreta Hotel in Céret. Again he has burnt dozens of his paintings. He must wipe them off the face of the earth. His hatred endures; he will track down art dealers who hoard his paintings and will buy back paintings from his time in Céret in order to slash them with a knife. Will sell a painting only if he is provided with two others from Céret to destroy. Poor Pyrenees!

Now he rides in a hearse, once again travels from Paris to the Pyrenees, past landscapes that chase each other and flash through slits and the small rear windows where they compete with his own images. The morphine helps the eyes glide past the black sheet metal to the overgrown landscapes outside. They pass through his closed lids. Day or night? Paris or the Pyrenees? He no longer knows. The destroyed paintings from Céret run alongside the hearse, try to catch up with him, to take revenge for having been slashed with knives and scissors whenever he was able to track down one or another. The morphine messiah is riding along, as are the ashes of paintings from Céret.

Once upon a time there was an occupied country that pretended only one half was occupied. The south was now called the Free Zone, or *zone nono*, and the occupied north, *zone o*. With good local knowledge and the aid of helpers, people were able at night to cross the demarcation line between *o* and *nono*. But the French air in the region is buzzing with German *Bekanntmachungen* and *Verordnungsblättern*, proclamations and official gazettes, monitored by the eagle with the spread wings and talons that clutch the hacked-up cross. They threaten draconian punishments for illegal crossings.

In June of '40 the wavy line with its two peaks appears in the paper. With a fingernail framed by stubborn bits of paint he can no longer scrape off, Soutine traces the line's two camel humps from the Jura Mountains to the Pyrenees, from the Swiss to the Spanish borders. In the camel's belly are Vichy and its decrees, and Pétain's appeals to collaborate with the Occupiers. For the good of France.

Chana Orloff, his neighbour, runs into him in the street. It must be the autumn of '40 and not far from the Villa Seurat where they have lived since both the armistice and the division of the country have come into force. She asks: Chaim, why don't you go south, to the Free Zone?

His answer comes quickly, as if he didn't have to think: There's no milk down there.

Had Marshall Pétain drunk all the milk in Vichy? Had the cows flown away? Did cows exist only in the occupied zone in the north? Were they not afraid of tank tracks and sidecars, of black jackboots?

He adores their animal warmth, the treasure of their udders, the flow of their soothing milk, which, when mixed with bismuth powder, temporarily puts to rest the pain in his belly. And he hates the cows that Chagall, having barely arrived at the Beehive in the Passage de Dantzig, used to brush onto his Vitebsk sky.

Why would I go there? There's no milk down there.

And with a shake of her head Chana turns away, wishes him good luck, pulls wings over her strong sculptor arms, says loudly and clearly, I'll be a seamstress in Jaffa, rises high above the Villa Seurat and escapes with her son to Switzerland. His old friends from Minsk and Vilna have begun to make their way south as soon as the Germans pushed through the Ardennes. In May of '40 Kikoïne finds sanctuary at his son Yankel's in Toulouse.

Krémègne moves to the remote Corrèze as if moving to the moon, hires himself out as a farmhand to get through the war. Soutine stays.

There's no milk down there.

On 3 September 1939, the day France declared war, he and Mademoiselle Garde were in the Burgundy village of Civry. He went to the village store and glumly looked for the rustling messengers of doom that were filled with black, smudged letters: *LA GUERRE!* But the war seemed to sleep through its arrival in the west. A *sitzkrieg* along the Maginot Line, all remains calm, people play cards on the ramparts, brim with good cheer and smoke. Nothing happens. Not a day goes by that the painter doesn't hastily open the paper. He distrusts the ominous calm, any calm. The war takes its time and first devotes itself to CASE WHITE as if it, too, were a painter. In Poland the future loot is being shared with Stalinland. There's no milk down there. The war continues to paint; CASE WHITE is followed by CASE YELLOW, the campaign in the west, on 10 May 1940. *Sitzkrieg* turns into *blitzkrieg*. Operation Sickle Cut, capitulation of the Netherlands and Belgium, advance to the Channel Coast. The exodus begins, seven million French leave the north and flee with their possessions to the south.

There's no milk down there.

The Maginot Line is bypassed on the south, German troops push through the gap near Sedan, break through the Ardennes on 14 May '40, tanks approach—the thrust into the heart, its beat audible from afar. One month later the caterpillar tanks forge into Paris and occupy the city without a fight. Finally, the armistice of 22 June in Compiègne, the beginning of the Occupation.

Lucky those who got away in time. Or who still know a place to run to. Paris's Golden Age is over. Henry Miller, already in June '39: That's the end of my long stay in the French paradise. Tonight I shall wait for Hitler's famous speech. The whole world sits on its arse and hopes for miracles.

Off to Greece, another five months to inhale Europe through ravenous nostrils, fill his lungs with light, pay a visit to Homer, say hello to Korfu, drink resinated Greek wine, gather like a bee the stuff of life for *The Colossus of Maroussi*, and then back to Brooklyn, his old home that opens its kind arms again to provide safe harbour for the rover. Enough sipping of quinquinas, little marcs, stouts and mandarin orange-lemon cocktails in his deluxe Paris exile. Enough *Amer Picon*. Enough bluster in Gertrude Stein's salon. Enough sparkling Picassos dazzling the eye. Golden years. Gone. In provocatively slow motion the tanks are rolling into the city once called the city of light and are extinguishing the light of those years.

Milk was everything to him. His meals consist almost exclusively of milk and bismuth powder. They are meant to tame the gushing of stomach acid. Wherever he can get milk, beautifully white, foaming milk, his pain can be soothed. The doctors have prescribed all sorts of medications, papaverine, histidine and whatever else they are called. Mademoiselle Garde picked them up for him, but initially he threw them out in a fury. He had faith only in the power of milk, with the divine condiment of bismuth powder. Heavenly white cow's milk, Sumerian moonshine, the only liquid that gives life. The only stream from heaven's udder.

He wants to remain in the occupied zone that includes Paris, and now finds himself a few map sections farther south. The city is the centre of his world; the Occupiers may have trampled it, but it still exists. Defiled, yes. Everyone felt it who crossed paths on the pavement with one of those jovially insolent gangs in their bulging grey uniforms or who heard the *übermenschen* bark on the Champ de Mars. Throughout the shafts and tunnels of the metro their noise reverberated, callous echoes of polished jackboots. Most noticeable, despite it all, a ghostly calm. Few Wehrmacht vehicles in the streets of the city corpse. Wan, dull, blind light. Standing legs akimbo on metro platforms, sitting triumphantly on fat arses in commuter trains. Giving the pale, slender legs of the woman on the seat across the smirking once-over. City corpse. Silence. Nightmare. The Occupation is invisible and omnipresent.

Black uniforms behind the doors of Doctor Knochen's SIPO-SD on the Avenue Foch, the Gestapo residing on the Rue Lauriston.

One day it would rise again, covered in scars, bent over from its losses, but still and once again desperately beautiful. Then the canvasses would return from the basements and tell of the brief thousand-year Reich.

There's no milk down there.

And the painter Chaim Soutine hopes that the whole nightmare will be gone one of these mornings. Gone like the time of his ulcer. While many clamber for the Mediterranean ports or crawl on all fours across the Pyrenees, wait for visas to escape to the United States, Palestine, Shanghai or South America, Soutine remains hidden in green-and-purple Champigny, not far from the Loire river and the town of Chinon. From there, hidden paths lead back to Paris, where he still knows doctors, and to the enchanted, sad kingdom of Montparnasse, its studios, cafes, scattered painters, to the merchants who still sell brushes, palettes or tubes. Who is demanding what prices. There they have his paint, his milk. No attempts whatsoever to cross the demarcation line at night. From Buenos Aires or Chicago, Paris would have seemed to have moved to a different planet. Why should he so quickly renounce a city that in 1913 was his life's one and only destination? And all those dreams he shared with Kiko and Krem in Minsk and Vilna of the art capital of the world? Already the Americans know of him; in December '35 the ARTS CLUB OF CHICAGO has a first exhibition; the poster reads PAINTINGS BY HAIM SOUTINE; they might have welcomed him with open arms. And the legendary Doctor Barnes from Merion, Pennsylvania, who in 1923 stepped into Zborowski's flat like a pharmaceutical thunder god—had he not prepared for Soutine's secret emigration by shipping his paintings? Part of him has long moved to Philadelphia. Wasn't each painting a colourful passport? The nightmare will pass. When it happens, he has to be here, for his leap back from the Loire to the Seine.

There's no milk down there.

Now everything is in short supply. Transportation routes are interrupted, the Occupiers requisition locomotives, wagons, lorries. Coal and electricity? Heating is limited to four hours a day and sometimes forbidden altogether. They survive on nothing. Rationing, that's life now, and people can't even get what is on the food ration cards. Request concerts that they sing for each other. Ersatz coffee made of turnip and chicory. Sugar is rare and sacred; ersatz reigns. Queues, shrunken opening hours.

They live on vegetables they must reluctantly appreciate. Roots and tubers with exotic names such as RUTABAGA and TOPINAMBUR torment them with their harsh flavours. The tuber called Swedish turnip makes them think of the North Pole. Swedes, goosefoot, Jerusalem artichokes, ersatz vegetables. A farmer in Champigny whom he and Marie-Berthe overhear cursing in his barnyard as they pass, They're going to choke us, those *boches*. I can't eat any more of that crap. They are going to choke us with it.

And with that he furiously hurls one of the tubers to the ground where it explodes like a pulpy grenade. War is vegetables. When he sees the two scurry past his farm gate, he becomes scared and falls silent. Smashed rutabaga smells of sabotage. Barter and theft, common in every village. Lucky he who has a rabbit hutch. But how he has to guard it. Day and night he has to lie in front of it.

And Soutine thinks of the hares, pheasants and turkeys he painted when he lived on the Rue du Saint-Gothard and in Le Blanc, of the drama of their deaths, their hides, their shimmering feathers, traces of blood. The colourful triumph of their deaths, blue hues in their black plumage, emerald green. And he thinks of those years of starvation in the Beehive, the herrings with the hungry forks. What bountiful, faraway meals!

Again and again the attacks; writhing, vomiting, racking. A diary of pain. Who counts the breaths. Pain has played a game with him, has mocked him. Sometimes it lasts for hours, then disappears all of a sudden, and the painter praises the milk and the bismuth powder, strokes his belly and gives thanks to it. Don't think you'll get rid of me that quickly!

Once, already in Champigny, he believes that the Occupiers have left and with them the gnawing pain in his belly. Suddenly peace and quiet, one couldn't even hear the tanks withdraw that night, no rattling caterpillars, no revving engines, no piercing orders, nothing. Overnight the Occupiers had vanished into thin air. An eerie silence blanketed the city that seemed strangely alien and must have been Paris. All signposts in German had been taken down, no more *ORTSLAZARETT*, no *WEHRWIRTSCHAFTS-RÜSTUNGSSTAB*, no word monsters like *INSTANDSETZUNGSWERKSTÄTTEN*, no Gestapo on the Rue Lauriston, no Doctor Knochen on the Avenue Foch, no barking goons doing drills on the Champ de Mars, no more German words in the streets. Nothing but silence over the city.

And Soutine jumps from his bed, suddenly understands everything, runs from the Villa Seurat down the Rue de la Tombe-Issoire, turns left and on to the church at Alésia, on along Denfert-Rochereau and past its astonished lion, and to the intersection at the Closerie des Lilas. Running feels immeasurably easy; he is amazed he can cover such distance without getting a stitch or starting to pant. Turns left, down the Boulevard du Montparnasse where all the cafes are packed—La Rotonde, Le Dôme, La Coupole—packed down to the last seat, and yet there is this incredible silence. No clinking glasses, no voices shouting across each other, no waiters rushing about. The cafes are as quiet as churches. All his old friends are there, including Modigliani, with a glass of gin (he too? the dreamers are the ones who are most astonished), and Kikoïne and Krémègne, Lipchitz, Zadkine, Kisling. They stare at Soutine in surprise, point their fingers at him and cry, We already know. Why didn't you get in touch earlier?

And Soutine is bewildered. Could he be the last one to find out? He cautiously touches his belly and realizes: his hurting stomach is also gone. The Occupiers seem to have taken it with them; it was in full retreat, decamped during the night, the war was won and the pain gone. Life could finally begin.

When Soutine wakes up, Ma-Be is still asleep next to him, softly snoring in their rickety bed, and he gets upset about his dream. He has always had bad dreams, dreams full of blame, of brothers bandying blows; dreams full of shame, inadequacy and doubt; of vanished painting materials and the compulsion to keep painting with his fingertips; dreams of collapsing studios made entirely of iron and glass, of fires in the Beehive.

And now this gorgeous, easy jog from the Villa Seurat to Montparnasse—how ridiculous it was, totally implausible. He should have guessed. He is upset he fell for the dream, is furious at the painters in the cafes who supposedly knew everything all along, probably also knew it was a false, deceptive dream.

And then, now fully awake, he imagines the painters splitting their sides laughing, pointing their fingers at him and raising their glasses to each other: He fell for it . . . ha ha ha . . . he really fell for it!

But that morning he really feels no pain; he touches his belly in search of it, but there's nothing. All he knows with depressing certainty is that this is not a permanent farewell. He is upset that he has recently been associating the Occupation with his ulcer. As if the *boches* had brought the ulcer with them. He knows only too well that the pain in his stomach had already started when Modigliani was still alive, that he had always been aware of it, in the Pyrenees and in Provence, in Céret and Cagnes and Vence, in the airy summer months near Chartres. His stomach ulcer had long kept him under occupation, even before anyone had any premonition of *L'OCCUPATION*.

But the Occupiers are still in the country, and for the last few weeks have been all over. On 8 November '42, the Americans land in North Africa; the Wehrmacht reaches the Mediterranean with Operation Attila; the black puppets in Vichy no longer have any say; there is no more demarcation line the painter could cross. His hideout in the country near the Loire is his green prison.

There's no milk down there.

They had heard about the invasion of North Africa on Radio Londres. And they aren't overly excited about it; war makes you suspicious. But only a few weeks later, in January '43, the BBC reports that the encircled troops in Stalingrad have capitulated. Wasn't at least that a sign you could trust?

Will the time of hideouts ever end? The devastation that carries everything away. 21 January '42. Wandering the streets, Marie-Berthe in front of a house entrance on the Boulevard Raspail, completely dishevelled, shivering with cold. She still has to quickly pick up a few potatoes for Soutine from an acquaintance. Then up the five flights of stairs in the Rue Littré, where Marie-Berthe's father lives, the old Aurenche. An indescribable mess. Several days' worth of dirty dishes. Hair, cigarette butts on the floor, ashes, balls of lint, scattered rubbish. The bed is unmade; the filthy floor has not been swept for ages. A few briquettes are smouldering in an iron basin. Barely a metre away, the room is cold as ice. Scarcity smothers the bourgeois comforts with a layer of ice, exhales bitterness.

Soutine only thaws out when he tells, grateful and happy, that the last time in that village he had painted a landscape with pigs. Enraptured by the animal's fabulous, unrestrained impurity. A young French doctor enters, gives him an injection so his stomach ulcer will be quiet for a while. He speaks calmly of the devastation caused by the Occupation that he faces day after day, the disintegrating bodies, the vermin, the effects of scarcity. Everything shrinks.

Suddenly doors are slammed. The old Aurenche enters the stage. A thunderstorm breaks, profanities and curses, kicks against the door. What a pigsty, can't you at least clean up your mess? The old Aurenche has had it. He throws them out. They will return, pleading, begging for shelter.

It has become dangerous to live on the Villa Seurat. The necessity again and again to change lodgings. Only a few are available. One night during the spring of '41 Ma-Be takes him to her old friends on the Rue des Plantes where she used to live with Max, to Marcel Laloë and his wife, the singer Olga Luchaire. Out of nowhere the bedraggled couple arrives on their doorstep; Ma-Be makes a strange gesture with her fingers, wordlessly asks to be let in. Barely inside, she gasps: You must hide him—the Gestapo is looking for him.

Ma-Be does not need to explain much; a spring mattress is quickly dropped on the floor in a side room, a raft on this river of misery that will not end. A mattress. Nothing else. He no longer paints. Everything wrests the brush from his hand, conspires with the pain fist that burrows in his stomach. Everything forms an alliance to prevent him: his pain and his cramps, the Occupiers and their humiliating decrees. For three months they live on the Rue des Plantes; Soutine drinks milk with bismuth powder and listens to Bach, to all of Olga's records, every one of them. The St Matthew Passion, no end of cantatas, the Goldberg Variations, the Art of the Fugue, everything. What good fortune to find refuge with a singer whose collection is her pride and joy. When the black disk no longer produces anything but the annoying scratchy sound, he lifts the arm and needle back to its thick rim.

Bach and milk, nothing else. For days. Music from the land of the Cyclopes, and milk from the land of the future. Big fat black disks, time and again placed on the turntable, and bitter, rationed milk. And there it was again, this unbelievable music that kept talking to itself with such determination as if nothing else existed, as if it could make everything else fall silent, every caterpillar tank, every boot's thud. Everything, except that spot in his stomach. That spot will not listen to music. Still, the sanctuary with its heavy black disks is a stroke of good fortune.

Each cantata an arrow against the black motorcycles and rattling caterpillars, ineffective weapons that ricochet around but are his only consolation. And he imagines that this music will still resonate when nothing will be left of the other but a pile of rusting junk.

Let Satan rage, rave, thunder.

But the line that follows Satan: The mighty God will make us unconquerable. From the gramophone words can be heard, a few of which he sometimes understands.

We had already sunk too low; the abyss sucked us fully in.

But understand how the barking Occupiers and this music can come from the same country, the same rivers—that he cannot. They are the same ears. The voices come from that country. Does Doctor Knochen never listen to Bach?

Look, look, it snaps, it breaks, it falls, whatever God's own mighty arm does not support.

And he listens for anything in that music that could yield a spark of life, could tame his despair. But: How doubt-filled is my hope, how wavering my anxious heart. Before the war, Henry Miller, his neighbour on the Villa Seurat, kept trying to lend him records of American jazz. He never gives up: Please, Monsieur Soutine, tell me what you'd like, I've got a lovely little collection upstairs. You are welcome to listen to anything you like. Upstairs, that's America, those black, sweaty magicians with their golden instruments.

Soutine politely refuses. For him, no other music exists. Bach. The end. Bach was like milk. And bismuth powder.

And in Clichy, at that weird doctor's who gave him the injection after he had collapsed on the pavement, they also talked about music. The doctor says, I think German music is parochial, clumsy, uncouth.

And the painter, But Bach is wonderful!

Long days without painting. Nothing but milk and Bach. Stretched out on his mattress, his eyes on the ceiling. In hiding with Bach. Who knows how near my ending is. And sometimes, after hours of these black disks, he hums a piece from his faraway childhood. It was the only thing he wanted to keep, those few songs he sang to himself, whereas he wanted to forget everything connected with Smilovichi. Only the little calf, he'd always keep that.

When Olga comes home, he picks her brains about Bach; she must tell him everything she knows. That he lost his mother at age nine, was orphaned at age fourteen. That his siblings died around him, one after the other, and that three of the seven children he had with Maria Barbara died shortly after birth; that seven of the thirteen children Anna Magdalena had given him he had to carry to their graves with his own music after they had already been joyful little creatures who had skipped on one leg, played hopscotch and praised the Lord. And still the Lord demanded to be praised. In truth, death always sat at Bach's table, followed him up to the gallery, wherever he went, sat next to him at the organ.

Soutine fights against an involuntary memory; he can't help but think of Sarah and Solomon's eleven children, of whom he was the second to last. He kept seeing Bach's children fly up to their merciless God, whom their father had to praise. Olga said, Of all the composers in the world, Bach was the one most besieged by death. Death vaingloriously considered himself a member of the family. Bach lived under a relentless occupation. Of the death of his first wife, Maria Barbara, he learnt upon returning from a work-related trip to Karlsbad. She was already buried. In tears he ran out to God's acre. So he had been here again. *Ich habe genug*, I have enough, he lets them sing. And: *Ich elender Mensch*, Wretched man that I am. And Soutine cannot get enough of the music, listens, his mouth agape.

Ah! This sweet comfort . . . refreshes my heart as well . . . that otherwise finds in anguish and pain . . . its endless suffering . . . and writhes like a worm . . . in its blood . . . I must live like a sheep . . . among a thousand vicious wolves . . . I am a truly lost lamb . . . and must submit to their rage . . . and cruelty . . .

But the days were endless for the man in hiding. A mattress jail. A life among the thousand wolves in the streets of Paris. The agony of feeling himself a burden to others, of taking up space, no matter their patience. Of lounging about, of not painting. For three months, he could step outside only occasionally at night. When Marc took the dog for a walk, he followed, slipping soundlessly past the concierge's loge and into the nightly Paris street. Some air at last, curfew air. Not a soul to be seen. They walked close to entrance gates and doorways, always prepared to step into the darkness inside in case someone were to come towards them in the street.

Oh, the power of concierges! A big eye for anything strange, a fine ear for echoes and steps. They heard all, saw all, cornered every mouse scuttling into a gateway. Professional honour demanded they not miss a thing occurring at the entrance, keep their watchful eye on all traffic. The caretaker becomes suspicious.

Do you have a guest staying with you, Monsieur Laloë?

Yes, a cousin of mine from up north is visiting; he'll continue his trip tomorrow.

Since the big exodus of May '40, that Stuka-perforated flight from the north when seven million people took to the road with billycans and mattresses, his reply could pass as an excuse. All points of the compass led through Paris. But nothing escapes the eye. Each time the false cousins with their dog ducked out late at night and returned shortly afterward, the concierge whipped back the large curtain of his glassed-in loge with a sharp swing and scrutinized the returnees. He wanted them to know he had picked up the scent; not a speck of dust would enter the building without his knowing. Non-resident visitors must register, their registration be submitted to the police, to be passed on further by the officers.

This can't go on; the strange-looking cousin has to go. Someplace with farmers, basket weavers, coopers, blacksmiths and innkeepers, but no concierges. In the summer of '41 they drive to the Loire valley without attracting attention. The Laloës write to a friend, Fernand Moulin, the veterinarian and stubborn mayor of Richelieu near Chinon. He undertakes to find shelter for the two refugees. He arranges to get them forged papers, stamped by the Prefecture of Tours, and recommends they move to Champigny-sur-Veude, a village nearby, and rent a room there.

Madame Coquerit sizes up the strangers. Folks like them arrive more often now that the north is occupied. She doesn't fancy the gentleman's accent. They are too dirty, a flea-ridden pair, what business do *clochards* from Paris have down here? And Ma-Be knows how to pick fights. Six times they change lodgings.

Once again he starts to work, with paints Marc sends his way. In the mornings, the astonished farmers see a ghost dart along their streets and country lanes, bent over and with long steps, as if trying to escape from his pain. He sneaks past the walls of their houses, his dirty shirt only partially tucked into his tattered trousers. Under his arm he carries a canvas he has tacked onto a board with drawing pins; he will paint trees, always trees, and a few children from the village. He groans: the land here is too flat, the trees too straight, I need crooked ones with branches and cracks. Alleyways, small hill towns and small mountain towns, all leaping upward, the same as way back in Céret and Cagnes. At least he has started to paint again.

On Christmas '42 the Laloës come to visit them in Champigny, in their new hideout, where no more records of Bach exist. He looks forward to seeing Olga, asks her again and again to sing cantatas for him. He listens to Bach again, in her voice. Blessed be the joy of recognition. Half a year later he will leave Chinon, a curled-up embryo in a hearse, in a slow-moving black womb, and no one knows how it will end. No more Bach to accompany him. Only Sertürner's poppy juice.

You can't live there; there's no milk down there.

Is it Ma-Be who sits next to him and dabs his forehead with the white cloth? Sometimes nodding off in despair, at other times opening her eyes wide with a start, as if someone had screamed to pull her from her sleep, as if sleep was improper for a person accompanying a living corpse to Paris for operation. Her white face is shadowed with dark bands. Street lights? Daylight? Her face is unrecognizable in this deceptive light, cut through by dark branches.

His eyes tremble; his lashes appear to pick up the movement of the grey, pleated curtains; suddenly a different companion seems to sit next to him in the hearse, his arms embracing his pulled-up legs. He sits slightly elevated as if on a wooden box or a stool. The painter has seen his face before, way back in his childhood. Impossible. Or is it? It is the old *rebbe* who murmurs and waves his hand in the deceptive light like an aggrieved puppet. His gappy set of teeth is visible; his jaws, which at first open and close several times soundlessly as though he were searching for a word.

No, Chaim.

And he shakes his head in disapproval.

No, and again: No.

Soutine knows all the reproaches, often heard them in his dreams in Minsk and in Vilna and even in Paris, after he had long escaped from the village. Everywhere the same raised voice, the rebukes, a litany like an old prayer that has long permeated his flesh and bones. This time the old man sounds even more incensed; everything seems to justify his indignation. It is too late for forgiveness.

I kept telling you. But you wouldn't listen, took off, ran away from us. It'll end badly for you, Chaim. Now you are on your way to His judgement; the Nameless One will know you did not listen to your father, not to your mother or your brothers, not to me. One must not paint. Painting is for idolaters who become intoxicated with the brightly painted statues of Baal and their filthy colours. It's an insult to the eye the way you smear paint on to our faces. He made us from mere clay, He alone, and breathed life into us.

Only the word he allowed, only the word. *Pirkei Avot* knows it, Chaim. With ten utterances the world was created. And then the book asks us, Why with ten when the world could have been created with a single utterance? The word alone creates the world, Chaim. Your paintbrush daubs a grotesque distortion and mockery of the world that He created. Can't you see how you have made everything crooked and twisted, landscapes and people, how everything trembles and teeters, as if the pain in your belly had done the painting, and not you? As if pain had created the world and not the Creator's calm eye and His utterance. As if an impious stomach ulcer had created the world! The creation must not be painted, Chaim, why should it? By the end of the week, the creation is there, having been made over six days and crowned with the *shabbos*, the day of rest for the Nameless One, who saw everything that He had made and, behold, it was very good. Have you forgotten the commandment? Forgotten the most important one, forgotten everything? You shall not make for yourself a graven image . . . or any likeness . . . which is in the heavens above . . . which is on the earth below . . . or which is in the water beneath the earth . . .

Does that sound so foreign to your ear? Do you no longer want to know any of it?

Lest you become corrupt . . . and make for yourselves . . . a graven image . . . the representation of any form . . . the likeness of male or female . . . of any beast that is on the earth . . . of any winged bird . . . that flies in the heaven . . . of anything that crawls on the ground . . . of any fish that is in the waters, beneath the earth . . .

And the old man mills the grain of his words with his jaws, bends over, lifts his head into the deceptive light, and is nothing but a rebuke. The painter continues to hear the *rebbe* sigh and exhort, but his small body seems to move away, shrink, merge with the pleats of the hearse's curtains.

But almost instantly he returns, his movements softer, almost feminine; he is turning into a woman. The painter does not recognize her. She could be one of several women, Garde, Ma-Be, or someone else? He does not recognize her. She is none of them.

What are you doing in this car? Who has brought you here? And why are you riding along? I have to get to my operation, don't you know?

He wants to say a word, but no word comes. The woman remains silent, merely nods and looks away. Then she gently runs her fingers over his arm, like Lannegrace; a tiny flash bursts into the hearse; relief sets in. The painter mutters as if with a mouthful of bread, as if chewing without teeth. She dribbles the poppy juice under his tongue. The pain in his belly dozes off.

He has heard the *rebbe*'s castigations hundreds of times in his dreams, has stammered muddled, incomprehensible excuses, has invoked Bezalel in the desert but has not once attempted to speak of his paintings, not a word. Has never pointed to his canvasses, never tried to explain why it had to turn out this way, why he couldn't help himself. He has turned the paintings around, leant them against the wall, deflected their gaze so no one could see them. Has explained nothing. Not in a letter. Not with a single word. There is no explanation for such paintings, you understand? The painting exists, nothing but the painting. And the word counts, but must not be spoken.

Moses is disappointed. Silent Soutine, that's what he will be called in the world of Montparnasse. *Muet comme une carpe*, mute like a carp.

All of a sudden he hears Henry Miller with his American French, his neighbour on the Villa Seurat.

I remember meeting Soutine for the first time in 1931. There was this fellow Louis Atlas, a New York business-man who traded in furs and had hired me as his ghost writer to write a series of articles about famous Jews in Paris. He paid me twenty-five francs per article published under his name in the Jewish magazines of New York. And so I finally got to meet Soutine in a cafe. I asked him questions for my article, his friends answered on his behalf, while he said not a single word during the whole interview but sat there lost in thought, wrapped up in cigarette smoke . . .

Smilovichi is tar. In his memory, people always make tar. His childhood is a shtetl with collapsing rotten shacks, rickety wooden walkways, stubborn dust and gurgling mud, depending on the season. Coughing children and hunger. In his memory, Smilovichi remains a grey place, a filthy hole. The overcast sky grey with smoke. Chagall will wave his arms and expound to their circle: The colours in that place are like the shoes of the people who live there. We all left because of that colour.

It was called Smilovichi, was located a few kilometres from Minsk, and the painter only wishes to forget the place. When in 1913 he lands in the Beehive on the Passage de Dantzig, where Chagall has arrived earlier and is dreaming of his childhood in Vitebsk, he flies into a wild rage. Chagall has dragged his shtetl all the way to Paris, all the houses, all the animals, the *rebbe*, the *shochet* and the matchmaker, the *moyel*, the sawmill and the horse traders. Everything Soutine thought he had left behind he faces again on a grey day in Paris—yes, even there days could be grey—in a blaze of colour in Chagall's honeycomb. Chagall hears cows bellow in the nearby slaughterhouses of Vaugirard and lifts them with his brush into the sky of Vitebsk. Then the war starts and Chagall returns to Russia to marry his fiancée Bella under that same sky. On his gurney Soutine wants to puke; nothing can drive him back there. No world war. Nothing.

To erase the place of his childhood in himself. No crumb, no straw, no smoke must be saved on the canvas. To cauterize the absence of childhood from memory. To burn the childhood canvas. The humiliation of having had a childhood at all in that poor excuse for a town that was none. He wants only the cities, Minsk and Vilna and the city of cities, where art nests in all its folds and corridors, on its boulevards and in its alleys. Living paintings everywhere; no return to the never-painted. The village was filth and pogrom, fear and trembling. In all his paintings, he wants to liberate himself from this Smilovichi; every brushstroke tries to brush it from memory.

Where is he now? Why would the childhood village have to drop into the hearse with him now of all times? The Pyrenees, Paris, then the Volma river, the area around Beresina that still remembers the French decomposing in spring mud. He is the family's whipping boy, the live sack everyone hits and kicks, the tenth and second-to-last child of his mother Sarah, who has grown weary from so many births. She floats through the rooms as if she were absent, tends to her duties like a ghost. She is silent. Always too worried, too exhausted to whisper some tenderness into their ears, as he has seen other mothers do. He is the tenth of eleven children, can you hear that, Doctor Bog, the second-to-last. Someone called us the hunger champions. The tenth and second-to-last. Divide a love by twelve, my good *Rebbe*. Her name is Sarah. She no longer speaks.

His first memory. Still in his cradle, he watches the play of light and shade on the wall as they tremble and take turns, dancing on white. He sees sunshine and shadow get entangled in the motionless, dusty curtains . . .

He wants to tell Ma-Be about it, or Mademoiselle Garde, or some third figure that briefly showed up in the hearse and whom he could not recognize. He slurs his speech as he gestures her to get close to his mouth. Bow down thine cool ear.

The house looks out on the market, and when the weather allows, his father Solomon, a tailor but mostly a mender of clothes, sits cross-legged like a Buddha in the lower window, where there is more light for the stiches, where the fine thread rises and plunges along his fingers into the fabric of a caftan. He hums, stitches, pulls; life is his thread. He sews mechanically, then pauses and turns a page without lifting his eyes . . . Rabbi Menachem Mendel of Vorki says a true Jew must master three things: upright kneeling, silent screaming, motionless dance. The customers come from the market and toss their trousers at him. Russians, Poles, Tatars, from the small village on the other side of the river.

When they hear of the pogroms that flare up in the tsarist empire and race through its shtetls, they know it will take but a spark and their featherbeds will be slashed and ripped open, their chests of drawers flipped over, their throats slit . . . They see blood spatter on feathers. They jump at names such as Kishinev, Gomel, Zhitomir, Berdichev, Nikolayev, Odessa. At night the gruesome names rattle through their dreams. After 1905, evermore names get added; after Bloody Sunday, the rallying cries of the Black Hundreds roar: *Beite Zhidov!* Slaughter the Yids!

Chagall is wrong if he thinks they left merely to escape from the grey smoke and the dirty shoes to look for colours. Just leave! Get away from the golem, away from ghosts looking to possess a living body and its voices, away from the dybbuks in the sinister stories of his childhood, keep only a few songs to hum, just to prove how far behind he has left all that, mocking reminders that that world has vanished. Yet he keeps painting children and the dreary misery of childhood where everything is but a dull promise that will never be kept. The faces of old men or women; rough, oversized hands clutching twisted toys, on tiny low chairs.

No one knows the path. No one will ever know. No one can know who the man is who rides in the hearse. There are only the paintings, those he has not shredded or burnt to ashes. No one knows him. No one can make him talk, least of all about his childhood. May his paintings talk, should they so choose. No one knows him. Only a single memory of his childhood exists.

I once watched . . . the *rebbe's* nephew . . . slice the neck of a goose . . . and drain the blood out of it . . . I wanted to scream . . . but his cheerful face . . . choked me . . . that scream . . . I still feel it here . . . when I was a child . . . I drew a portrait of my teacher . . . I tried . . . to rid myself of that scream . . . in vain . . . when I painted the carcass of the ox . . . it was still that same scream . . . that I wanted to rid myself of . . . I have yet to succeed . . .

He expects the sky to turn black, that very instant, and the Nameless One to hurl lightning bolts to stop the blade that cuts with a quick, practised move the neck of the goose, cuts through its flesh, its cracking vertebrae, its tough muscles. In a moment, He will stay Abraham's hand, already raised to kill his son Isaac. But nothing happens.

Everything remains calm that bright afternoon in Smilovichi, and the *shochet* gives him a jaunty smile. The blind horror on the child's face makes him laugh. The Nameless Himself seems to laugh at the killed goose, laugh at all the blades that cut through throats and at the warm blood gushing to the ground where the raspberry-red splashes combine with the grains of dust. He runs from the courtyard and hides in the cellar. He stays a long time down there afraid of the laughter, of the blade, of the blood from the goose's neck that drips on him, then rains and gradually fills the cellar, like God's laughter.

The morning of Yom Kippur, the Day of Atonement. The ritual of forgiveness, brought about by the goat that is driven into the desert to carry away all the community's sins. A rooster has to be bled on the threshold of the house to cleanse it of evil. The *shochet* holds the white rooster in his outstretched hand, head down, above the threshold. Then a sharp cut, the last twitching flap of the wings. The children stand next to it with wide-open eyes. Later, in Le Blanc, when he hangs a pheasant in the brick chimney big enough to hold a person, it is always the Day of Atonement that refuses to be forgotten. But there is no relief to be had.

Early on he starts to draw; each scrap of paper is another temptation; he draws quick sketches when he is by himself, his eyes every so often anxiously checking the door in case someone will suddenly enter, rip the scrap from his hand and give him a thrashing. He draws with charcoal on the walls of the stairwell to the cellar. That, too, gets him a beating. At night, when he is half-asleep, his big brothers shout into his ears: We mustn't do that! Don't you get it? It's not allowed.

And they pull his ears and rip the blanket off him. They put stinging nettles in his bed to stop him from drawing. They wake him in the middle of the night and box his ears.

He steals a knife from Sarah's kitchen, sells it in the market and spends the money on a coloured pencil. For two days he is locked in the cellar without bread or water. Two days without light. To exorcise the colour. He runs into the forest to escape from the scolding, hides until his hunger drives him back home. Again he gets a thrashing; it is the old drubbing ritual, his back and buttocks hurt, but he finally sits at a table and is given black bread, which he loves, and a jug of water, which he gulps down as greedily as an animal. Where does this scar come from, Doctor Bog? The scar on his chest comes from a broomstick his eldest brother shoved him with so fiercely he fell over backward.

He often skips *heder*, runs into the forest and grabs a short pine branch to draw on the sandy forest floor, hurriedly draws a face, crosses it out, draws another. He plunks himself on the ground, lies for hours, gazes at the sky; the black tips of the trees are waving from the left and from the right and from above. There is no orderliness in the sky. When you lie on your back and look at the sky, everything drifts upward; gravity is gone, everything floats up and the wind-blown branches dance along. His eyes are pulled upward, too. Only with difficulty do they find their way back.

For his brothers, it is like a prayer; they believe they please the Nameless One when they beat him. You shall not make for yourself a graven image! They want to beat that thirst out of of him. But he can no longer stop. His father runs to the *rebbe*, what shall I do, he's sick, doesn't want to become a cobbler or tailor, wants nothing but draw and doodle. He runs off into the forest. He is one big worry.

He is supposed to become an apprentice in Minsk with Solomon's brother-in-law, who also is a tailor. But he is too clumsy. Needle and thread? A whole life hanging by needle and thread? Not his. He gets shipped off to a photographer; at least he should learn how to retouch. But that's not it, either. Photos know nothing of his secret. But there is a certain Mr Krüger in Minsk, who teaches private lessons in drawing and promises success within three months. It must have been 1907, he's no longer sure. His friend Misha Kikoïne, the one from Gomel, is already there, too. They want to draw, nothing but draw.

The first money he ever has comes from compensation for injuries suffered. And is for travel. In the summer he returns from Minsk to his shtetl. There are rumours that even in synagogue he keeps doodling on odd bits of scrap. He draws the *rebbe* in prayer, whose sons fly into a wild rage and threaten him with furious gestures. He is barely back out in the street when one of them, the butcher, calls the boy over and takes him to the back of his store. Suddenly the butcher wraps his arm around the boy's neck and pushes down so hard he almost suffocates him, pressing him sideways against his own belly, and with the leather strap in his other hand lashes the boy's back, his buttocks, his legs; his red face is firmly pinned under the butcher's arm. He sees the butcher's blood-smeared apron and the dead, dripping animals hanging off the hooks and feels he has become one of them. Will the angry butcher slaughter him, too? He wants to scream but can't.

I don't want to drown in my own blood!

Even now in the hearse he can feel the chokehold around his neck. Then all of a sudden the arm lets go; he drops to the floor. He plays dead. He will learn to become a living corpse. The butcher picks him up with rough movements and flings him out into the dusty courtyard. His brothers find him, carry him home like a sack. For days he vomits the red juice; he has too many bruises to count. This time they went too far. His mother complains bitterly at the commissariat; oh, Sarah has suddenly found a voice! But they tell the young woman to get lost, the great tsar has nothing to do with it, some trivial business among the Yids, best to leave it to their own court to deal with the misdemeanour.

Twenty-five roubles indemnity and compensation for injuries suffered. You understand? Cash in hand.

With the money he leaves the village before dawn, and will never see Smilovichi again. The time has come. Kiko and he set out for Vilna; even Minsk is no longer an escape. They are sixteen and want nothing else. No prohibition on images can stop them, but the feeling of an ancient guilt stays with them forever. They know they are doing wrong. They experience a liberation, though not from shame. He will carry it all the way to Paris.

They move closer to the art capital of the world with each small step they take in Vilna's alleyways; it is 1910, and they attend the Academy of Fine Arts on Universitetskaya Street. For three years. It is there that they meet the third member of their group. His name is Pinchus Kremen; he comes from Zhaludak and has a permanently sad face. They are proud of their student uniforms, which already give them enormous importance. Their limping landlady, widow of a railwayman, charges ten kopeks per bed in a room for six students. Classes with Professor Rybakov are deadly boring, just a diversion from their true path, but they competitively practise for the city that will embrace the three painters with open arms. Paris is expecting them, they are certain. Paris can't wait to have them. They paint everything they see around them, dog carcasses, wretched courtyards, funerals; the lined, trembling faces and clenched hands of old women chandlers.

Play dead, he says to Kiko, who lies down on the floor. He covers him with a sheet and places candles around him. Pretend to be dead. But death won't let itself be painted; it is too early. It is good to start to practise early. You can't paint death. It won't let you, you understand? Try again later, with hares, pheasants, turkeys. Try to paint their deaths; that will lead you to it.

At night they sneak outside and discover the town in the pale light of its gas lamps. Sparse milky light in the night streets of Vilna. In spite of its filthy corners, deep puddles, scarred streets and walls reeking of saltpetre, it is a fore-taste of the one and only city that awaits them. They save every kopek for the big journey. They endlessly retouch pictures at the photographer's. Kremen is the first to leave, it is 1912, and the other two envy him, promise soon to join him. Kiko follows a few months later. This time, Soutine is not the second-to-last one.

It seems to him as if the hearse has taken off and now soars above Vilna, the Jerusalem of Lithuania, as if through its transparent undercarriage he sees Naberezhnaya Street, Arsenalskaya Street, Antokolskaya Street. Far below he sees Gediminas mountain and the castle of King Sigismund the Old, the Church of St Anne's, the Church of St Peter and St Paul, the Chapel of Ostra Brama, the Gate of Dawn; he does not feel dizzy but is astounded at how clearly he can recognize everything. The Moses statue on St Stanislaus Cathedral they often went to and stood before in silent awe. And he sees three miniscule art students walk through the streets, Kiko, Krem and Chaim. Oh, the confluence of Vilenka, Vilia and the Lithuanian Neris!

And finally the unforgettable moment when Doctor Rafelkes, to whose home the poor students are invited for dinner on Friday nights, presses the travel money into his hand. His young daughter has chosen a better catch, no longer responds to his shy glances. The greedy eater, who has no table manners and always sits in morose silence, has to be gently pushed out. His Russian passport gets issued in Vilna on 20 March 1913, according to the Julian calendar. Later he will often stroke it as one would a clever black cat.

Ma-Be, where are we going? To Raspberrytown? Paderborn? Smilovichi? Let's turn around. Let's not go there.

He moves his wrist, waves it in the empty space.

Better go back to Chinon, to Lannegrace, back any-where but not there. Not back to the place of birth. No path leads back there. We are no longer there, not even in our memory. No one is waiting there for anyone.

A BEEHIVE AT THE CENTRE
OF THE WORLD

How well he can see everything. He is still flying, sees far below a face pressed against a train window. It is his face. He sees eyes that avidly take in landscapes not seen before and now framed by the smoke streaming behind the locomotive. Once again he is twenty. He finally left Vilna in the spring of 1913. He travels down into his forty-nine years of life, is in transit for two days and two nights, stares at the lights dancing past him outside. Landscapes never seen before. The benches are hard; the smell of rank sweat and pungent urine from the nearby privy hangs in the air, but tremulous anticipation exhilarates him that everything will start anew, that the journey will at long last lead him to the place where the greatest miracles will embrace him.

He is hungry as never before. The few bread crusts of his provisions, the herring wrapped in newspaper, the pickled gherkins are soon devoured. His hand squeezes Krem's letter; he reads it over and over.

We live very poorly, but many speak Russian, Yiddish or Polish; you won't feel lost. There are no Cossacks here; they'll leave us in peace. We shall paint! The ramshackle palace we live in is marvellous and is called *La Ruche*.

Once again he arrives in Paris, in 1913, again twenty years old. In the beehive of his memories he travels up towards his arrival in the art capital of the world. Kovno, Berlin, Brussels, hurried changes of trains as if half-asleep; nothing counts but the destination. When he arrives at the Gare du Nord, he drops from the train like an egg from the halves of its shell. Around him, nothing but a world abuzz with new words, called Paris. He sets out right away, approaches pedestrians and stammers *La Russe*, points at Krem's letter and gets sent underground. Below are endless paths of a sour-smelling labyrinth, so he decides to climb back up into daylight and continue on foot.

Blind with exhaustion he rushes along the streets, stammering *La Russe*, again and again *La Russe*. A lost bee trying to find its hive. By chance he runs into a painter, who instantly understands.

La Russe? What Russian woman are you looking for? You mean *La Ruche*, don't you?

He shows him on the palm of his hand where he needs to go, not north to Le Bateau-Lavoir, where Picasso has built his nest; he crosses out the north. The palm's life line is the Seine, cutting the city in two, keep going south; he understands only *Momparnass* and *Voshirar*, ask again once you are there. He is not surprised to have run into a painter, thinks that everyone here is a painter; I've landed in the paradise of painting, whose streets may well be filthy, stink of urine and be covered in horse droppings, but this is it nevertheless. He wanders the streets for hours and by two in the morning stands before the wrought-iron gate.

In his mind Kiko and Krem have been in the city for an eternity even though their farewell in Vilna was only months earlier. They are way ahead. He who arrives a day earlier in paradise can be expelled that much less easily.

Krem and Kiko are delighted, Vilna is far away, they have reached their final destination. He can barely stay on his feet, but gets invited to the table in the middle of the night where five or six fellows have already taken their seats and scrutinize the newly arrived painter. He has hardly sat down when he dives into the bowl of boiled potatoes, polishes them off and asks for a piece of bread. The others haven't had time to help themselves and look sadly at one another.

It's the tapeworm, the newcomer stammers.

He never has enough to eat. Never have they seen such hunger. He will paint meals in this place, of bread and herrings, and will beseech them to make him feel full. Full at long last, full for once, full for good. Nevertheless, the feeling of hunger stays trapped on the canvas he has pleaded with to fill him. Skinny fish, a green onion, wrinkled apples, a soup pot and a tattered artichoke he has picked up from underneath a market stall. Never have they seen such hunger.

Where is he lying right now, on what ancient, stained mattress, two coils of which have poked through the fabric at an oblique angle, tossed on the pavement by the poorest of the poor in the Vaugirard quarter and carried by lice-infested painters to the Beehive? Or is he lying on a board that each evening is balanced between two chairs in Kiko's studio? On a bier, pushed into a hearse? It is all the same to him; he is twenty. He is off to another planet called Paris. He is expected for his operation.

The Beehive is a world unto itself, as he soon realizes when Krem tells him its story. It sounds like a fairy tale. The good-hearted sculptor Alfred Boucher emerges from a cloud in a carriage the Queen of Romania has given him as a token of her gratitude for the magnificent bust he has made of Her Majesty. He has heard about the artists' residences and their communal studios in Paris, and his dream knows what he wants. Finds himself a property among the dirt puddles of the Vaugirard neighbourhood. A wasteland of weeds, rubbish, debris. Nobody wants the junk; the land is cheap. Just having been decorated with the Grand Prix of the 1900 World's Fair, he buys up—with the exhibition barely dismantled—fragments of the Fair's pavilions that are being sold dirt cheap: beams, boards, iron scraps, window frames. Using what's left of the world, of the Woman's Pavilion, of the buildings of Peru and of British India, he builds his pitiful artists' paradise, which he names *La Ruche*, the Beehive. The pavilion of Bordeaux wines, whose metal scaffolding was constructed by Gustave Eiffel, forms its core.

The madman with that gigantic tower?

He's the one! The whole thing looks like one gigantic brick beehive, but its small studios that taper towards the central stairwell are called coffins by the painters.

Soutine listens to Krem, mouth wide open. Time will pass before he gets his own coffin.

Boucher likes to imagine the studios as a hive's honeycombs for artists united in the shared effort of producing the golden honey of art. In his pocket he lugs around a book he never wants to let go of: Maurice Maeterlinck's *The Life of the Bee*. Rent is so low it is almost non-existent. And the dens without water or gas, amid the smell of urine and turpentine, rotting wood and vomit, are his ideal of a city. It is dark in the Beehive; stinking garbage piles up in its hallways. Only candlelight and dim paraffin lamps. Sometimes the smell of butchered flesh and death wafts over from the nearby slaughterhouses. Tendrils of a sweetish, deathly aroma.

The paradise will always be squalid, you know. It's right next to the slaughterhouses. Soutine crashes with one inhabitant or another.

One month after his arrival in Boucher's strange beehive, in July of 1913, Kiko bursts into the studio, out of breath, at almost midnight. He swings his right arm with a conductor's flourish and exclaims: Chaim, get dressed, quickly, we are off to the opera!

The opera? Are you drunk? *Vypil, chto li?*

It is the eve of 14th of July, the French national holiday. Kiko has learnt from someone on the street that on this special day there's a performance of *Hamlet* free of charge. A sung *Hamlet*, a *Hamlet* opera. He can still remember how excited they were. That they revelled in it, as if intoxicated. They don't ask questions, they race off, he hasn't even changed out of his paint-stained rags. Line up at four in the morning for the free tickets, goof around on the pavement, cadge cigarettes, and someone lets them have a sip from his bottle of red wine. They feel no tiredness, as if waiting in itself were already a pleasure. The queue on the pavement looks endless; they'd never all fit into the Opéra.

Kiko is the one who utters it, the magic word. Kremen longs to forget even his childhood language, adds two French accents above his name and from now on wants to go solely by the name of Krémègne. All of a sudden they stand on the grand staircase with the huge lanterns on the left and the right, are aflutter at each stair that takes them closer to the box office, full of trepidation that the double window will be slammed shut: all tickets gone, try again next year. But no, they get their tickets, hold them in their hands like a precious treasure, and in memory the night before will merge with the great spectacle.

All he remembers now in the hearse is their blind excitement, the green and pink marble, the red velvet, the immense chandeliers. They tried to make out the history inscribed on a plaque, the good fortune of the thirty-five-year-old, utterly unrenowned architect Garnier, who came out on top of all his competitors; they recognize the name of Napoleon III, read *Second Empire*, and words that make no sense to them. They admire the arcades and statues on the temple's outside, and the dance they represent.

As if he had built the Opéra just for us, the greatest theatre in the world, a thousand storeys high, a new tower of Babel—and we're suddenly right at its centre!

When they enter the interior, they are blinded by the giant chandelier in the centre that weighs several tons; like thousands of stars it hangs above them before it finally goes dark. They experience *Hamlet* helplessly; they forget to breathe. When the performance is over, they slowly drift back outside with the trembling river of people, sit down on the pavement right next to the grand staircase, dazed with happiness and excitement; for minutes they cannot say a word. It is as if Paris had greeted them with this *Hamlet*, of which they understood not a word. As if the city had shaken their hands and welcomed them. It was he who said to Kiko: If we don't manage to accomplish something in this city, then we are truly good-for-nothings, do you understand? Completely useless.

And Kiko, suddenly serious: The Republic, Chaim, has invited us to see *Hamlet*. Do you understand? Here, there are no Cossacks. No looting mob. One day the pogroms will disappear from our dreams. But this evening will remain forever ours. There will never be pogroms in this city, you understand . . .

And in the hearse he jumps as he hears these prophecies. They are talking about Minsk and Vilna and laugh out loud—so far away seems that world that they escaped for good; they know there can never be a return. Even brick-red Vilna is now on a different planet. Everything over there seems pathetic compared to this *Hamlet*. A few fragments of songs have remained:

Maybe I only build castles in the air.
Maybe my God does not really exist.
In my dreams I feel lighter, in my dreams I feel better,
In my dreams, the sky is bluer than blue.

And Kiko, the lucky devil, will father two children with Rosa, will paint colourful landscapes, magnificent still lifes, radiant flowers and women, hymns to joy, to light. For years he will wear two odd, different-coloured shoes, one red, the other yellow, which he found at a flea market. Rosa will take in and feed Russian crackpots, nihilists, anarchists, rebels, who hand her baffling pamphlets; Kiko's studio will be kept under surveillance by the French police; in the Beehive, too, spies will keep an eye on those

Eastern European strangers. But the entry in his file will be mild: harmless Bolshevik.

And Soutine will become none of it, neither some family's Bolshevik nor an ambassador of joy, but will never leave behind the shame of having been born, or the label of a god-forsaken painter of misfortune. The issue is neither good fortune nor misfortune. The issue is colour or non-colour. White with blue and red streaks. Veronese green, turquoise, scarlet and the colour of blood. The death of colour that cannot die, and the resurrection of colour. The issue is colour applied too abundantly, colour that blisters or is hatched; bristling, tormented, triumphant colour.

Colour does not reconcile with reality; no, if you believe black and white to be harsh reality, and colour, paradise—no, everything is once again different. Irreconcilable colour bends to no law; it by itself is the rebellion against and the resurrection of matter and the flesh. Paradise will be white, will not know colour. But at what cost.

They had arrived, Hamlet had assigned them their seats, and they were ready to earn their stay in the centre of the world, to prove themselves worthy of the city. Even if the city suspiciously eyes them in the streets, these strangers, or at the police prefecture where he has to register, apply for his residence permit, stammering his few words. And at the grumbling market women on the Place de la

Convention. They loiter at the market, impatiently lie in wait for it to close so they can gather up vegetable scraps.

Hands off! They're for my rabbits! Has anyone invited you to help yourselves?

Tattered cabbage leaves, frozen potatoes, withered chard, which they use to boil their everlasting soup in the Beehive's big cast-iron pot. Sometimes one of them walks over to the slaughterhouses where bellowing can be heard from at night, begs for a bone with marrow to submerge in their broth or for a lump of mysteriously crimped entrails. They can get a can of bouillon for two sous, and whoever has one, as well as the patience to wait for the market to close, can survive another few days. Chagall teaches them how to cut up a herring: the head for the first day, the tail for the next, with a bread crust and a glass of tea.

In the Beehive they are called the Russian colony. Archipenko, Lipchitz, Zadkine, Chagall, Dobrinksy, Kikoïne, Krémègne, Soutine. At the shout of *Dîner russe!* they assemble for the feast. Sometimes they invite the French, too, even if they are Cubists: Léger, come eat Rrrrussian foods.

What was that weirdly tough, stringy meat they boiled for hours in a pot with strong, home-made rotgut vodka? Cat meat, cut small, cat fricassee. Divine cat meat. It stank and burnt your throat. No cat was safe from them; they cleaned out the Montparnasse neighbourhood all the way to its southern periphery. And the rats and mice who enjoy life in the Beehive love the Russian *dîners*. Only one cat was taboo. Residing at the entrance to the Beehive, Madame Segondet, its big, short-sighted concierge, is good-natured and passes out a bowl of soup if the newcomer looks starving. Her husband nails damp boards into dens that make up new studios in the wasteland of Vaugirard. Madame Segondet's tabby enjoys eternal life.

At night he works with Kiko as a freight handler for a few sous at the Montparnasse station. They unload entire carriages of seafood from Bretagne. They so reek of fish that Madame Segondet's cat amorously brushes against their legs when, exhausted, they return to the Beehive in the early morning. They paint signs for the automobile exhibition, work for Renault in Billancourt at its ravenous conveyor belt.

But all of a sudden the world is cleft apart. General mobilization. White sheets of paper that rain down on Montparnasse. Soutine receives his residence permit on 4 August 1914, the day war is declared. They volunteer to dig trenches, want to give back to France for having taken them in. And are soon sent home for being too weak.

No one buys their paintings, a state that continues for years. They remain a bunch of unkempt Russians, Poles, Jews who fled the pogroms, obsessed with painting in spite of the commandment against it, spared homelessness thanks only to the blessed Boucher. Now that war has broken out, people eye them that much more suspiciously when they hang out in the cheap cafes. Just imagine, our boys are at the front while this trash sips its *café crème*.

People spit in front of their paintings. The angel Boucher had dreamt of the emergence of a new academy, but they don't want to become out-and-out idiots or paint in academic style. Boucher lets them be, promotes them when their paintings get slandered as revolting, horrible daubery. All they want is to survive, bear the hunger and the bees' wretchedness, pull through. One day their path will lead them out of this squalor, and once they have managed to reach the Cité Falguière, they will have completed the first lap. Those who can afford it abandon the utopian beehive as fast as their legs will carry them and leave behind, saddened, the blessed Boucher. O you jumping lice, who has invented you?

Then there is Indenbaum, whom everyone calls the good Samaritan. Even now in the hearse Soutine sees his reproachful face and hears his plaintive voice:

I wanted to help Soutine, too, but he was insufferable. Each time I bought a painting from him, he came up with some excuse to borrow it back and then sold it to someone else. Seven times he played that comedy and I let him fool me. One afternoon, at La Rotonde, he desperately wanted me to give him thirty francs. At the time, that was a lot of money for me. I left him standing, but he ran after me all the way towards *La Ruche*, repeating his stupid litany:

Give me thirty francs, give me thirty francs, give me thirty francs, hey, hey, hey!

When we got to the Place de la Convention, I bought two herrings and said to him: Now you are going to paint a *nature morte*. He went up to his studio and two hours later brought me a little painting of three fish on a plate with a fork. He hadn't invented the third one but had rearranged the second one. I gave him thirty francs and put his painting up on my wall with four drawing pins. Three days later he asked me to lend him the picture. Once again I said, all right, only to discover it at a Russian émigré's, a photographer. The scoundrel wouldn't stick a plate in his camera, and his customers who had paid in advance never got to see their portraits. Delewski was hiding a small painting behind his back.

Do you want it?

It's already mine.

I had recognized Soutine's herrings.

He's just sold it to me, wanted five francs, but all I gave him was three.

This time I swore to myself never again to buy anything from Soutine.

Indenbaum walks away, shaking his head. But they no longer stop, those voices; they enter him, whisper, scream into his ear, muffled only by the gentleness of Sertürner's poppy juice. He pulls his head deeper between his shoulder blades so as not to hear the furious voices.

A Russian peasant with a flat face! Only the nose sticks out like a fleshy cube with flared nostrils! His bulging fat lips! The spittle in the corners of his mouth! The rare time he smiles, he bares his gross, greenish teeth! The brute! Unwashed oaf with no manners! A ragged palette on legs, always splattered with paint! What a hideous sing-song voice! Looks like he always stares into space the way dogs do! Loudly slurps water from a bottle! Eats with his fingers, rips his food apart with bared teeth!

He wants to slam his hands against his ears but cannot move them. No matter whose voices they are that whisper at him in outrage or scream at him in fury in the black Citroën, they all sneer at him and heap accusations upon him.

Worthless friend! Perfidy personified! Defiler of your own paintings! Apostate! Violator of the prohibition against images! Mute blasphemer of God's law!

Yes, that too. An outsider, among both his own kind and among other outsiders. The startled, suspicious look on his face; the tormented, dark, burning eyes. Always getting caught out at being still alive. Suspicious of himself and of his paintings, which endlessly betray him. A prisoner in the dungeon of his body who bangs against the walls and will be released only in his final flight over the Montparnasse Cemetery.

No one knows the path. No one will ever know. No one can know who the man is who rides in the hearse. There are only the paintings, and only those he has not slashed or burnt to ashes. No one knows him. The ravenous man who leaves not a crumb for others. The klutz with the delicate white fingers whose tips gently touch the corners of his mouth. The eternal ingrate who drives all his friends to bitter resentment. Who leaves nothing but ruinous chaos in his wake and will not return. No one understands him, no one. A ray, standing upright, lost cartilaginous creature, dead pheasant, ox skeleton!

Nothing exists but the frightful singularity of life. But the multitude of voices intersecting in this beehive, the embarrassment of dreams, the false memories. Read this, dear sons! Life is unique. Half is invented, the other half made up to match. The dreadful fear of going missing, of suddenly disappearing. When will he have his conversations with Doctor Bog? When will Doctor Livorno recite the entire Book of Job for him? Where did it end up, that twice-sold icon of hunger?

He has by now escaped from the Beehive, has arrived in the Cité Falguière, in that studio with tattered wallpaper. He rages against the walls, which he wants to slash open, too; something's got to be hiding behind them, the ultimate secret of painting, the absolute image that can never be destroyed, not even with knife blades.

One woman visitor gets a fright when he calls himself the murderer of his paintings.

Whatever you see here is worth nothing, is just muck, yet is still better than the paintings by Modigliani, Chagall and Krémègne. One day I will murder my paintings, but they are too cowardly to do the same to theirs.

Everything murmurs into the ear of the painter's living corpse in the Citroën as it slowly rolls towards Paris: Traitor! Defiler of your own paintings!

The *rebbe* and Zbo, the disappointed friends—they all rebuke him. Never have they seen such hunger. And Soutine runs out of the house in a fury.

Suddenly the hearse stops. The painter opens his eyes. Gloomy light, the curtains move, there must be a breeze. Where is Marie-Berthe? A moment ago she wiped his brow with a damp cloth, opened the little bottle of Sertürner's tincture and dribbled a few soft drops on his tongue, as Lannegrace had instructed.

Marie-Berthe has disappeared. He is still on his gurney in the hearse. The two drivers are still there. He slightly bends forward towards them. He realizes it is other men who smile at him. Where are the right ones, the two undertakers, the young one and the chubby one? Are you members of the Chevra Kadisha, do you belong to the Sacred Fellowship? They merely smile.

The hearse has stopped. His ear strains listening to the sounds. They are encircled. Outside, motorcycles clatter, dogs bark furiously. Have they tracked us down, have we landed right in front of their machine guns on these obscure, narrow country roads?

The backdoor is jerked open. A chieftain clad in black leather glances inside, flashing and mute; triumphantly he slams the door shut again. When the door was pulled open, the painter caught sight of a belt buckle in the centre. It showed an eagle. And sharply embossed, fixed with a metal seal: GOTT MIT UNS, God with us.

It's him! We've got him!

The pack howls. Do the intruders speak the Occupiers' German or the militia's French? The painter's corpse struggles to find out. He strains to catch a few snippets, but all he hears is hissing and rolling gutturals, croaky stuttering and a commanding tone, yowls and whines, rattling and clicking. This was not German; he had heard enough of it in Vilna to know. Were they the *Gitlerovtsy*? Darnand's militias? Russian Black Hundreds that had come all the way to this place?

He figures he can hear 'quick march!' but no, that's not it. Then fierce barks, yelps, persistent and furious, as if someone had tossed part of the prey to the hounds, who cannot decide whether to noisily relish the scraps or bewail the end of the hunt. Either way, there was the smell of wet dog fur and the sweat of a thousand dogs.

A horde of tall men in black leather—this the painter can clearly discern through the now glassy sides of the hearse. Has the poppy juice drawn them here? No, those were real noises and jumbled spoken sounds; the hearse was full of them. The leather men bare their teeth and roar at the hearse.

You won't get away from us that easily!

Their faces are full of scars and cuts. Weird metal pieces have pierced their skin, and their bulging eyebrows, lips and nostrils are deformed. Atrocious tattoos climb all the way to their necks.

Vikings, Normans! flashes through the painter's mind, and he remembers a Sunday he came across a book at the *bouquinistes* along the Seine whose illustrations made him shudder. So that's what they looked like, he thought that Sunday. They had sailed up the Seine and razed everything, desecrated churches, massacred the peasants. No, these men here are no Vikings, but they look, he thinks, somehow northern and cold. They have hideously gaping jaws that are rent open by their language, and they must have metal joints because their movements are abrupt and angular. Their voices are piercing, their sounds no longer human.

The motorcycles roar into life, boots kick against asphalt, and soon the black Citroën continues, surrounded by several engines. The wheat fields grow black; crows obscure the golden straw, the stubble where nothing is left to glean. Not one comprehensible word has been uttered.

How long does the journey take? He cannot tell. Minutes or hours later they arrive at a black gate that slides on a track and is hastily opened by swarming guards. He has been expected. The black raven rolls across the track, judders. The wolves in their leather coats try to enter but are shoved back; rifle butts bang into knees. Hooded men in white come running with a stretcher from a long white building that looks like some hangar or factory. They remind him of the Michelin Man made of nothing but tyres. They run up to the hearse, reach for the painter, move him from his gurney onto their stretcher. They carry him towards the white hangar.

The black mob must remain outside the sliding gate, howling and foaming at the mouth, baring their wolf fangs, shaking their fists. From his stretcher the painter can see one of them lift his leg and piss on the iron bars; he sees the sharp jet before white racers dive to carry him through several white sliding doors deeper and deeper into the hangar whose ceiling is coming down. What is this—a clinic, a hangar, a factory? Everything is white, the rushing men with their stretcher, the silent figures with white caps that scurry past. The black-leathered accomplices are locked outside the sliding gate.

White, white at last!

Where did he end up? He lies in a clean white bed, with a white sheet folded back over his chest. His hands rest on an immaculate white blanket. White all around him, nothing but white. White light from a blinding light bulb on the ceiling. No other patient next to him, only white walls. Have days passed, weeks, seconds?

He tries to remember, but he is not where his memories are. Where is he? Where he is.

O music of cones and colour receptors! The combination of equal intensities in the red, green and blue cones steers his rapt eye straight towards the white paradise. O colour of immortality and infinity, colour of enlightenment and holiness! Doctor Bog will explain it to him.

The painter had searched for the absolute colour, had cherished it, though never in its pure state, never unalloyed. Purity has no appeal for him. He multiplies the colours he mixes in; conjures up bloody, fine streaks and fibres, arcs and delicate loops, tiny purple streams, small blue veins, as if every white dress were a magnificent skin. It reminds him gently of the beloved colour of milk.

The collar, the cuffs of the village idiot? The surplice of the altar boy, the jackets of the pastry chefs from Céret and Cagnes, the ceremonial dress of the little communicant? His Woman Bathing, the gathered-up white chemises that have absorbed the reflections of the water and each and every colour? That most colourful admixture of absolute colour! Is there not a painting by Rembrandt that he particularly loves and enviously strives to emulate? Hendrickje, bathing in a stream. A woman stepping into water and raising her white dress, exposing her thighs.

Nothing but heavenly impure rivulets in the colour of purity. Nothing but glorious impurity in the absolute colour. His dark paintings secretly rejoice in the bruised white.

What is black? The non-colour, the darkest colour that absorbs all rays of light and reflects none. The black, snaring non-colour we have to move into. The colour that reigns in the dark stomach.

What is white? The brightest colour, reflecting all visible colours and giving off the most rays of light. The comprehensive colour, the unalloyed absolute colour containing all others. The colour of the sky in front of the blue. Of a sky that is but a big, bloated white stomach.

But here—in a hangar, a clinic?—everything is different. A pure, blinding, cold white is all that surrounds him, which surprises him. He has slid into a white shoebox.

BELYI RAI! BELYI RAI! someone yells into his ear.

He was carried into a room; many hands reached under his body, lifted him off the stretcher and gently lowered him onto a white hospital bed. He allowed it to happen and sank into a deep sleep. Memory tells him that this was no sleep but retribution, a gentle revenge.

And he sees the place on the Creuse River, the house Zborowski had rented for the summers of 1926 and 1927 to lure the painter. The town was called Le Blanc. He marvels at the name. So, White is actually a town and has withdrawn to this place. He feels well there, and in a shed paints strung-up pheasants, turkeys, guinea fowl. Paulette Jourdain, Zbo's assistant, has to track down the most beautiful specimens the farmers have, accompanying him to the markets and farmsteads. Blue neck feathers enrapture him.

An extraordinarily beautiful hen!

The farmers turn away and wave their hands in front of their eyes to signal to the other vendors their customer's mental state. The painter has eyes only for the magnificent hen with the bluish neck feathers.

The town with white in its name had given him a foretaste of paradise. It was chock-full of strung-up dead pheasants he obsessively captured on his canvasses. Their glorious, colourful, feathery deaths. Their last triumph, their deadly plumage, the fleeting brilliance of their stunning colours.

In Paris, a Russian who had arrived from Berlin slipped him a sheet of paper after they had started talking in La Rotonde. Actually, it was only the Russian who talked; Soutine was either mute, as usual, or grunted, grumbled and ground out his objections through a cloud of cigarette smoke. The painter would have liked to have talked about the impossibility of pure white. White is not white, he wanted to say but cannot seem to. He wants no white ever to be left white, do you understand? Wants to mark purity with impurity and soil it, make it come alive. Pure white is destructive, hostile to life; it is the ultimate nothingness. The vein of colour is rebellion.

The Russian did not give up, pushed the poem across the cafe table; Soutine is to read it, to get the point.

Paradise . . . a wide, empty land . . . covered in deep snow . . . phantom of a white sky . . . silence and whiteness . . . there, above a downy lake . . . breathing the sweetness of the cold . . . shines the while soul . . . of the young forest . . . there I will feel bliss . . . in the sparkling of the frozen net . . . I will glide on . . . entranced by the eternal white . . . and like an arrow from beneath branches . . . fly into space . . . on brilliant, light skis . . . float down from white mountains . . .

The Russian stood up abruptly, almost yelled at the painter and left the cafe with a shout: BELYI RAI! BELYI RAI!

He lies there and tries to think but can't form a clear thought. Is he in Le Blanc? Paradise is a wide, empty land. The Pyrenees of his memory, too, are now a biblical landscape covered in deep snow. Hip-high snow, tall as summer wheat.

Do days exist here? Either way, they pass without his noticing a change in light. No one shows up, no doctor, no interrogation officer. Only a pale nurse scurries in, brings him food. He is still hungry, but he no longer ravenously devours his food as he once did in the Beehive. He accepts his meals gratefully and is too shy to speak to her, to ask her questions.

He has never known how to approach women, pay compliments, charm them. He swallows his words, gets muddled, remains doggedly silent. Once he stammered into the bewildered face of a maid in Clamart: Your hands are as delicate . . . as plates.

And he is astonished by the meals. Pale noodles, white cream sauce, strewn with snowflakes of cheese, white chard, white pike dumplings, cauliflower, white asparagus, Béchamel sauce, white veal, cream cheese, cloud-like milk soups, rice pudding. White peas. And no carrots. They had removed the yoke from the egg.

But no, that's not all. One day—but do days exist here?—he is given white strawberries, such dainty little fruit; incredulous, he gazes at the tiny scars in their white skins.

May he get out of bed? Apparently not.

Once again he is in the centre of the world, albeit on its margin, in the world that he watches from a quiet corner of La Rotonde and in which he lies in ambush for a generous patron to treat him to a *café crème*. The rest of the universe was irrelevant; the world existed only here, among those few streets and the three cafes where the most significant things unfolded. Three temples in this holy district: Le Dôme, La Rotonde and La Coupole. An enraptured chronicler or tipsy evangelist offers his thundering truth and Soutine pricks up his ears: Anyone who has ever set foot in our cafe is forever infected with what we painters call the plague of Montparnasse. Neither syphilis nor any other disease, but something much worse: an epidemic of all-consuming longing for what right now is the most interesting place in the world.

Not ferretting out a generous patron does not spell the end of the felicity. In his mind's eye he sees Libion, La Rotonde's silently gesturing landlord with his quivering moustache, sitting behind the bar. Even during the First War, this temple wafting with the aroma of coffee affected normalcy. Soutine quickly draws a few snuffles of air in through his nostrils. O those paradises of *café crème*! May others gush about quinquinas, mandarin orange-lemon cocktails, Amer Picon, Curaçao and Gin Fizz, Soutine's stomach demands only one drink: a soothing coffee with foamed milk. For hours one can sit behind a cup, stir the emptiness and warm oneself at the stove. Libion, Libion! Admittedly, sometimes half a dozen police on bicycles show up, surround the temple and roar: Raid!

La Rotonde is the stronghold of the Russian revolutionaries, a small Bolshevik island, a narrow Eldorado for deserters and pacifists who don't want to croak in the trenches. Opponents of the war are stigmatized as defeatists, but in La Rotonde they can freely curse the war. Libion sticks a few patriotic posters on his walls, as an immunization of sorts.

Yet already the next war in the long chain has arrived. Once again the painter sees himself at the margins of the centre of the world; he is heading somewhere, in the year of 1943. The great epoch has long passed; now even the centre is full of sorrow, even the centre is an occupied place in an occupied country, and every second person—as everyone knows—is an informer or a carelessly camouflaged Gestapo man. Paris seems to be their favourite breeding ground.

The centre has become a mere dream from which the painter is absent. He has become invisible; the Gestapo guys can snoop around the corners of La Rotonde all they like. Soutine now lies in the white paradise and there, too, is at the margin, just as he used to be at his customary place in the world of Montparnasse.

How many faces have shown up in these cafes, how many strange figures from Chile, Japan or Lithuania have come to these small, noisy temples, attracted by the fragrance of coffee and the bitter juices of anise and vermouth. How many conversations, how much jealousy and how many oaths of vengeance has he overheard without saying a word.

One such conversation he has always remembered. As always, he is in his corner lying in wait for the generous miracle patron. The corner means safety; having no one behind his back reassures him. Some poet whose name he has forgotten or who is still to be born advises sleeping with one's head in a corner because there it is harder for one to swing an axe and hack the sleeper to pieces. Hence: square the circle. Those who came in horse-drawn carriages from Minsk and slashed first featherbeds and then throats, triggered remarkable reflexes in their victims. Animal flight instincts, glances quick as lightning out of the corner of one's squinting eyes, jumping power (jump from the window to stand a fighting chance!), nimbleness, zigzagging—the divine art of a hunted hare.

The taciturn man hears more because his voice does not need to drown out that of another. The silent man is all ears. His place is on the margin of the centre of the world. All of a sudden three men entered, glanced around, briefly looked for the right spot and sat down at the next table.

The painter tries to make out what they are talking about. One moment they speak French, the next, German. Occasionally his Yiddish lets him understand the odd word. Hadn't some joker in Vilna claimed that German actually derived from Yiddish? One of the men must be French; the other two may have come from the collapsed Austro-Hungarian Empire, from Galicia or Bukovina?

The waiters flutter hither and thither like butterflies, clink glasses and cups, and shout imperious orders above people's heads that the man behind the bar receives wordlessly and obediently. The painter has ears only for the conversation at the next table from which he catches the recurring word 'Farben'. They are talking about some connection between colour and pain. The man with the local accent exclaims, Wonderful! In French colour and pain are so close. And several times he rolls his *bon mot* around in his mouth.

Just listen to it: *couleur* and *douleur*.

The conversation is about some letter that appears to have been written in German and that the local man is to translate into French. A letter from an exile, or from an exile who has returned home. Apparently the letter is about a certain painter, and he would have loved to know whom. Painters are curious and jealous creatures because for them there is always only one in any given generation. You may bow before the Old Masters; you may venerate a Rembrandt or Courbet or Chardin, but when it comes to the living, one word about another painter is one too many.

He cannot catch the letter's author, only some 'Tal' comes up repeatedly and taunts him, nor can he figure out the identity of the painter whose name may not have been mentioned anyway. One of the two German speakers reads out a sentence: *Warum sollten nicht die Farben Brüder der Schmerzen sein, da diese wie jene uns ins Ewige ziehen?* And why shouldn't colours be the brothers of pains since both the one and the other pull us into eternity?

The man with the French accent proposes to turn the brothers into sisters: *Et pourquoi les couleurs ne seraient-elles pas les sœurs des douleurs, puisque l'une et l'autre nous attirent dans l'éternel?*

At that point a glass is dropped and crashes on the floor; a fierce curse cuts through the sudden, seconds-long silence; the thread of the conversation is briefly inter-rupted, and the painter has to concentrate if he wants to overhear any more of the increasingly quiet conversation. Speak up, will you, Soutine wants to shout even now from his white sheets, but his tongue is absent.

If in French *couleur* and *douleur*, colour and pain, lie so close to each other, one of the three throws in, what do you think of the strange proximity of *Farben* and *Narben*, colours and scars, in German? While colourful wounds in the one language are painfully visible and present, throb in one's skin and in the fabric of language, they tell in the other language of past injuries, closed-over wounds, of subsequent memories of pain.

The painter jumps. For in his language, colours rhyme with yet another word.

Vi an ofene vund . . . Loz mikh nit azoy fil mol shtarbn vi der harbst in toyznt farbn.

Soutine mumbles something that sounds like the smacking of lips on the brim of a cup. Like an open wound . . . Do not let me die as many times as autumn in its thousand colours. Listening, he converses silently with himself. Silence is coffee with milk. It soothes his ulcers. He understood barely half of it. But *couleur* and *douleur* he instantly grasped, as if they were signals just for him. Colours and pains are sisters, of course they are. They are incurable, even when colours eventually turn into scars.

No, colour has to embody them simultaneously, both the throbbing pain and the lasting scar. And in the end, the dying. Everything leaves behind scars, do you understand, leaves visible traces. Everything. Immaculate bodies may have existed in Greek statues, in ancient Egypt, or with Modigliani. For Soutine, there are no immaculate bodies, only mutilated, gnarled, battered ones. Nothing in life has remained whole; nothing can be restored. These are the only principles he will admit to. He makes colours rub against each other, chafe, adore, damn and curse each other, elevate and cut each other down, until they stammeringly release their scarred blessing.

The painter at long last and against his habit of dogged silence wants to turn to the right and approach the three with a surprised shout, but it is too late. The conversation has suddenly been wound up, the letter of the returned exile been tucked away, and the three men rise and don their hats.

Where might they be now? He has no idea. How could he know. He painfully, slowly, tilts back his head, believes briefly that he still rolls along in the hearse and wants to whisper at the two drivers: Can't you call those three back? Can't they sit down just one more time? I didn't even get the half of it. Too much noise in here, too much clinking of glass.

But his tongue is not in its place, can't be raised, can't be dropped. If there is a tongue left at all. No whispers from the centre of the world penetrate this place. Montparnasse has fallen silent. And on its margin are muteness and silence and a ride towards operation in Paris.

Soutine mumbles as he talks with himself. He has just been at the centre of the world. Now he lies under his white sheet and does not realize he is being watched. The white door has an opening with a slider that can be pushed up from the outside. There, a pair of eyes awaits, has been observing him for some time. Softly the slider is lowered, and the opening in the door closes. He is again completely and utterly alone in his white paradise.

On one of his trips to the capital, when his feet take him almost automatically to the intersection of the Boulevard Raspail and the Boulevard Montparnasse, right across from La Rotonde, someone comes his way, recognizes him and hisses: *A mentsh on glick is a toyter mentsh!* An unlucky person is a dead person!

Soutine, what are you doing here, are you mad? Scram! The Gestapo has already bagged dozens of painters. The place is teeming with spies. Why on earth did you come here?

A glick ahf dir! Good luck to you!

And he spits on the pavement as if in a coded greeting. And Soutine turns on his heel, leaves without haste, his big, dark-blue hat pulled even farther over his forehead, his head deeper between his shoulders. Uses only side streets.

Those Barclay hats! Soutine has loved them since pharmacist Barnes with his dollars cured Zbo and him of starvation. The elegant blue hat is magic; Soutine is convinced it makes him invisible. In the past, everything was different. When Zbo nudged the ragged painter to wear a hat so as to appear more respectable in front of patrons, he had grumbled: I can't always walk around looking like the tsar!

He knows himself invisible on these dangerous trips to Paris. Clutching his forged papers in his pocket, he briskly walks to the doctor and then off to his secret lodgings. Superstitious, he avoids the big intersections where the Occupiers have planted their signposts, staking claim to the capital's territory with their German word monstrosities. The signs spatter the imperious phonetics of a consonantal eruption: a black, intimidating curse.

He makes a diversion around the Sixteenth Arrondissement, where the Occupiers have requisitioned many buildings: the Hôtel Majestic on the Avenue Kléber, seat of the Military Command; and the gorgeous Haussmann palaces on the Avenue Foch, where SIPO, the Security Police, and SD, the Security Service, reside, and on the Rue Lauriston, where the Gestapo has its headquarters. The people of Paris soon experience firsthand who has taken up which quarters where. The SS chiefs have installed themselves on the Avenue Foch: Oberg, the butcher of Paris, responsible for the execution of hostages and for deportations; Lischka, SS Lieutenant Colonel and SIPO-SD chief; and Doctor Knochen. Doctor Knochen? Yes. Senior Commander of the Security Police and the Security Service. Doctor Knochen? Yes, responsible for . . .

He no longer visits the Laloës so as not to endanger them. Their suspicious concierge still glowers at him in his dreams. The hat has become a necessity. He goes to Marie-Berthe's father on the Rue Littré in the Sixth Arrondissement, a side street of the Rue de Rennes, but takes diversions and avoids the cafes where someone might recognize him, might give him away with a greeting.

Old Aurenche, a retired tax official, is less conspicuous than the painters. Quietly he opens his door, says nothing, nods and with a gruff gesture points the painter towards the sofa. Neither says a word. His daughter's acquaintances have always struck him as dubious. Having put his doctor's visit behind him, the next morning the invisible man sneaks to the Montparnasse station and takes the train in the direction of Tours. Paris meant nothing more than a doctor's visit and new supplies of papaverine and bismuth powder.

Since 20 October '40, he has been registered in the Tulard files as *Juif*. His number is 35702. When he leaves the sub- prefecture of his arrondissement with his registration card, he pokes fun at the botched stamp on his photograph, telling Chana Orloff, They have smudged my Jew.

He never wears the yellow star. Or is his star also invisible? After 7 June '42, the sign must be solidly sewn on and visibly worn; failure to comply risks arrest. In exchange for the star, recipients must trade in one coupon of their monthly clothing ration. Jews in the Reich did not have to surrender clothing coupons for the star. They had no clothing ration. And soon the collection of stars begins; roundups follow roundups at ever-shorter intervals. Afterwards, the transfer to Drancy or Pithiviers, Compiègne or Beaune-la-Rolande, the transit camps around Paris. Attaching the star with a safety pin or snap fasteners is forbidden. Sew it on, impossible to tear off; sew it in, if possible under the skin.

From the very start he was determined not to wear it. The painter Chaim Soutine is forever invisible under his hat. And so is his star.

Once he takes fright when a woman stumbles from a gateway into the street, her face pressed into a big white handkerchief. It must have been after July of '42, during the flood of mass deportations: first the 'foreign' Jews and, shortly after, even their children. He stops abruptly on the pavement, face to face with the woman in the middle of the street. He is paralysed with terror when she turns and addresses him as Monsieur Epstein.

She sobs, her speech is choppy, again and again she presses her eyes into the white cloth. She is obviously so desperate she either no longer knows to whom she is speaking, or has simply gone mad with agony. She has not even looked at the left side of his chest where nothing is sewn on, but has simply addressed him. Unable to control herself, she bursts out: Monsieur Epstein . . . What will they do with the children? If they deport the adults for labour, why take the little ones? Please, Monsieur Epstein, please tell me . . . it's such ghastly nonsense, what good are two- or five-year-olds in a labour camp? Isn't it monstrously stupid for a country at war to do such a thing? What's the benefit? It's all so pointless, what good can it do to arrest women and children . . . It doesn't make sense, Monsieur Epstein, why don't you answer me . . . an atrocious machinery that wants to grind us to dust, please tell me . . .

And the mute painter Chaim Soutine stands paralysed and peers out from under his elegant dark-blue hat into the terrified, sobbing face. He cannot utter a word, takes a slow step backward in order to begin his escape.

If the woman recognized him as someone who should have worn the jagged sign on the left side of his chest, how could he walk past any of the Occupiers? Abruptly the woman had called into question his invisibility. He has unexpectedly become visible on the pavement, albeit as Monsieur Epstein, yet visible nonetheless. Alarmingly visible.

At the end of the Alley of the Swans, upriver, on the left bank of the Seine, rises the Vélodrome d'Hiver on the Boulevard de Grenelle, not far from the Eiffel Tower. In the past, he used to go there to watch boxing matches and catch-wrestling for his Sunday entertainment. Since then, the winter cycle-racing track had been degraded into the city's holding pen for the victims of the mass arrests: a gigantic dark maelstrom into which they are indiscriminately thrown, so as to later drop from a railway car more dead than alive in some unpronounceable place in Poland. In the roundup of 16 and 17 July '42, the Paris police force under orders by Leguay, deputy of Vichy Chief of Police Bousquet, drove the arrested Jews there like cattle.

The painter can't help but remember Kiko's enthusiastic exclamation; it was 1913 and he had only just arrived in the city of his dreams: Here, there are no Cossacks. No looting mob. One day the pogroms will disappear from our dreams. But this evening will remain forever ours. You understand, there will never be pogroms in this city . . .

This time the Cossacks spoke French; the police prefecture's Circular No. 173–43 ordered the arrest of all foreign Jews. More than 13,000 in Paris alone. Half of them are instantly carted off in buses requisitioned from the city to the Drancy camp north of Paris; the others are held in the Vélodrome d'Hiver. Many, however, remained undetected in the Big Roundup. Among them an invisible painter. Ever since Mademoiselle Garde went there two years earlier and never returned, he would no longer obey any decrees or have his registration of October '40 renewed. From the stadium with the wintery name people vanished into the void, into an eternal winter. From the holding pen a path led directly to death.

Disappear, he pants in the hearse, find yourself a refuge. Go into hiding, now, right away. The Black Hundreds are on the prowl, you hear me, children, quick, off into the woods, don't take anything, just hide, leave everything behind, they are coming on horse-drawn carts from Minsk . . . run as fast you can . . . Kiko . . . the Cossacks . . . do you hear . . .

He can no longer remember when he last saw the velodrome. Did he actually ever stand again on the Grenelle Bridge after 17 July '42 and look across to the Vél d'Hiv and the Alley of the Swans, the needle-like island in the Seine? Or did he merely send his eye, that is, his soul? Rumours were racing through the city. And he loathed himself for being unable to imagine the horrible events in the sports arena. Never could he paint it. It was beyond his power.

Seven thousand people were crowded into the rows of seats, screaming, lost, hitting out in a panic, or apathetic with hunger and thirst. Below, in the velodrome's centre, a Red Cross tent with a single doctor and two nurses. Women giving birth, people dying, people with fevers. Five days without food; a single hose with water is fiercely besieged. The sanitary installation is blocked up and unusable; faeces and urine drip from the bleachers onto those lying below. The sharp orders by the guards, who speak French this time. A trembling old man rises and calls out with his last strength, This is a huge misunderstanding! *Vive la République!*

And collapses. No air supply, a place to suffocate, full of straw, fear and moans. The July heat, the sweat of the penned-in crowd. A pungent stench. Hearts suddenly stop; by the evening of 17 July a hundred suicides have been counted. And they would be proved right: only *one* path led out of this place. Yes, he did loathe himself for being unable to imagine it. He had heard of families who flung themselves from windows to escape the deport- ation. And of a woman, mad with anguish, who threw her four children from a window. In Smilovichi, there is no longer a living soul.

The penned-in masses often stood before him in his dreams, staring at him with questioning eyes, seeming to expect something of him. For them, he was not invisible. But he remained outside; the maelstrom had not swal- lowed him. Now, in the Corbillard on his way to Paris, the morphine whispered into his ear that he had actually been there, indeed most certainly, he had witnessed every- thing, could swear to it.

The bridge seemed to float, as did the Alley of the Swans; everything had begun to move. There are no more swans to be seen; they were caught long ago and wolfed down by the occupied city. All the swans vanished from the city this way. Once, though, he saw black, charred birds. Whirring wings that disturbed the air above the Seine. When he saw them rise into the sky, the velodrome was blown up before his eyes. It had been built a few years before his arrival; Parisian workers were crazy about cycle races and flocked to it in large crowds.

His eyes now watched it erupt into the sky, which would indeed happen in the future, long after his death, blown away with all the beams and planks that had drunk blood and urine. Bits of rubble whirl through the air; the iron reinforcements stick out like the ragged skeleton of a giant monster. Blown away. At this moment he could have painted it. A landscape burst wide open.

He has gone into hiding with Ma-Be. He has made himself invisible. He is in Champigny. He is in the Pyrenees with his poppy juice. He hides under a blue hat. In Raspberry-town, not far from Smilovichi. In the Passage d'Enfer. In Kremenkikominsk.

A glick hot dir getrofen! A leben ahf dir! Happiness has struck you! May you have a long life!

Barely has the poppy juice begun to take effect when he feels himself swell and expand as in the grotesque self-portrait of 1922 where he is nothing but giant lips, a massively distorted ear and a distended piece of shoulder. He is now again invisible under his invisible blue hat.

Meanwhile there has been some news in the German embassy on the Rue de Lille where Abetz resides. The personal data of the detainees have been checked against the Tulard files. The painter Chaim Soutine is not caught in the roundup of 16 and 17 July '42. Two weeks after the mass arrests and the inferno in the Vél d'Hiv he is still nowhere to be found. The time has come for a special operation, Monsieur Soutine. A search warrant goes out from the Rue de Lille.

German Embassy, Paris

30 July 1942. No. 305/43 g

CONFIDENTIAL

To the Head of the Security Police and the SD, for attention of Obersturmführer RÖTHKE, Paris, 72 Avenue Foch.

Subject: Measures concerning Jewish artist Soutine.

With regard to the aforementioned case, I herewith confirm our phone conversation of Tuesday the 28th. As you know, the instructions come directly from the personal adjudant to Herrn Reichsmarschall H. Göring. First, the French authorities are to be informed, i.e. the Commissaire aux Questions Juives and the Chief of Police. Their active cooperation is requested. Due to highest-level secrecy, no details are to be discussed with the French authorities. Second, any works by the Jew Soutine found during the investigation are to be seized and immediately shipped to Berlin. A speedy execution of these instructions would be appreciated.

By order of Achenbach

A silver uniform bends over the typist's shoulder and states curtly: With a T please, not a D. A man remembers his brilliant Latin classes back home in the Reich. *Adiuvare. Adiuvo, adiuvi, adiutum.* Damn it, I do remember. To help, support, assist. *Adiutor*, hence adjutant. And he puffs up his chest.

The secretary has written so many such ordinances that the hunted perfidiously sneak into his spelling. 'Adjudant' it says indeed, with the *Jude*, Jew, in the middle, in the vice grip of Ad and Ant. They can't even leave the spelling alone but sneak into the words and subvert them from inside. The personal adjudant tails Reichsmarschall Göring. Then the ring of an urgent phone call interrupts and the D stays where it is.

And it is precisely this Jew with a D in the middle, who sneaks into words and eavesdrops from there, who has an informant in the French police. Let's call him Armand Merle. Why not? Merle is the blackbird, and that bird sings beautifully. Because now the French authorities begin to wonder. Ship them to Berlin—all those works by the Jew Soutine? Has the number-one art thief suddenly changed his taste? One begs to differ: the number two. Hitler himself has ordered vast confiscations of works of art for his Special Project Linz. Rosenberg controls the loot from the western and eastern occupied regions. By collaborating with him, Göring tries to snatch up a few choice pieces for himself. The impassioned art thief is planning the 'North German Gallery' for his Carinhall country residence in the Schorfheide forest district near Berlin.

Eleni's bright, excited voice comes through the phone. How did she manage to locate the letter from the German embassy? What connection did she have to what archives? She won't tell.

You have your secrets and I have mine. But the document is there.

She is on the trail of the riddles, has assembled the pieces of the puzzle and can't wait to let the baffled recipient of her message finally see the whole picture. She is always one step ahead of him.

So Deputy Police Chief Leguay assigns one of his inspectors to the investigation and requests the creation of a confidential dossier about the wanted painter, possibly to figure out the Germans' mysterious interest in Soutine. Why did they want to have his paintings? What did they need them for?

No. No risk of that. He won't show up in the 'North German Gallery'; Clarinhall has no room for degenerate art. The Old Masters will hang there.

He's going to hang them?

Eleni bursts out laughing into the phone. In Hitler's Linz collection? Hardly. No change of taste there. He wants to grow a thousand years old and stay encircled by the same old paintings.

Encircled?

Do they want first to ship the paintings and then burn them? Compete with the painter who's rumoured to burn his own works?

There is actually a note on the back of his *Little Girl in Blue*: FOR BURNING. And then the stamp of a German art gallery. Legible, illegible? For burning. Do the art thieves for once have the same plan as the painter? One day I will murder my paintings . . . he said to his visitor in the Cité Falguière between the walls with the tattered wallpapers.

Reichsmarschall Göring used his numerous visits to Paris to help himself to works of art. But Soutine's degenerate paintings? Not in demand.

Oh yes, Eleni interrupts, as a means to procure foreign currency. Why burn paintings that can fetch plenty of foreign currency in the American market? Why burn when the Wehrmacht is advancing into the Russian bowels and each caterpillar tank is precious? With Barnes's collection in Merion and the 1935 exhibition in the Chicago Arts Club, Soutine's market value has been rising steadily, you realize? Let the Americans and his fellow believers buy his paintings and bankroll the eastern front. The art market is what it is; it flourishes in times of war. Don't forget, at the end of July '42, when the search warrant is issued for the painter, the Sixth German Army is advancing on Stalingrad. Why heat the air with worthless paintings if they can fire up artillery pieces? Heating fuel, yes. But everything for the war effort. So, off to Berlin with his tormented canvasses.

I loved Eleni's voice, could listen to her for hours. Read me the phonebook and I will listen to your voice. There are voices that transform your auditory ossicles. Your jubilant stirrup, your anvil, your hammer. Your bony labyrinth, your sentimental organ of balance. And her sweet little cochlea. She was on the trail of the riddles, and her dark Mediterranean eyes had seen things none of us had anticipated. She was the fairy of the secret archives.

In the milky future, invisible bloodhounds and sleuths obsessed with their antennae will appear, and they will use their own paths to drive to the operation. They will submit politely deferential queries to archives and beg for minor bits of information. They dream of getting themselves locked into the archives for nights on end, of twice turning over every miserable scrap of paper and wearing out every pencil and other blessed writing tool in alien registration offices and police headquarters, of slurping cold tea in basements and document dungeons. Oh yes, a police museum does exist, the Paris police headquarters' museum at No. 4 Rue de la Montagne Sainte-Geneviève.

Thousands of gestures will be useless, many notes unusable from the outset, but at some point a little piece of paper will appear that seems to have been waiting just for them, that has duplicitously kept itself hidden. It might be a letter by an informer, a residence permit, the meticulous trace left by a routine bureaucratic measure. Or a search warrant by the German embassy on the Rue de Lille.

Soutine has no idea of these machinations, but Sertürner's poppy juice knows of Armand Merle. The painter hears from a neighbour on the Villa Seurat whose path he happens to cross as he leaves the train at the Montparnasse station, that several times French plain-clothed officials have shown up.

Thursday, 10 December 1942, 4.30 p.m. Investigation into the wanted individual Soutine Chaim, *artiste-peintre*, resident of 18 Rue Villa Seurat, Paris 14. Proceeded to the above address on the afternoon of 2 December. According to statements by neighbours interviewed, Monsieur Soutine had not returned to this address since the end of spring or summer of the previous year. Recorded statements offer no new leads regarding Monsieur Soutine's present whereabouts.

All that Henry Miller has left behind on the Villa Seurat is a pile of papers and a few letters. Let the Nazis wipe their arses with them, he had whispered to his neighbour Delteil as he was hotfooting it before the war broke out.

Everyone is looking for a painter.

Witness interrogation at Gestapo offices in Chartres, 21 April 1943. Second interrogation of Madeleine Castaing, resident of Lèves near Chartres, in the case of: Proceedings against Chaim Soutine. Present: SS-Hauptsturmführer Uwe Lorenz, head of SIPO-SD in Chartres; Jean-Yves Meyer, interpreter; and Frau Ingrid Elster, typist. Witness warned about consequences of making false statements.

He still lives on the Villa Seurat, but because his studio cannot be heated he spends his days during the winter behind closed curtains in a small hotel room on the Avenue d'Orléans, sweating under his raincoat as he lies on the bed, his eyes fixed on the ceiling. He no longer sets foot outside. His ulcer prevents him from sleeping. He speaks in a staccato, is doubled over in pain . . .

Can you tell us the name of that hotel, its exact address?

No, sorry. There're so many small hotels, you know.

He kept changing his lodgings. His friends told him to move into the Free Zone, but he refused. For a while he stayed with friends and then left Paris in June of '41. I have not seen him since.

Not even at your place?

My place was requisitioned by the Wehrmacht. How could I have guests in my home?

Terminated: 1330 hours. SS-Hauptsturmführer Uwe Lorenz.

Read, approved, signed: Madeleine Castaing.

She lied and had to lie. A painter makes himself invisible; they can look for him all they want, they will not find him. Neither the Occupiers, nor their helpers. Neighbours and acquaintances are interrogated; Inspector Merle gathers up their statements like tiny crumbs, finds nothing useful among them. Soutine has dissolved into thin air; he has become invisible once and for all. Whoever can still see him must have good eyes indeed.

Hidden in the hearse, Soutine is riding towards Paris; his entire life has led him there, always to Paris. From Minsk and Vilna to Paris. From Céret and the Pyrenees to Paris. From Cagnes and Vence—always back to Paris, as if the city were the eternal magnet whose attraction he can no longer escape. A motif in his paintings from Cagnes, a minuscule walker, barely recognizable, staggers towards his misery on twisted paths, moving upward towards his destination, on an ever-ascending road to wherever the void or God or the white paradise awaits him. The red stairway at Cagnes! It, too, already leads up *there*.

He rides in a black hearse, make Citroën, model Corbillard, to Paris. Is he riding there to die? Of course not, the poppy juice chases away the thought. He rides to the country of milk. He rides into a future that will not come. He rides into the white paradise. He is not to wake up as long as the poppy script, discovered by Sertürner, writes forward, the poppy juice of literature . . . He is to remain anaesthetized, to not feel pain.

Bing! The first ever exhibition dedicated to him alone, in June of '27, flashes in front of his eyes; he sees his paintings hang in the Galerie Bing. Yes, at the Bing. His first. Since Barnes showed up in 1923, since the pharmacist snatched up his paintings in a frenzy and scattered dollar bills in his studio, Montparnasse, aka the world, knows the meaning of Soutine's name. He is seen as having made it, as having arrived for good. What a triumph. Finally arrived.

Arrived—where? The people in the gallery are starting to get anxious. The painter is invisible. A person prances through the crowd turning heads in astonishment. He goes out onto the pavement, desperately looking in all directions for someone.

Where is Soutine? The opening is about to begin, but he is not there? The crowd is densely packed, barely able to catch a glimpse of the paintings. And he is not coming? Is hiding somewhere. Or roaming the quarter, watching from afar the small groups of people pushing their way into the Bing? Someone runs to his studio in a panic, down to Parc Montsouris near the periphery. No Soutine. Nowhere near or far. He is not there. He is not coming. He is invisible.

Now, too, the painter writhing on his cot does not want to show up. Death hosts an opening; the painter is expected. But Soutine does not want to appear. The Bing misses out. Skipping his own death, boycotting it. The morphine tincture whispers into his ear: You remain hidden, you ride on, incognito. Just don't try to wake up. May the anaesthesia last forever. Let death gaze at its own paintings. Opening or not—a painter disappears. And wishes to remain invisible.

He lies in his hotel at 25 Avenue d'Orléans. The faded curtains are pulled. He lies on his bed in his raincoat, sweating, no longer taking it off. He wears his blue hat. Lies on his bed and stares at the ceiling. For days on end. The Villa Seurat has become too dangerous. He no longer sets foot outside. Goes into hiding. He lies in the bleak hotel room on the Avenue d'Orléans. He rides incognito in a hearse to an operation in Paris. He lies on a white bier in the clinic of Doctor Bog. He is back in the white paradise.

DOCTOR BOG

Have days passed, hours, minutes? Seconds-days? Weeks-minutes? Time has long ceased to play a part. He lies there, entirely calm, breathes steadily, his hands placed on the white sheet. The light in the room is blindingly white; since his arrival, he has not noticed any change in day or night. The slider in the white door is softly pushed up; again a pair of eyes watches him attentively. A round, still face. But then the handle is gently pushed down and a stocky man in white enters.

The painter has his eyes closed but feels he can see the face through his lids, just as earlier he saw the landscapes north of the Loire through the black metal of the Citroën. His gaze has moved and slid outside. As on the day he stood on the Grenelle Bridge and stared across to the Vélodrome d'Hiver, which blew up in front of his eyes—in the future.

He must be a doctor, all clad in white. Probably the head doctor. Well nourished, chubby, in these times of war. He adjusts the delicate, white-laminate frame of his glasses and introduces himself in a low, not-unfriendly voice, the corners of his mouth flickering with a lone, melancholy twitch.

Bog. My name is Doctor Bog. Dear Soubin, if I may call you that?

I am called Soutine, Chaim . . . no, Charles. Here're my papers, where are they, here . . . please . . .

And with both hands he begins to fumble down the sides of his torso under the white sheet for the forged documents that Fernand Moulin, veterinarian and mayor of Richelieu, had got stamped for him at the Tour Prefecture. They are nowhere to be found, and for the first time the painter is confused.

We don't want to let a tiny little letter become an issue here. Names are irrelevant in this place. We only deal with cases. I don't have a name, either, even if in an emergency they call me Doctor Bog. So there, dear Soutinhaim. You can stay in bed and relax. Get some rest. Take it easy . . .

The painter morosely mumbles something about the vanished papers and stares at the ears of the god in white with the self-satisfied smile.

You no longer need your papers. We have a file on you.

When the painter looks up, a snow-white canvas for the demonstration of medical explanations suddenly stands on white metal feet behind the chubby medicine man. The painter Soutinhaim wonders how he would have painted the white god on this canvas, how the bald moon head and the bulging lips, and how the pop eyes behind the oversized white glasses and clenched hands.

He remembers Fouquet's portrait of Charles VII, which he so often visited in the Louvre, remembers the time he proudly carried home a rolled-up reproduction of that favourite of his, that Sunday's trophy. This is how he would have painted Doctor Bog, but of course all in white, in nothing but white. By the way, where are we here?

The doctor sits down on a chair and fixes his diffident gaze on the patient.

You know, in this place we have no failed surgeries. We have a wonderful assistant here: Doctor Kno.

The painter jumps at the the two consonants the name begins with, which remind him of some other name's curt, military monosyllable. Kno. He has encountered the calamitous combination of k and n and o before. Where that might have been he can no longer recall. So Bog and Kno are colleagues, or at least head and subordinate. Doctor Bog continues his genial monologue.

Actually, here we operate only in the rarest of cases. In your case, it will no longer be necessary. In the meantime, consider yourself healed.

And the god in white dreamily strokes the big preserving jar full of liquid that sits on a white side table next to him.

Healed? Me? Without operation?

Entirely without, we no longer need it. In the past, we wouldn't have passed up on a stomach such as yours. Do you realize what I have in this beautiful jar?

No, the painter replies.

It's not your stomach, Soutinhaim, yours is still inside you, but it is a stomach. Or, rather, a lovely little mountain range of mucosal folds, cut open so we can see the many little damp valleys held together by a light mantle of connective tissue. This little gastric-mucosa mountain range has come from Chicago and will return there. You know, don't you: The Arts Club of Chicago, 1935, your first exhibition on the American continent?

The painter is baffled; for the life of him he can't think of anything to say.

You'll be surprised, Monsieur Soutinhaim. This is the first stomach that Billroth resected, beautifully preserved in 1880 in fragrant formalin. The partial gastrectomy was a stroke of genius. The resection of two-thirds, right? The two variants of gastrectomy according to Billroth are still among the most popular exam questions.

And what does this stomach have to do with mine?

You know, my dear Soutinhaim—and he winks at him impishly with his right eye—every single stomach has something to do with all the other ones. And what we especially love here is the medicine of the future.

Of the future, the painter wanted to repeat before he remembers that in the past nothing good ever tried to come his way from the future. That is why this word, too, makes him jump.

Certainly. And now take a look at this pretty white device. Looks quite complicated, doesn't it? It's something special. Admittedly a smaller version of its kind, though still the size of a large desk. Have a little patience; we shall push it on its dainty wheels close to your bed. It's a scanning . . . electron . . . micro . . . scope. Save yourself the question. It'll show you instantly the spiral form of Helicobacter pylori.

Of Helico . . . ?

That's a gorgeous gram-negative, microaerophilic rod bacterium; let's call it, for simplicity's sake and somewhat intimately, your Helicobacter. Because its preferred settlement area, if you want to call it that, was your stomach lining. It's a spiral-shaped, curved bacillus that uses flagella to propel itself.

Flagella?

The painter tries to imagine a rod that lashes itself forward, but he has no success. He squirms and slides about in his white bed. The white canvas behind the smiling god has gripped his attention. At last he cranes his neck and stares at a strange square the device offers him, and recoils at the sight. With his left elbow he knocks over a whole container of white pencils that crash to the floor with a clatter.

For a long time, Doctor Bog continues, it was thought that no bacterium could survive in gastric acid—which is a thousand times more acidic than citric acid. But you'd be amazed: The little guy from the ghetto has! A curved, spiral-shaped bacterium, about six thousandths of a millimetre long and half a thousandth of a millimetre wide, with two to seven flagella at one end. Its helical shape along with the flagella is assumed to give it a survival advantage by allowing it to pass quickly—think of a kind of outboard engine—through the potentially lethal gastric acid and instead lodge itself in the stomach lining and stomach cells, where it forms the enzyme urease.

Enzyme urease? The painter remembers the curious Russian spoken by the people in the small Tatar village on the other side of the Volma river across from Smilovichi. The last scattered descendants of the Golden Horde.

It breaks down urea and in the process creates ammonia, which, compared with the acid, is strongly alkaline. Helico- bacter pylori surrounds itself with a kind of alkaline cloud that will protect it from decomposition by the acid. Rather clever, don't you think, Monsieur Soutinhaim?

The painter is still stunned by the image of the tiny rod with its flagella.

Simultaneously, it forms a toxin that together with the ammonia attacks and so damages the stomach cells that they produce more acid. The stomach lining becomes inflamed as a result of this increase in acid, and in turn becomes even more vulnerable to the acid. In effect, the stomach produces something that dooms it. Just like your artist friends in Montparnasse. That's how you ended up with your splendid *ulcus ventriculi*, dear Monsieur Painter. Don't forget: thanks to its spiral shape and flagella.

And what about . . . my particular . . . stomach ulcer? the painter would timidly like to ask.

Nothing unique about it, Doctor Bog answers, almost bored. Here, you know, we prefer very rare diseases; they are simply more interesting. *Epidermolysis bullosa, systemic lupus ertythematodes, porphyria cutanea tarda, takotsubo cardiomyothapy* —they are the kind that send us into ecstasy. Dear Soutinhaim, yours is just a banal stomach ulcer, nothing exquisite. For 60,000 years our Helicobacter has resided in the stomachs of humankind and has remained so well hidden for so long. It wasn't discovered until 1983, imagine that! The stomachs of half of humanity offer asylum to the bacterium; half the crown of creation has been infected. In countries with poor hygienic conditions it's even ninety per cent. Ninety per cent!

The painter is mystified. For 60,000 years? And 1983? A crazy date.

Do the names Barry Marshall and John Robin Warren ring a bell?

No, the patient replies. I am familiar with El Greco, Tintoretto, Rembrandt. Are these two also painters?

Doctor Bog ignores the question.

As for the transmission, my dear Soutinhaim. We are not so sure. Faecal-oral, oral-oral or even gastro-oral.

The god in white, playing the pipe organ, savours the sequence of these sounds, cannot get enough of them, enjoys repeating them, his index finger stabbing the air in three directions.

That is, via excretion and subsequent ingestion of contaminated water or food. Possibly also via infected gastric mucus in vomitus, you see? Even blowflies are being considered.

Now the painter is visualizing clouds of black-green blow flies; Europe was full of them, from Norway all the way down to Italy.

You often felt bloated as if after a meal that was too rich—what a delicious irony fate has served up for you! That you often went hungry in your life we know very well; it says so in your file. A feeling of pressure in the upper abdomen, nausea to the point of vomiting, lack of appetite, weight loss, acid reflux. And then of course the piercing and burning pain you surely know only too well, at the centre of your upper abdomen. How often you jabbed your finger into your belly to greet your pain and curse it . . .

The doctor dreamily chatters away, pleased with himself and his medical science:

Pain begins shortly after ingestion of food, because the gastric wall and hence the ulcer get stretched and extended. In addition to these stomach symptoms you probably also had indications of recurring smaller haemorrhages and, consequently, of anaemia, right?

The painter's face has actually turned pale; he is dizzy from all the unexpected happenings in his belly.

A direct indication of smaller haemorrhages is tarry stools, black and sticky, caused by blood getting in contact with gastric acid and being decomposed by it. That makes you think of the tar smells in Smilovichi, right? My dear Monsieur Soutinhaim, let's talk colours instead, shall we?

Colours are the sisters of pains, the painter says and wants to tell Doctor Bog of the conversation he once overheard in La Rotonde. But the head of medicine continues to hold forth and does not listen.

In a gastroscopy the ulcer tends to show as a reddish defect in the mucosa, most often covered by fibrin threads. Cell debris, fibrinoid necrosis. Distinctive RED and a streaky WHITE—that would mean something to you, wouldn't it? So much for the florid ulcer. When the ulcer has healed, the initially highly vascularized red scar turns into a fibrous white scar—as if the healing gastric ulcer had chosen your favourite colours for its portrait, right? The altar boy's surplice, the groom's uniform jacket, the pastry chef's handkerchief. As if the ulcer tried to flatter you even as it disappeared. You, Monsieur Soutinhaim, would be the painter best able to paint the stomach ulcer. And finally, there comes the white, as it does after all significant things in this world. The colour of the healed stomach ulcer. And then the culmination of the process: regenerated single-layer epithelium growing over the former ulcer!

The painter grimaces, with his sleeve wipes a drip off his nose and audibly sucks in air.

So all that milk . . . I drank over the course of my life . . . has done . . . nothing for me?

Soutine's face reflects the woefulness of futility.

See, dear Monsieur Painter, the history of medical errors is what amuses us most in this place. We sometimes laugh our heads off when we aren't otherwise too busy. For decades you kept drinking milk, scooped in your bismuth powder, stirred and hoped for the best. Meanwhile, the acid continued to flow, poured into your stomach and made you double over with pain. The sharp burning in your upper abdomen, the nausea attacks, the tarry stools—we know only too well how you felt. Your doctors prattled on about shattered nerves and poor nutrition, prescribed papaverine, histidine and the odd turpentine preparation, bismuth salts and other antacids, and then sent you on your merry way. You figured your ulcer was the price you had to pay for your drinking binges with your painter pals, for the errors of your ways before God and for your poor childhood diet, the filthy food. And you know what? This tiny spirally squirt was to blame. Helicobacter pylori.

Then all that milk hasn't helped one bit? the painter asks again, shyly persistent.

Don't underestimate our cows, Doctor Bog replies. Milk buffers gastric acid. It soothed your discomfort. Be grateful to the cows. Thank them, thank them, Soutinhaim. Were it not for them—what would your life have been like? Even more pain, as if you didn't have enough already. In a certain sense, you couldn't be helped. No one can be helped. But now we take care of you.

So there's a cure?

Oh yes, there's always something like a cure. For everything. Even if it's called exitus.

This pointed word gives the painter a fright.

Relax. Here, you won't even be put under our jolly knife but will receive a triple therapy. Shortly my assistant, Doctor Livorno, will see you and ask you a few simple questions. By the way, he used to have tuberculosis, the white plague—yes indeed, that bacillus identified by Koch—highly infectious and, in his day, incurable, but today is feeling great. It may amuse you to know that milk contaminated with bacteria was the cause. And when was the BCG vaccine first used? You'd be surprised. Almost exactly one year after Livorno's demise.

Bewildered, the painter stares at Doctor Bog. Demise? And is feeling great today? But of course such things are not incompatible in this place.

Doctor Livorno enters the examination room timidly and awkwardly, turns his face away and merely asks: Triple?

Yes, French Triple. The combination of a proton pump inhibitor with two antibiotics. Nothing more beautiful than that. Pantoprazole, Clarithromycin, Amoxicillin.

The painter wants to counter this tempest of words, but all he can think of are the names of the terrible pogroms that afflicted the nights of his childhood. Kishinev, Gomel, Zhitomir, Berdichev, Nikolayev, Odessa. He holds back, though, and replies to Doctor Bog's slightly contemptuous smile: Terra di Siena, Veronese green, crimson, incarnadine.

Doctor Bog tiptoes away, leaves the room, and presently Doctor Bog's assistant approaches him, smiling mildly, his once black hair now entirely grey, transformed by the milk of old age, and whips out a snow-white piece of paper.

The painter cannot believe his eyes. The face, those eyes, the lips—it can't be true.

Modi, you—here? What are you doing in this clinic?

Doctor Livorno generously pretends not to hear the question. The white-clad assistant, who has Modigliani's facial features but a perplexing impassivity utterly unimaginable for the Italian painter, asks no questions, puts aside the white sheet of paper and indifferently starts to chant a strangely otherworldly recitation: The cattle were ploughing and the she-donkeys were grazing beside them . . . tremendous fire fell from heaven and burnt the flocks and the youths and consumed them . . .

Again, the painter slides about restlessly on his white sheet. His belly is hard as a plank. But the pain is gone; the pain has disappeared. Not that he misses it—but the absence of pain is always unusual. The decades-old pain, the spasms, the twitches, the burning, the vomiting. The burrowing inside him, the fist of pain, its slow twists.

He looks straight at Modi, who has turned pious and is adopting a solemn expression to recite something else, but the painter interjects, Is that Lautréamont? You always loved him! Do you remember that passage about the louse?

But his partner in the conversation ignores the second half of this question as well and replies brusquely, Concentrate, will you. No distraction, young man. *Yungermantshik!*

And the listless Modi begins to chant again, though not the way he used to in the old days when he belted out his Dante, but rather with a cotton-wool voice that seems muted by sedating bromide medications.

Chaldeans formed three bands . . . spread out on the camels . . . and took them . . . and slew the youths . . . with the sword . . .

Doctor Livorno's face takes on a questioning expression, as if he wants to know whether the patient recognizes what he has heard. Does any of it ring a bell?

Your sons and daughters were dining . . . and drinking wine . . . at the home of their firstborn brother . . . when, behold, a great wind . . . came from the other side of the desert . . . and struck the four corners of the house . . . it fell upon the youths . . .

You surely recognize that, don't you, Livorno says with an accusatory grimace.

No, not at all. None of it.

He merely gives the pseudo-Modi a smile and asks,

Would you like me to sing you the little calf?

But Doctor Livorno doesn't allow himself to get distracted and continues to chant: From my mother's womb, I emerged naked . . . and I will return there naked . . . If the scourge kills suddenly . . . he will mock at the calamity of the innocent . . . The tents of robbers prosper . . . and those who provoke God . . . are secure . . . to whomever God brought it with His hand . . .

The painter closes his eyes and pretends to sleep. He has no idea how much time has passed. His operation was successful or unnecessary, Doctor Bog said. His pain is gone. He marvels that it has left behind no pain. And no suture. No scar. How did they penetrate his body? Without leaving a trace? He feels light. Has the god in white not told him to consider himself healed? Healed! A curious condition. A pain-free feeling of astounding lightness. Dubious, tentative, paradisical.

His pain had once been like a second pulse; he had felt for it, auscultated it with his fingers, cursed it. His pain had belonged to him like his breath, his sweat, his bodily fluids. To say he was now missing it would not be accurate.

How could he be missing it? But now something that used to belong to him like an organ, a limb, a nagging feeling is no longer there. He feels amputated, amputated from his pain. Yet it seems so absurd that he forbids himself to contemplate it. One moment he briefly believes it is still there, but it is a delusion. There was nothing there. His stomach was painlessly absent. And he thinks about Doctor Livorno's odd demeanour and monotonous recitation, which are so different from the way Modigliani, like one possessed, used to recite for his painter colleague Chaim Soutine Lautréamont's louse episode and Dante's forest of the suicides. Now he appeared so strangely serene.

And smote Job with severe boils . . . from the sole of his foot . . . to the crown of his head . . . then he took himself a potsherd . . . to scratch himself with . . . and he sat down in the midst of the ashes . . .

The painter has shut his eyes and stubbornly continues to pretend to sleep. In his ears, however, Doctor Livorno will not stop. He chants softly and dreamily into the white colour.

May the stars of its evening be darkened . . . it shall hope for light . . . but have none . . . neither shall it see . . . the rays of dawn.

MODI AND THE FLYING WOMAN

Stop, don't jump! Don't jump! Don't jump!

The painter wants to shout, get up from his gurney, but Marie-Berthe's hand gently pushes him back down and turns over the soft cloth on his forehead.

Stay calm. No one wants to jump from the running car . . .

Not from the car, from the window, the woman up there, hold her back . . .

Ma-Be recognizes the dream he has often told her about. Each time she wonders, Why do you always see women jumping from windows?

Not women, one woman . . . Jeanne.

When the hearse hits a pothole in one of those interminable country roads and the vehicle judders, Soutine suddenly sees a young woman jumping from a window on the fifth floor. It is on the Rue Amyot, he is sure, and yet it is not there. Somewhere else. But the movements remain the same. She climbs on the windowsill, her back facing the street, and steps back. This step he sees again and again, and his horrified gaze and his scream cannot wake him up. The morphine messiah will stop on the pavement of the Rue Amyot and shout, Stop! Don't jump! Don't jump!

But no matter how long he stretches out his hand, the woman can no longer be stopped and smashes onto the cobblestones with a dry thud. No one hears her splintering bones; no one sees the blood trickling from her mouth. There is no one left. The Rue Amyot is utterly empty.

Why does she do it, the painter mumbles, and Ma-Be does not understand.

Yes, he did have a friend, the least likely of the whole rag-tag gang. Amedeo! In the war year of 1915. Amedeo. An Italian the gods loved: at age eleven, they gave him pleurisy; at age fourteen, typhus with a fever-induced delirium lasting more than a month that kept him suspended between life and death; and at age sixteen, tuberculosis that made him cough up blood. Really, with that name? Loved by the gods? Some cynical gods for Modi *le Maudit*. Modi the accursed. Soutine will not be able, later, to forgive him for dragging him along into his intoxications. Accursed alcohol, spurring on the deadly acid of his stomach lining.

No one could have foreseen it. Modi and Chaim. In-between two bouts of intoxication and his towering rage, this camouflaged aristocrat who bedazzles and seduces the world takes under his wing the timid tongue-tied man who has never mastered the art of eating politely. Monsieur Montparnasse shakes his head. The son of a ruined timber merchant from Livorno and the son of a mending tailor from Smilovichi—the most outlandish pair of friends he has ever seen. Monsieur cannot get over his astonishment. The former laughs loudly, endlessly recites his Dante, or, rather, belts him out in a rolling Italian that explodes with delight in its own sound. The latter sits mute in a corner, clutches his head, licks his lips and is amazed at the spectacle.

Modi, forever drunk on absinthe and cheap booze, his whole life an intoxication. He smokes hashish and opium and insists they are the only available treatments for his tuberculosis. Yet always spick and span. Not a day without stepping into the old, banged-up bathtub. Clean and proper he goes hunting in the Montparnasse cafes. He is capable—of everything; with a flick of the wrist he can toss anything onto the paper, but it has to be fast, fast as life, a sketch never taking more than a few minutes. In the cafes he lies in ambush for the chance patron who will push a glass of gin towards him in exchange for a pencil portrait. He pays with his pad. The disgusting ease with which he tosses a few lines, a head, eyes, a nose, an arrogant mouth onto the paper.

For the strange friend from Smilovichi each painting means a crushing agony that generally ends in destruction. Cleanliness won't solve the problem of interacting with those out there. Soutine builds a tight wall of bodily odours against the world. He will not relinquish his protective barrier. Whoever comes too close will turn away in time. Strong smell is a weapon against the intrusive world.

The inventive Modi even shows him how to deal with lice and bed bugs, how to keep their pesky roommates at arm's length. At the Cité Falguière he pushes the two sagging mattresses close together and builds a wall of ash around the mattress island. But then he claims that the clever critters climb the ceiling to drop down on residents who keep a candle at their side and a book in their hands. Ingenious animals, so much smarter than we are!

Soutine can no longer hear. Foujita, a guide for the blind and their fellow lodger at the Cité Falguière, takes him to Laënnec Hospital. Let's see what we've got here. So many tiny bedbug eggs! The doctor marvels and fishes a whole bedbug nest from the painter's ear.

Soutine can hear again. In his hearse, he still hears Modigliani's voice. It is right there, next to his bent arm where his left ear rests in the palm of his hand. Soutine listens. The voice speaks.

There exists an insect . . . which men feed at their own expense . . . This insect, which does not like wine . . . but prefers blood . . . would . . . be capable . . . by means of an occult power . . . of becoming as big . . . as an elephant . . . and crushing men like ears of corn . . . The head is given it as its throne . . . Look at his countless family . . . which he so freely bestowed on you . . . and which is advancing . . . that your despair should be less bitter . . .

What? You don't know Lautréamont? the voice shouts into Soutine's ear. Did you read nothing but the Talmud in your damn village?

Where was it that Modi, rolling his R's, croaked Lautréamont's bitter paean to the louse into his ear? In the Beehive? In the Cité Falguière? Modi talks himself into a trance and ecstasy when he recites the *Songs of Maldoror*; they are his gospel, his daily glad tidings, his diabolic litany. He never goes anywhere without the tattered little book in the side pocket of his stained, dark corduroy jacket. He races about his studio and glances with blazing eyes at his listener; he becomes Lautréamont's fallen angel, the satanic seducer who takes revenge and aims to punish God for having created failed humankind. Soutine still hears Modigliani gasp Maldoror's sentences, hears him cough, whistle and croak them. A dybbuk has taken possession of him. His tuberculosis speaks Lautréamont's language.

O louse with the shrivelled-up eyes . . . as long as humanity tears its own sides apart . . . with disastrous wars . . . as long as divine justice . . . hurls its avenging thunderbolts down on this selfish globe . . . as long as man denies his creator . . . and not without reason . . . snaps

his fingers at him . . . combining insolence and disdain
. . . your reign over the universe will be assured . . .

He bathes in the black floods of Maldoror with the scornful singsong he rattles off in rapt disgust. Modigliani's
mouth is full of Maldoror. Again and again he reproaches
Soutine for what he hasn't read and forces him to read.

How free Modi is when he recites. As if free of pain,
when he is nothing but voice. His tongue licks the eternal
salt block. Opium and poetry. For minutes, Baudelaire
cures his tuberculosis. As if released from everything,
magnificent in his embodied pain. Spellbound by the
croaking grimaces, Chaim squats on the mattress on the
floor and looks up at Modi who raves and roars the paean
to the louse.

O son of lewdness! . . . Lewdness, queen of empires . . . keep
before my hate-filled eyes . . . the sight of your starving off-
spring's imperceptible growth . . .

He sits glued to the spot, understands almost nothing,
but what little he understands frightens him. Where does
this freedom come from? How can Modi with these poisonous litanies mock the scriptures of his childhood,
Torah and Talmud, all the fathers' book burdens? The
Songs of Maldoror was his bible with which he frightened
the venerable, bearded Italian rabbis of Livorno and his
own clan. They block their ears.

Even as the hearse carries him to the white paradise, Soutine feels guilty and cursed for having lent his overwhelmed ear to the drunken preacher from Livorno. Modi no longer knew who he was. Pushed him to drink, to become intoxicated, ordered him to finally read some books.

It is time to get drunk! Baudelaire screamed into his ear. And he had to obey and pass on the scream.

He declaims Dante with a glass-shattering voice and waves his arms on the Montparnasse Boulevard so the startled passers-by jump out of his way, and he sucks on Baudelaire with pursed lips like on a citrus fruit. The death of lovers! *La mort des amants!* We shall have beds round which light scents are wafted, divans which are as deep and wide as tombs.

Only when he recites Dante's *Inferno*, with the anguished cries of the damned, does he sound even more venomous, even more compelling. Canto 13! When they have crossed the river of blood and reached the forest of the suicides who had been transformed into wild shrubs bruised and fed upon by the harpies, his wheezing and moaning makes his listener jump.

Why do you break me? Modigliani howls through the Cité Falguière.

The traveller through the beyond tears off a twig, whereupon blood issues forth and a voice erupts from the bush; Pier della Vigna's wounded soul cries, Why do you tear me? Is there no pity left in any soul? Men we were, and now we are changed to sticks.

And Modi croaks and writhes in his only half-staged tubercular pain. Words and blood well from the broken branch. Modi himself is the broken twig; he is the suicide's tormented voice. He is Dante's bleeding lung. He is the universe's tuberculosis. And Soutine has opened his eyes wide, sits on the bedbug-besieged mattress and bites into his sleeve. Dante caws wildly in the direction of his painful stomach wall. Modi is his own king, King of Livorno. He needs no other.

Modi's shamelessness. He paints in public, just as he loves in public. When he has been drinking, he strips and exposes his divine body to English ladies who turn away aghast. And how shamelessly he paints his naked goddesses, who offer the viewer their breasts, their thighs, their dark tousled triangle. The shy salesgirls and the country girls who have come to the city to try their luck he hustles to his studio and undresses with a deft routine. Antonia, Adrienne, Rosa, Louise, Victoria, Marguerite, Almaisa, Lolotte—nothing is left of any of them but her pose on his canvasses, her pretty face and her naked body on sofas and daybeds. Her dazzling breasts, little black grove, her beckoning sex.

Everyone remembered Modi's first exhibition and the scandal caused by his paintings. He was living with Zbo and Hanka after his break-up with Beatrice Hastings. Is painting in their living room, with Zbo providing him with paints, brushes, liquor and models. Leave him alone, let him get drunk. In 1917, nudes follow one another in feverish succession. He makes firm bodies stretch, swell, show off their pink, shameless nudity. Zbo organizes the exhibition in Grete Weill's gallery in December of 1917. The day the exhibition opens, the district commissioner, whose office is on the opposite side of the Rue Taitbout, wants to close it down. He has watched the crowd in front of the gallery windows. People stop, stare at the nudes, their outrageously exposed pubic hair, their triumphant sex. Shake their heads and cannot tear themselves away. Tumult is in the air.

We are in a world war, and this Montparnasse gang puts their smut on display!

Modi's paradisical shamelessness, Chaim's incorrigible, incurable shame. The nude model strikes him with panic and fear and leaves him paralysed. Only one nude portrait exists, from 1933, that someone has titled Eva. Do not paint the nude, don't, but rather her hastily covered nakedness. Not the black triangle so celebrated by Modigliani, but the feeling of shame flitting across the face. At the moment of the expulsion from paradise.

All lightness is a burden for the other one from Smilovichi. They are sitting around the table at Zborowski's at 3 Rue Joseph-Bara; Kisling is there, too; they are eating minestrone prepared by Lunia Czechowska. Modi has had enough, wipes his mouth with his sleeve and jumps up.

Chaim, I'm now going to paint your portrait.

He grabs his palette, walks to the living-room door and, with sweeping, swift strokes, begins to paint Soutine's portrait straight onto the door: Chaim under his battered hat. Smack onto the door, for the fun of it, for digestion. Everyone is amazed, licks their lips. And Hanka Sierpowska, Zbo's partner, who cannot stand the filthy painter, now meets him every morning on her door. One of Modi's jokes. Shameless, swift as the wind, for digestion. Soutine is now resplendent on the door and looks into all the guests' soup plates. When Hanka complains, Modi replies that the door will be worth its weight in gold one day, far in the future. And Hanka: But until then we'll have to live with it.

Modi paints at least four portraits of Chaim, who paints none of Modi. It's Eleni who one day, on the phone way after midnight, in the Rue de la Tombe-Issoire, points it out with bated breath: Have a look at his right hand!

She was referring to a particular portrait, from a private collection. Ringfinger and little finger side by side, together spreading away from the other two, index finger and middle finger, which also lie tightly side by side. She had seen hands similarly spread with a gap in the middle on tombstones. In Prague or Krakow, she can't remember exactly. The hand of the *kohanim* giving the benediction, of the priests who after the destruction of the Second Temple were scattered all over the world.

Modi turned Chaim into a priest, gave him the *kohen*'s hand for the priestly benediction, you see that, don't you? The hand of a painting *kohen*: a shining paradox, because no priest of the Temple would ever violate the injunction against representation.

But why did Soutine refuse to paint a portrait of Modigliani?

Because he couldn't imagine him as an old man. Whenever Soutine painted people, his models visibly aged in front of his eyes. They sat before him for a few hours and during that time became ancient men and women. In their faces the years had already done their work; they had dug deep into wrinkles and furrows, warped people's bewildered mouths, made the cheeks droop and the nose dominant, while the ear had forever been ancient. And the familiar death announced its arrival with silenced steps in these faces. The young Paulette Jourdain, Zborowski's assistant, often sat for him. She was eighteen, and he painted her as a woman as old as the hills, deeply marked by life.

Paulette, don't move, stay as you are, no more movements.

It took hours; the painter was elsewhere, perpetually dissatisfied, digging into the paints, abusing the canvas. And the model, painfully petrified. Even the children are ancient, and so are the dolls in their hands—age-old, excavated toys. The children are wizened foetuses, prematurely cast out into the world. Stillborn ancients. Twisted mummies, sticky with the sweat of the paint. Why does Soutine deform the bodies of his models? some curious person wants to know. And Modigliani replies: But he doesn't. During the session the model becomes what he sees, the invisible behind the appearance. The human being, mistreated by life, having long been marked by death. The revelation of our ultimate, final state.

Soutine dreads painting a portrait because he knows the model will age distressingly fast in front of him as soon as he touches the brush. He is afraid of his own aging machine. His dark eye already sees the physical decay of the person sitting before him, hands twisted in a panic, sees the terrified faces of ancient men and women who are ashamed to still be in this world.

Have you noticed? Eleni asks. Among Modigliani's portraits there is not one old person, nothing but toned, youthful goddesses and firm, unfurrowed men.

And you know what? Soutine never painted Modi because he knew he would have rapidly aged under his hand. Modigliani himself knew that he would die young, and Soutine knew that he had no right to read into Modi's face the old man who would never come to be. This is the one he did not dare to paint: the youthful Italian god from Livorno who did not wish to grow old, who knew that his tuberculosis would be proved right, as would his constant intoxication. Chaim looked at Modi sideways and knew:

He will never exist as an old man, cannot be imagined, or seen, as one. Soutine was distraught—with everyone else he saw the furrowed face of the ancient person well before their time, yet Modigliani's alone he could not reach. With him, he saw nothing. His face does not exist in the world's gallery of ancient faces that since time immemorial have kept watch over us. So he did not even try.

Prince Modi! Why did he bolt so early in the year of 1920? Soutine was not in Paris; he was in Vence where Modi had lured him in 1918. He got the news down there, also that of Jeanne's suicide, who, eight months pregnant, had thrown herself from a window. All of a sudden ash had been mixed into the South's luminous colours.

He reached his destination early, at thirty-five. To live short, fast, short, fast. No endless journey in a hearse through all of France's provinces. No ageing, no torpid maturation, only absinthe, ether, hashish. The tuberculosis did the mixing. He was not in Paris, had Kisling tell him everything, every detail. No death has shaken him as much. He is determined to never have another drop because each reminds him of Modi and of the worst binges his stomach ulcer was ever expected to cope with. For years he will remain angry at the eternal drunk.

Modi didn't drink milk. But whatever he could get his hands on: high-proof absinthe, the green fairy, that thujone concoction of wormwood, anise and fennel. Also *mominette*, the cheap potato hooch. Drank to speed everything up, to speed himself up. When he drinks, the gentle, charming, prudent prince becomes a fury, spoils for a fight, lashes out. The green fairy sends him hallucinations, terrifying deliriums. One morning he wakes up because someone plucks his sleeve. He wants to move but can't. Feels his knee against his chin, lies curled up on the side of the street in a rubbish bin. Two laughing street sweepers have woken him up. A god in a rubbish bin! A crumpled bundle, a hungover god.

Soutine memorizes every detail in Kisling's report. In the hearse he sees before his mind's eye Modi's funeral; the entire Montparnasse circus has gathered to pay Modi their last respects. Kisling sends pneumatic dispatches to all their crowd. Gathering on 27 January at 2.30 p.m., in the Charité, where he died, burial in the Père Lachaise Cemetery. Modi's brother Emmanuele had sent a telegram: Bury him like a prince, let him not want for anything—an Italian funeral procession, please, with flowers, horses, tears, song.

The procession moves past La Rotonde as if past a temple, with huge crowds on the pavements on tiptoe to see the vehicle and the Italian whom they all love but whose paintings no one wants. At all the intersections police officers stand to attention and salute. Probably a lawmaker, a senator.

Death picked up his scent early. Sniffed his body the way a dog's nose would, looked for access, went for a fitting organ for the project. Heart, lungs, brain, stomach, take your pick. Death loves variants. Sometimes he pants in haste, at other times feigns calm. He enjoys playing games, accelerates, slows down and smothers. He is choosy and loves variety. Death alone is god. He finds himself a certain painter from Livorno, selects tuberculosis. The painter eagerly helps with the job, drinks excessively, sniffs ether, smokes opium. Or he opts for one from Smilovichi, picks a stomach ulcer as his gateway. Go for it. We'll give ourselves three decades. Will wait for the Occupiers. Meanwhile, will order a hearse.

The fake state funeral would have delighted Modi. Soutine would have arrived much too late. And his old friend will not come to his own secret burial. His will not be a state funeral.

And what about his little Madonna? He first met her in the Colarossi Academy on the Rue de la Grande Chaumière where she was a student. At a masked ball in the spring of 1917. She is nineteen. Gentle face, wide mouth and nose, a small Byzantine icon, two clear forget-me-not-blue, almond-shaped eyes. Two plaits, left and right, with a copper tint, arranged into two dark snails. Pale, waxen face, contrasting with the dark hair. Teal dress, Veronese-green headband.

Modi sees her climb straight out of the paintings of his Italians and into the wreckage of his life. For four hundred years he has dreamt of her. After the hell with the unpredictable, extravagant Beatrice Hastings he is looking for different women, submissive, quiet, gentle sufferers who don't create scenes. A slender, moving statue with an unspeakably sad expression. She does not laugh; she appears to dream, is absent, shy, not from here.

She reminds him of that girl in Rimbaud's childhood. Modi had pressed the *Illuminations* upon Chaim. Take this. And finally read it. Read the childhood, read *Enfance*. She is the girl with the orange lips Rimbaud saw at the edge of the forest. It comes back to him now in the hearse, as his ear listens on the palm of his hand. That whole passage. Knees crossed in the clear flood that rises from the meadows. At the edge of the forest—flowers of dream chime; burst, flare. Nudity shadowed, traversed and clothed by rainbows, flowers, the sea. Indeed, she is the girl with the orange lips Rimbaud saw at the edge of the forest. She is the little dead girl behind the roses.

Jeanne, the little Madonna, runs after her Prince Modi, hauls him home when he is drunk. Her parents are horrified, try to hold her back, while her brother André in the trenches up north roars with rage that his fragile sister has fallen in with that rake. One day she disappears without leaving a message, leaves her family to live with him. With that tubercular wreck, drug addict, a foreigner to boot, and a runaway Jew from Italy. And his gentle Jeannette wants only him and no other.

The family has no idea where she has gone. In July '17 she already lives with him in an L-shaped room under the roofs on the Rue de la Grande Chaumière. One bed, one chest of drawers, the narrow studio. Zbo hopes that Modi's life will calm down. But Modi can't stop getting intoxicated, flying into destructive fits of rage. During summer, they swelter under the metal flashing and tar paper; during winter, they lack the coal to heat their icy kingdom. In November '18 Jeanne gives birth to a girl. Giovanna. She wants him to marry her; he hates her for it, does not want family ties shackling him. The hand must be free to paint, you understand? She gives up everything, including herself, to keep him. She sits for him, cleans up his vomit, adores him with mute devotion. Jealously she watches his models. Soon Thora Klinckowström, the beautiful Swede, appears in his paintings. Or Lunia Czechowska, whose husband Casimir he ignores completely. In the summer of '19, while Jeanne and her baby stay behind in Nice, he loves Lunia. For Modi, his prey is always single. She waits for him.

He is a living wreck, but his hunting instinct will not weaken. Escaping the Spanish flu was easier. Losing his teeth one by one, getting pulled deeper and deeper into a black maelstrom. Painting, his last desperate excitement that wants to leap across to the model; a last leap or, rather, a last mounting. He no longer feels alive except when he drinks or paints, or both at once. He knows he has begun to die. But when? Minutes ago, or years?

He lives, even though he was already twice dead. Resurrected, with respite. When he is sixteen, everyone gives up on him when his tuberculosis breaks out. No one has survived that long. Already in 1900 his doctors give up hope. He is dead. Two decades later he lives on, a holy drinker spitting blood. O Calmette, O Guérin, O BCG— the year after his death, the vaccine becomes available; ships arriving too late.

He is babbling about a ship that will take him to a beautiful country. And he keeps confusing it with Italy, where his mother waits for him and the vainly hoped-for cure. He is looking back; forward no longer looks like much of a cure. His mouth froths; his screams and curses rend the remaining canvas.

And Jeanne keeps guard and watches. A cat noticing out of the corner of her eyes everything that revolves around her one and only. Modi spits blood and drinks to numb the pain. The bitter juices hasten his tuberculosis. Whatever he can get his hands on. The disease feels encouraged by the hunger and the cold. And he whispers to Zbo, Wouldn't it be magnificent if we could contemplate our own corpses? I leave behind the muck. I know whatever there is to know.

He has become a madman who has trouble breathing and feeds on his tubercular hatred. Indeed, the bacilli of hatred form an alliance with his tuberculosis. He hates Jeanne's submissiveness, her self-surrender, her mute passivity, her complicity with his self-destruction. And he hates her twice rounded belly. In his last portraits he paints her ugly, shapeless, sad.

On the Rue de la Grande Chaumière she watches her beloved die without calling the doctor. It is January. The tuberculosis has jumped to his brain; the bacilli find their path. The stove remains empty; there is no coal. Tiny droplets form on the walls, combine, run down. The small windows are steamed up, the L-shaped boat is no longer steerable, it drifts over the roofs of Paris. Water has to be fetched from the courtyard, but Jeanne no longer descends so as not to take her eyes off her darling even for a second. There are still some candle ends, and oil lamps. She has reserved his dying for herself; it belongs to no one but her. Modi no longer runs away. He will be hers for ever.

They are entirely alone. Ortiz has gone away for a week, Zbo is in bed with influenza. Jeanne crouches next to him on the mattress, harvests every second of this sight. Calling the doctor, what for? He is here, with her. She gazes at her prince for a long time. Mute. So this is how one dies. She wants to fly with him from this muck into heaven, as they had agreed. They had a pact.

When Ortiz returns, he finds Jeanne still in the same position, teeth chattering with cold, in an indescribably filthy apartment. Empty bottles, open tins of sardines under a layer of ice. Oil sloshing at the bottom of the tin. The two mattresses, pushed close together, are streaked with oil. For eight days they ate nothing but sardines in oil, picked the slippery fish from the tins and shoved them into their numb mouths with their fingers. No hot meals.

Chaim got Ortiz to tell him Modi's last words, and he listens to them over and over during his journey in the hearse. *Cara Italia*, he said and pressed Jeanne's hand. *Cara Italia*. She was his wordlessly suffering Madonna, she was his little, shrunken mother, she was Livorno and the swallows and the Mediterranean. Yes, she kept shrinking until she resembled his mother. And time and time again: *Cara Italia*. He alone could do that—this eternal, accursed love for the fantasy country called *Italia*. Why on earth had he not remained in the paradise he forever longed for? Stay where you are.

And now that he unmistakably hears the *Cara Italia* echo in his ears, hears Modi slurring his words, Soutine is again aware of one thing: He has always cursed his village; even now on his gurney he wants to spit, never wants to see it again. Would rather revisit the Pyrenees where he ran miserably from hill to hill with his easel. Never again see the stinking village with its dilapidated wooden sheds, or hear the name Smilovichi, which hounded him in his nightmares, punching away at him. But Modi. That's what he stammered when Jeanne lay down next to him on the mattress: *Cara Italia*.

It is a January evening in 1920; he leaves La Rotonde, it is pouring with rain, his studio is close by—why does he not go there? He keeps going, mute and blind, gets to the Rue de la Tombe-Issoire (God, how I tremble when I write this name!), winds up at the Place Denfert-Rocherau, sits at the feet of the Belfort lion, and a cough rocks him, surges through him in this queer, rainy night. He coughs and writhes, spits his blood at the lion's paws. Then he staggers towards the Rue de la Grande Chaumière, climbs the steep staircase to his studio, flings himself on the bed next to Jeanne, who is eight months pregnant. And again spits blood, again and again. Nobody has so much blood.

Tittering, chattering swallows above the Mediterranean. *O Livorno!* This crown of screams and shrieks I give to you, poet with a billy goat's head. Early in the morning of 22 January, Ortiz knocks repeatedly at the door, then runs and hurls himself against it until it bursts open. The Chilean told us. Amedeo on the bed. In Jeanne's arms. Wheezing quietly, calling her *Cara Italia*. Ortiz calls a doctor who instantly arranges for Modi to be taken to the Charité, the paupers' hospital where *clochards* do their last round before making their exit. By the time he reaches the corner of the Rue Jacob and the Rue des Saints-Pères, he has lost consciousness and will never re-emerge from his Mediterranean. Two days later, on 24 January 1920, it is over. Saturday. Tuberculous meningitis. It is 8.45 p.m.

How late is it, Ma-Be?

Relax, it doesn't matter, close your eyes, we'll be there soon.

How often has she whispered it already: We'll be there soon. Time has been taken over by the morphine tincture. She takes care of the rest. The hearse leads the way to Paris, past Paris, beyond Paris, as if the entrance to Paradise can no longer be found. Some clinic is hiding there, appears to expect him and conceals itself from the eyes of the Occupiers. All he knows is this: it is not the Charité. Soutine stops wondering how late it is, whether it is day or night, or dusk. They drive endlessly, endlessly slowly; it is the longest day of his life.

And two days later still. A shadow flits over the pavement, a white shadow, tiny, skinny, extinguished. Jeanne Hébuterne. She is twenty-three. She knew him for barely three years. She has lived a mere three years. She was with him in Nice and Vence. Zbo had sent him to the south, to Vence; his palette was to brighten in the magnificently brilliant sun. He was to escape the Spanish flu raging in Paris, and the cannonade. In every life there are many good reasons to flee. From 23 March 1918, a glorious spring day, to well into May, Paris is being pounded by Big Berthas. Twenty-one shells hit Paris on that first day, fired from the St Gobain forest, 120 kilometres away and 16 kilometres behind the front.

And in January of '20 Jeanne again carries her rounded belly in her hands. She walks the way heavily pregnant women walk. She is led down the hallways in the morgue through an underground maze to Amedeo, who was supposedly loved by who knows what gods. When she sees his body, she cries out just once, like a mad animal, mad with grief. She stays with him a long time without saying a word. She remains standing not far from the door, does not kiss him, only stares at him for long in an effort to understand the dead riddle that has intruded into her life. Cuts a lock off her hair and places it in his hand. Then she steps backward towards the door without taking her eyes from her beloved.

Montparnasse knows everything. Nowhere does a rumour travel faster than here. There is a pact; she wants to fulfil it. It's all she has left. She spends the night in a cheap hotel, with Paulette Jourdain at her side. The maid finds a knife under the pillow. She once drew a portrait of herself in which she rammed a knife into her breast. Oh, the strength of a wrist. Little Madonnas have infinite strength. Has only one of her paintings survived? The sight of a courtyard, deep down, in which a thorny, bleak tree dozes away, viewed from high above, from the roof. Some day her other pictures will emerge, decades later, from among the effects her brother carelessly left behind. No one expected any; little Madonnas are not meant to paint. But Rimbaud's girl with the orange lips was an astounding painter.

Jeanne is calm; she has seen him die and there is nothing else to see. There is nothing else to know. The next day, the 25th, her parents and brother pick her up from Zbo's flat, take her from the Rue Joseph-Bara to the Rue Amyot where she grew up. Nothing is said. The reproach is mute and fierce. They have known all along. Jeanne is deeply walled inside the silence she has erected around and within herself for years.

At three in the morning she rises; the brother, who was to watch over her, has fallen asleep from exhaustion. She walks on ashen soles through the flat like a sleepwalker—no human being walks as silently—goes into the living room, does not bump into furniture, opens the window, climbs on the windowsill. Turns around, turns her face to the flat's interior so as not to have to face the street, and flies backward from the fifth floor, inside her the second child. *Cara Italia*. We will have her with us over there. She watches the windows slide up in front of her, who would have thought there are so many; endlessly she falls, the windows are rushing towards the sky, she does not see the street her head will hit. Rough cobblestones. A dull thud, but also a cracking, like the cracking of a dark, stringy nut. She lies on the cobbles, a doll with torn limbs; blood runs from her skull over her face, a delicate, thin trickle.

How long does she lie there? Two, three hours? In the morning, a street sweeper with his besom and his wheelbarrow discovers her when he starts his job. Tenderly he lifts her up, takes her in his arms, looks up at the building, rings all the bells. The father opens, Hébuterne. He does not want to accept his daughter's body, does not want her in his house, that broken doll. Let her go look for her Italian, who still lies in the morgue. The father tells the street sweeper to take his daughter to the Rue de la Grande Chaumière, to the studio where she lived with Modigliani. Gently, the man lays the young woman into his wheelbarrow. He places his besom across her.

In the hearse, Soutine tries to visualize her path, the streets her small, delicate body will have seen. The path is long; all paths to the operation are long. He turns into the Rue Lhomond, walks towards Claude Bernard, continues even farther south to the Boulevard de Port Royal, turns right and straight onto the Boulevard du Montparnasse. The man is strong, is used to burdens; the gruff man at the door has given him a few banknotes; this is a job. Soutine sees the streets in his mind's eye; how often has he run through the canyons at night when there was no sleep to be had? In his morphine dream he runs behind the street sweeper, behind Jeanne's light body. At last, the Rue de la Grande Chaumière. But the concierge at No. 8 won't let him enter; he needs a permit from the police, over in the Rue Delambre, crosses once again the Boulevard du Montparnasse. And up under the roof. Ortiz opens the door. The street sweeper lays the young woman on the bed, stands there sheepishly, fingers his cap, stares at the body with its blood-streaked face. Ortiz gives him a coin and he leaves. It is still icy cold, it is January. Jeanne does not need a morgue.

The next day is Modi's funeral; she lies alone on the bed. They want to bury her, alone, in the cemetery at Bagneux, without her lice-ridden painter friends. No one is allowed to attend. Now she belongs to them again. The little Madonna is put to rest in the suburb south of the city. No one is there to call out *Cara Italia* after her. Everything has gone silent. The burial, too, is silent. Ten years later, she will grab her odds and ends, become a gentle dove and fly into the city to the Père Lachaise Cemetery, into the grave of her prince. The tombstone speaks Italian.

Many times the painter will slip into the Rue Amyot, trying not to be seen. No one will ever know he was there, no one will watch him. He alone knows what he does on the opposite pavement. He looks up to the window that Jeanne flew from that night; he clearly sees her jump, slows her down with his gaze, looks at the street she must have hit, tries to intuit the exact spot. But the cobblestones remain silent; the blood that ran from her skull has long been washed away by the Paris rain. One time a window opens in the house next door; a young woman climbs onto the windowsill. He cries out: Don't! Don't jump! Don't jump!

Only then does he notice that she is holding a rag to clean the window and that a colleague of hers inside the flat is hanging on to her so she won't lose her balance. The two women laugh at him with good cheer when he cries out; he understands only too well their little Polish teasing when the would-be window-jumper hikes up her apron, leisurely and genially baring her thigh and the hem of an underskirt. The painter blushes, pulls his hat farther over his forehead and scurries off.

He does not envy Modi, nor Jeanne's flight; not that last pirouette for him on the ice of the January puddles, nor the flight backwards of a lonely airborne body in the cruel blue sky of his love. But the flight will never again vanish from his dream. He will tell Mademoiselle Garde about it and forever remember her shocked face. Jeanne flies from the window in the Rue Amyot, past endless floors, and the painter merges with his dream and the gurney in the hearse, where he lies on his left side, doubled over, an embryo with fingernails stained with paint.

A PHARMACIST FROM PHILADELPHIA

Doctor Bog enters the white room and somewhat brusquely addresses the painter, who quietly lies in his bed of flowers: You are healed, Monsieur Soutinhaim. You no longer need operation. All is well. The French Triple was successful. The holy trinity of proton pump inhibitor and two antibiotics. Helicobacter pylori will trouble you no more. Your stomach ulcer is gone, so don't mourn it. Think of that white, beautiful milk; venerate the cows; think back with nostalgia to the bismuth powder. Revel in your white freedom from pain. You can stay here as long as you like. Let me repeat: You are healed! Healed! You may keep your memories; they are yours to do with as you please. Bask in them, magnify episodes that matter to you, tweak them to your heart's content, or delete them in a fury—it's all allowed. Keep what you think is worth keeping and destroy images you want to sweep from this world. Get some rest. Isn't it wonderful to dwell in this white place? You have reached your destination. You even have a right to be here. I should add one thing, though. There is one thing, and one thing only, you must not do:

Here, you must not paint. You understand? Never again. The consequences for you would be horrific. I shall ask Doctor Kno to take the minutes.

Shortly before his final slipping away, Modi breathes into the ear of his dealer, Zbo: Don't be sad, I am leaving you a genius painter!

Zbo looks incredulous. No one puts faith in the revelations of the prophet from Livorno. He is probably already in a delirium where his naked goddesses, eyes closed in rapture, welcome him to a resplendent Mediterranean country. *Cara Italia*, O sweet home!

And it was Modi, too, who had quietly coached Soutine in the Cité Falguière: What you need is a dealer, Chaim.

It was he who in 1916 introduced him to Leopold Zborowski, the son of a landowner and student poet who in 1914, one month before the outbreak of the Great War, had arrived in Paris from Krakow full of lust for life and who was soon to forget the Sorbonne. A happy-go-lucky outsider who lived the high life on tick and had a weak heart. First he keeps buying rare books from the *bouquinistes* to resell, then the first canvasses arrive and are piled up in his living room. Kisling, his neighbour on the Rue Joseph-Bara, takes him into the world of the Montparnasse painters. In March '16 he becomes Modigliani's dealer. Contract: fifteen francs per day, plus paints, canvasses, models . . . The Italian paints in Zborowski's living room, daily from two to six. And one day he drags along Soutine and introduces him to Zbo.

A first-class painter, you'll see.

Zbo looks down his nose. He loves Modigliani, in front of whose canvasses he raptly stammers: What poetry! From a drawer he fetches a candle to show off his marvels to his visitors, fishing them out of a pile, passionately fondling them with both hands and eyes, nodding his head in rapture over Modigliani's naked beauties. What poetry! Look at them!

And he loves Utrillo, but not this awful, smelly oaf from Belorussia. Looking at his paintings makes his hair stand on end. Where is the poetry here? Nothing but hunger, distorted things and contorted faces; only distress, no feast for the eyes. Small people who stare in fright at the utter desolation of the world.

But Chaim clings to Modi; increasingly they show up together, two halves, inseparable in their hungry misery. The handsome Italian from a fine family and the uncouth oaf who snuffles and smacks his lips at the table and wipes his mouth with his sleeve. Hanka Sierpowska, Zbo's partner, cannot stand this guy who is hypersensitive, quick to take offence, and whose shyness is but a fragile shell a ferocious fit of rage can blow apart at any moment.

Why do you keep dragging in that unwashed Yid? Hanka hisses.

Modigliani says he's an incredibly gifted painter. And that he has some miracle in store for us.

Hanka curls her lip and rolls her eyes each time Zbo repeats the sentence.

There's no way we're going to see that miracle. His paintings are as repulsive and filthy as the man himself.

And Hanka stomps her dainty aristocratic foot on the wooden floor.

Zbo tries to get rid of him as soon as possible, sends him to the Pyrenees for three years, from 1919 to 1922, so he won't have to see him around and jeopardize his peace with Hanka. At the end of 1919, he signs a contract with Soutine. Five francs per day. And now off with you to Céret, famous for its cherries. *Céret est célèbre pour ses cerises!*

Two years later Zbo has yet to receive a single painting. He makes the journey himself, finds Soutine dejected and ready to burn all his paintings. The courtyard of the Garreta Hotel has already seen too much black smoke. Zbo manages to wrest most of the paintings from him. And returns to Paris with 200 paintings in a rented lorry.

As for Soutine, he in turn hates Zbo, who humiliates him, delays or forgets to pay him, sells his paintings without giving him his share. Who lets him feel: You are not Modigliani! Who sends him to the Côte d'Azur, to Cagnes and to Vence, anywhere that is far away. And then the miracle happens. Because miracles do not like to forget their soil . . . and keep their addresses.

Three years after Modigliani's death a thunderbolt strikes Montparnasse. In December 1922, Doctor Barnes appears in Paris, an American billionaire about whom people whisper that he started out as a paperboy and became exactly the kind of self-made man America has always admired. Son of a butcher from a blue-collar suburb of Philadelphia, he breezed through his studies with lightning speed and at age twenty was a Doctor of Medicine. He has invented a cure for universal conjunctivitis: Argyrol, a serum he now dribbles into the eyes of newborns. With the antiseptic Argyrol he has made his fortune and built a pharmaceutical empire. The eyes of the world thank you. God bless America!

He has another illumination when he realizes that the world consists of more than inflamed eyes and his miracle drug. And that pharmaceutical empires are as mortal as Chinese emperors. He embarks on a quest for colourful eternity, assigns himself a mission and travels to the capital of painting. Shortly before the Great War he had already taken the trip to Europe to buy dozens of paintings by Renoir and Cézanne as well as Matisse and Picasso. In 1922, he builds a museum for his treasures in Merion near Philadelphia to instil a sense of awe in the employees of his Argyrol factory and to cleanse their eyes with the beauty of art. Both white and black workers are welcome in his company; he is a liberal employer who has the well-being of his employees at heart. He has loved African art ever since his mother took him to the Methodist services and he connected with the dark-skinned children. The antiseptic is not the be-all and end-all, either. Lift up your disinfected eyes on high and see the paintings hung in several rows on top of one another. The treasury is almost full when the pharmacist's hunting instinct reawakens.

Praise be the eyes' illumination! In December 1922 he shows up again, preceded by a rumour that thousands of dollars will roll through the narrow streets from the Boulevard Saint-Germain to the banks of the Seine. He does the rounds of the galleries, joins forces with Paul Guillaume, the collector and dealer of African art, strides down the Rue Bonaparte an American Napoleon. Stern gaze behind his glasses, at times wide and affable, accompanied by sudden bursts of laughter. The pharmacist's eye is strict and demanding, the art addict's impassioned and enraptured. The whole of humankind depends on the lust of the eyes, on extraordinary feasts for the eyes. Albert Coombs Barnes is fifty. He is not interested in buying daubs; he is looking for the geniuses. Montmartre and Montparnasse are electrified by the entrance of the American Croesus, and the art dealers prick up their ears when the dollars jingle in the alleyways. Whom will it strike this time, who will be the lucky one?

America invented him and he wants to give back to America: a paradise for the eyes, stuffed with masterpieces of modern art, with the best that good hard dollars can buy. At Guillaume's, he happens upon Soutine's *Pastry Chef* and does not trust his pharmacist eyes. The little apprentice is stupendous: art has never known one like him. Pastry apprentices were overlooked until now. Guillaume discovered him when he went to some painter to look at a Modigliani. His eyes fell on the incredible confectioner and screamed inwardly: Masterpiece! Outwardly, he appeared unmoved, so as not to drive up the price.

Red, an unbridled celebration of red: vermilion, crimson, purple, amaranth, cherry red, madder red, scarlet, ruby . . . It is the pastry chef Soutine painted in Céret: his name is Rémy Zocchetto and he is seventeen years old. With the misfortune of an enormous right ear sticking out and with a red handkerchief hiding his left hand as if it were a stump. A large blood-red stain on his belly marks the spot where stomach ulcers dwell. A painting that will change Soutine's life. Indeed, it is his conquest of America. Barnes is beside himself with excitement.

Wonderful, wonderful! . . . Show me more!

For two weeks, Guillaume has to chauffeur him around town in his shiny automobile, a Hispano-Suiza, to make the rounds of the galleries. The hunting instinct awakes anew every day, forever insatiable. He wants to see the dealer of the *Pastry Chef* now, right on the spot. Zborowski is caught off guard, has no clue initially why Barnes would come for this hideous Soutine, tries to sell him Modiglianis, which since the Italian's death have been bringing in tidy sums of money. No, not this time.

I want to see paintings by that Soutine, do you understand?

The pharmacist from Philadelphia is becoming impatient. The bewildered Zbo bends down and drags the canvasses out from underneath his worn-out sofa, one after another. He peeks sideways at the crazy American, as Guillaume signals Zbo with his eyebrows.

And Mr Argyrol continues to stammer: Wonderful . . . wonderful . . .

Barnes gets into a frenzy and buys up more than fifty paintings, though some in Montparnasse even whisper of seventy and yet others claim a hundred. Montparnasse's rumour mill is a gigantic magnifying glass. There he stands right in Zborowski's living room and announces with the stentorian voice of the almighty pharma god: This one, and this one, and this one . . . as if the week had more than seven days. He pays peanuts, fifteen, twenty or thirty dollars at most for a painting. His first bout translates into fifty-two Soutines. For a few bottles of Argyrol to disinfect one's eyes. But pharma gods create myths, a new aura of desiring and of being desired.

Montparnasse now has its American fairy tale and it gets shared feverishly. Everyone trips over their words as they pass on how the American entered the scene and with one hand fished Soutine from the pond of the sodden painters of Montparnasse, while the other held enough dollars to buy anything he fancied in the world. The silent man from Smilovichi used to be forever pitied, someone so hungry he could barely keep going. Now envy and resentment appear, the loyal companions of someone in demand. How many unrecognized geniuses have waited all their lives for a pharma god who, like Barnes, would enter their caves and grungy studios, point his index finger at their canvasses and declare loudly, This one, and this one, and this one . . .

When Doctor Bog entered the white room, the painter Soutinhaim couldn't help but immediately remember the entrance of the American billionaire into his life. The healer of all kinds of conjunctivitis! And the pharma god had his Soutine loot shipped out of Le Havre. As early as 1923, the paintings manage to leap across the ocean. A first overseas embassy now exists in the villa in Merion near Philadelphia.

The numb painter wants to rise from his gurney and whisper into the ears of the two drivers of the hearse, I also had a chauffeur once, do you hear me? And Zbo's luxury automobile was always at my beck and call.

But his voice does not reach the drivers, who are looking for narrow lanes through tiny villages. His voice is far away; he has dived deep into the downy, cottony memories Sertürner's morphine tincture is granting him.

Zborowski, the Polish poet who is transforming himself into an art dealer, who loves white suits and white shoes, has finally acquired an automobile and employs a chauffeur, Daneyrolles. Modigliani's early death had made the collectors keen on his paintings, and since

Barnes's foray the Americans are flocking to him and leaving bundles of dollars on his living-room table.

Daneyrolles! Yes, Soutine can see him clearly before his closed eyes. He has himself chauffeured all the way to Nice without a stop, doubled over and asleep on the back seats: a painter embryo in a Lincoln Le Baron. Zbo sends him to the Côte d'Azur when Paris is too grey.

Vence or Cagnes, the light is magnificent, Zbo says.

The Spanish flu is over, these are the Golden Twenties. But Soutine hates this blinding, confident light; he is as desperate as he was in the Pyrenees. He wipes out whatever he paints, wrecks canvasses, slashes them.

I'd like to leave Cagnes, this landscape I can't stand. I'll have to paint a few wretched still lifes.

He is alone. He goes around in circles. Nothing keeps him there. He wants to get away. He hates the sun. He hates Cagnes. And he hates himself. He hates that he hates himself.

He is in every painting, the small, teetering rambler on the yellow country road who can barely go on. Or does he already lie on the road? A drunk? Someone who stumbled? Someone crushed by life's wretchedness? There is a huge plane tree in the village square of Cagnes; he has to paint it again and again, as the darkest tree ever, towering over the universe, a fringed, menacing black mass. Soutine to Daneyrolles: This tree is a cathedral!

There, too, the same hapless dwarfish figure will appear. Tiny icon of forlornness. Chauffeur Daneyrolles, though, has been given an additional, secret mandate by Zborowski: to keep an eye on the painter and collect his work. The surveillance of an artist. Once he has taken Soutine to the edge of some forest or to a quiet street in Vence and the painter has put up his easel at the right distance and has started to paint, Daneyrolles fills a little bucket with water from the next fountain and sets out with his sponge to wash first the bonnet of his Lincoln, then leisurely the doors and, with almost demonstrative slowness, the door handles. Then he polishes the automobile with his chamois until it shines beyond measure.

For hours he polishes his car, all the while taking sidelong glances at the painter, monitoring his every movement. When another desperate storm breaks and Soutine mutilates his canvas in a shrill fury, Daneyrolles is to distract the painter, calm him down, accompany him for a little drink to the next pub. The chauffeur will then sneak outside, diligently gather up the ruins, stow them away in the boot of the Lincoln to hand over to Zbo. The latter will take them to a restorer, who will need surgical skills to re-assemble the shreds into a whole.

Zborowski invites the visitor from the future into his small flat on the Rue Joseph-Bara.

Take a good look at what Soutine gave himself permission to do!

Zbo points to the portrait of the old actress. The canvas lies on the floor, lacerated, as if he wanted to cut the flesh of his model's arm off the bone.

I'll have to spend another fortune with Jacques to have him restore the painting.

A few days earlier his old friend Miestchaninoff had to wrest his own portrait from Soutine's hands because he was no longer satisfied and wanted to destroy it. When the painter finds a good number of his paintings in Zbo's flat that he thought he had destroyed, he uses a moment he is not being watched to quickly snatch up the canvasses and shove them into the living-room fireplace. Flames erupt, smoke spreads everywhere, neighbours come running, the fire brigade is called, police officers stand around, a report is written.

And an enraged Soutine has long fled the scene.

Daneyrolles, the chauffeur: He wants me to read! He recites Rimbaud for me! We have discussions about gladiator fights and about the soul that involves itself with our earthly affairs without leaving heaven, about Seneca's letters to Lucilius!

And in the summer of '28, Daneyrolles drives him to Bordeaux, to the art critic Elie Faure, who is writing the first serious book about the foreign artist, describing him as a religious painter whose religion is colour itself. But he's wrong! the painter wants to get up to disagree. And then there is Faure's daughter. Soutine wants to banish the memory, no, he does not want it, does not want to remember.

Dershtikt zolstu veren! May you choke on it!

Daneyrolles and his spotless Lincoln, yes. The rides to Nice, yes. But not Marie-Zéline. His shyness and clumsiness make a hash of his marriage proposal. He has never figured out how to talk to women. Modi seduced them with his voice; he would hum and whisper poetry into their ears that sent shivers down their spines. They started, closed their eyes—and already he had his hand on the arm, making contact, after the ear, with the skin. She does the rest. Soutine shoos away the image of the tenderly demanding, whispering Modi, who only makes him more embarrassed. He waits until he finds himself alone in the room with Marie-Zéline. A long time he remains silent; she starts to find it scary. Finally a hoarse word comes from his lips: Mademoiselle . . .

Yes, Monsieur Soutine, please go on.

He examines the carpet she stands on as if he has lost something: a coin, a pencil, a scrap of paper. He desperately searches the floor for what he has not lost. He dares not lift his eyes and look at her. Mademoiselle Faure herself has begun to check the floor around her legs and for the life of her cannot detect anything. Beauty bewilders him, punishes him. In the cheap brothels, Modi would quickly snatch up the little jewels, who would follow him to the room giggling, while Soutine picked the ugly, shapeless ones whose features spoke of early drinking and poor nutrition, whose skins told of lives full of defeat.

Monsieur Soutine, please, what is it you would like?

Mademoiselle Faure, someone . . . would . . . wants . . . to . . . propose . . . to you.

And she laughs this light and carefree laughter that defeats him. A laughter as if from a different planet, an airy, delicate laughter that says life is way too light.

Oh well, who is it? Three days ago, a pilot proposed to me. And I accepted, you understand? One day he'll even let me fly with him, carry me up into the sky.

The painter is so embarrassed he wishes to disappear into the carpet. He bolts from the room. Rejected. With a pilot he cannot compete, even though he no longer wears his paint-stained blue overalls but a suit from Barclay's. The shame stays the same; it will not accept a disguise. Shortly afterwards, the pilot crashes, and Soutine gets into a row with the most knowledgeable critic who has ever cast an eye on his works.

Es brent mir oyfn hartsn. It burns my heart, he wants to stammer in the white paradise.

And another pilot crashes. Zbo likes to live large now that Barnes has bought the sofa treasures off him. His simulation of genuine wealth looks deceptively real; heedlessly he blows what he takes in. His gallery on the Rue de Seine opens in 1926, but its success lasts barely two or three years before the rush is over. With the year 1929 comes the stock-market crash, the financial crisis. The Americans stay away and the demand for art is gone. Mister Argyrol battles the inflammation of American eyes in vain.

Zbo speculates on the stock market with no luck at all and at age forty-three in March of '32 dies lonely, ruined. His weak heart won its case. Money is just money, meant to be blown, and that's all there is to it. Wealth is a pack of lies and houses of cards are meant to collapse. When it comes to throwing away money and talent, Montparnasse is the centre of the world. His white dandy shoes no longer have an owner. A shared, anonymous pauper's grave. Life is never anything but pretend wealth. It lives large, then stumbles.

Soutine now lives in the Passage d'Enfer; one needs to cross only the Boulevard Raspail and is at the Montparnasse Cemetery. He is frightened of the address: Passageway to Hell. Names make him superstitious. How short the paths here are, and yet how endless seems the journey to the final operation.

CARCASS OF BEEF AND DOCTOR BARDAMU'S LETTER

Doctor Bog enters the room with measured steps wearing his splendid white garb and a pensive expression, steps up to the artist's bed, barely looks at his face and immediately begins to talk: Blood is a very special juice.

And he adds in a dreamy, slightly reproachful murmur: Heinrich . . . Heinrich.

No one hears it clearly. Sometimes Doctor Bog had a whiny voice when on his rounds he unctuously told the painter about medical progress throughout the whole wide world. He never talked about the war. Still, he seemed to grumble in his white paradise. The clinic obviously provided him with little real reason to rejoice. Apparently, not everything there went as well as he would have liked. It was only when he showed the painter Billroth's resectioned stomach that a fleeting smile crossed his face.

The painter Soutinhaim lies under his clean hospital sheet as though in a bed of snow and remains silent. He is determined to stay silent in this place, too. Just as he has all his life. Put each word on the snow scale. Not even a small flake from the artist's life. Nothing but the paintings themselves. Doctor Bog is not to prise out any more than that crazy Henry Miller did, who in the early '30s was to interview him for some two-bit American rag. A cloud of silence. Only there was no cloud of cigarette smoke in this place; he had to do without. Silently the painter stares at the white blanket, his hands beside each thigh as if lying at attention. But he hides his fingertips in his palms to prevent Doctor Bog from seeing the traces of paint that frame his fingernails. He clenches his hands into fists. And remains silent.

Unruffled, Doctor Bog muses on, not letting any stubborn painter's silence put him off his stride.

Is blood comprised more of life or of death? It certainly, Doctor Bog serenely continues, supplies this laughable envelope of a body, sometimes firm, at others times wizened, with nutrients and oxygen, flushes it with hormones and other magnificent substances, controls the cells' harmony. And yet, blood is also flowing, circulating death. Because, you know, those twenty-five quintillions of red blood cells that drift in it like mad rafts are dead cells. Nothing but losers. They have lost their genetic material, almost all their cellular organs. They are a deep-red death. Blood tells a never-ending story of dying, of unrecoverable losses.

And please don't tell me now, Monsieur Soutinhaim, that you can't bear to see blood. What about the bleeding beef carcass, the window displays of the butcher shops in Céret, the butcher boy who shimmers in all hues of blood red, the flayed hare lying on the table as if crucified? Everyone knows that for you there was no Sunday entertainment more thrilling than going to watch catch-wrestling at the Vél d'Hiv cycle track. The grappling and choking of human flesh, the burst brow ridges, the blood on the wrestlers' singlets, the drawn-out moans coming from the tangled knot of flesh. Where was I? Oh yes, the red blood.

Now Doctor Bog smiles with some satisfaction as he tells the painter about the astounding death in the life cycle of red blood cells. But he is actually more delighted with the white blood cells. For they are fifty billion living, fully functioning cells. They defend the body against infections. Like tiny guards, they are on watch in the tissues, and wait. Eventually, when they have waited undeployed in bone marrow for too long, they commit suicide. In a white paradise, all blood cells ought to be white because there, death no longer exists, Doctor Bog says. Red blood is, in effect, death's domain. A gigantic dead river flows through the living body. Can you imagine?

Soutine, the painter, remains silent, and silent. He thinks of the cut on Ma-Be's forehead when their angry landlady in Champigny brusquely slammed the door in her face. He thinks of the rooster bleeding to death over the threshold of the house on the morning of Yom Kippur.

Once dead, they still make themselves useful. Just like artists, right, Monsieur Soutinhaim? Red blood cells fulfil their function long after their death. For one hundred and twenty days they tirelessly transport oxygen from the lungs into the body's tissues until the spleen's or the liver's phagocytes gobble them up. Every day 200 billion of them fall victim to this massacre. 200 billion, Monsieur.

Doctor Bog pauses for effect, sinks with grand seriousness into a demonstrative thoughtfulness. Then he starts and continues, Isn't it strange that people know so little about that special juice that circulates inside them? That they are so deeply shocked when it pours out? As if they didn't realize that it exists inside them, this moving stream of sheer death held back by tissue and skin. The outermost layer of our skin, too, consists of dead cells: our body's envelope is a velvety cemetery. There is a conspicuous amount of death inside the human body at any given moment, don't you think? Today I won't even mention your stomach lining!

And the word *perforation* that the doctor in Chignon had uttered so emphatically enters once more into the mind of the painter, who listens because there is nothing else he can do in his white sheets. But he remains silent.

Doctor Bog continues to speak of red, dead blood for a long time. He also says: Those five litres are a small world wherein life and death lend each other a helping hand. Death, an efficiency expert, floats in the fragile life stream, clinging to its oxygen-laden red rafts.

The painter remembers how he once called out, before slashing new canvasses, I don't want to drown in my own blood!

He lets Doctor Bog continue his self-satisfied musings. He no longer listens. A gentle slumber carries him away from his white sheets. When at some point he opens an eye, Doctor Bog is no longer there. He dozes off again but is startled awake by fierce knocking and a forceful voice shouting in the hallway: Department of Health! Department of Health!

The painter gets a fright. Here, too? But nothing happens. Nobody bursts into his room. Did he really hear that voice? The ear likes to deceive us. With hissing sounds it suggests the noise of departing locomotives. It tortures with tinnitus and acute hearing loss. No, somebody really did shout Department of Health outside the door. He thinks of the beef carcass. It is still drifting towards its decomposition. He had it delivered from the Vaugirard slaughterhouses, which he knew only too well since his days in the Beehive. He built a special scaffold in his studio on the Rue du Saint-Gothard, fastened it with ropes, such hard work, the butcher boy had to help. For days he stands in front of it, wrestles with the beef carcass; the flesh begins to stink, loses its bright red colour, goes brownish, dries further with each hour. It needs to be freshened up!

Paulette Jourdain, patience personified and go-to girl delegated by Zborowski to assist the painter, hauls bucket after bucket of beef blood to his studio. One in each hand. Her soft, chubby palms show the red imprint of the handle. The painter prattles about Rembrandt, keeps running to the Louvre like a madman to gape at the Old Master's beef carcass there. And in the meantime an impossible stench spreads that makes Paulette grimly breathe through her mouth.

Monsieur Soutine, I'd rather not go there any longer.

She is embarrassed when the slaughterhouse workers eye her with distrust. She can read the suspicion behind their brows. What does the girl need all that blood for? What's she doing with it?

It's for a large sick man, she had stammered.

The painter grabs the bucket, pours the blood over the brown cadaver. He rejoices because the beef carcass shines again, death triumphs, regenerated by the fresh blood. It trickles down in small streams and through the floor planks until the people who live below start to scream and call the police. They suspect murder and mayhem. The stench is unbearable. The whole place stinks to high heaven!

Suddenly there is a fierce knock on the door. The painter hears it again, just now, in the white paradise.

Who is it?

Department of Health! Open the door now!

The painter gets a fright; he is deathly pale. An official with white apron and white cap enters and wants to impound the ghastly stinking beef carcass. Green flies buzz about the studio. Soutine is aghast because his painting is not finished. In the corner, Rembrandt crows triumphantly.

Paulette pleads on behalf of the desperate painter: Can't you see he is painting it? He needs it to complete his painting. Please!

The health authorities have mercy. They draw their syringes and inject ammonia into the battered flesh of the cadaver. With a few moves they teach him how to preserve animals without fouling up the building. From then on, he walks through the world gratefully carrying formaldehyde and ammonia and an assortment of large syringes in order to preserve the triumph of death in all its blood-red freshness. Turkeys, hares, pheasants also arrive. He has several beef carcasses delivered to his studio and each time he fixates on another distinct aspect of juicy death: a small lump of yellow rancid fat, the contortion of a limb or the blood clots on the undulating surface.

It is in 1925 that for the first time ever he is able to rent a proper flat, and it is only steps from Parc Montsouris. In addition, he rents a large studio close by, in the Rue du Saint-Gothard, where he paints the animal carcasses. *Boucherie Soutine*, the neighbours hiss. Soutine's butchery.

Again and again he runs to the Louvre, hastily buying the admissions ticket. He has to see Rembrandt's *Slaughtered Ox* . . . and Chardin's *Rayfish*, Corot's landscapes, Courbet's half-red *Trout* and his *Burial at Ornans*. One after the other, for hours. His secret visits are a ritual. To see everything. As if they were the girls who parade scantily dressed or half-naked in the *maisons closes*, one after the other and all at once. He always visits the same paintings; he cannot get enough of them, trembles with desire and awe as they drive him to despair, his eyes eating up the canvasses. He wants to devour them, carry them in his gut home to the Rue du Saint-Gothard to wrestle with them.

The guards recognize him, signal one another behind his back with alarmed gazes and pointed gestures, fearing a robbery; the stolen *Gioconda* is still on their minds. Or they fear an attack; plenty of nutcases hang out in museums and hatred of art is more common than the kissing disease. They don't know that he destroys the paintings of one artist alone . . . But never his gods'.

Department of Health! echoes once more in the hallway.

He now lives in a flat and has a studio. But the crises deepen. Pain makes him double over, attacks him suddenly, appears without warning. In Clichy, too, in the Rue d'Alsace, some time in the early months of 1928. He has collapsed in the street, is picked up by a butcher and carried to Doctor Destouches like the bleeding half of an ox. Destouches? Louis-Ferdinand Destouches? The name does not yet ring a bell.

How can he hear Destouches's voice in the hearse? Are the dying omniscient? At the end of the whole operation the man now bleeding to death can no longer distinguish between what he has experienced in his life or has only heard about. Did it happen to him, or to someone else? A life is more than one's own set of memories. Is this memory really his, or is it a foreign invader? Who separates the foreign from one's own? Surely not Doctor Bog. Does he hear all the voices that have spoken to him throughout a lifetime? Where is the recording device located? How inexhaustible is his ear? Or does Sertürner's poppy juice mix together the memories and the voices, the foreign sounds and his own experiences? Are dubious memories playing tricks on him?

Doctor Bog would know.

Destouches writes to Inspector Armand Merle, who is handling the investigation, and in the future any reasonable person will regard this letter as an invention. But chance is not rational, Eleni says, and for good reason. Doctor Bog triumphantly waves the piece of bumf; he has the evidence in his hand. Tenderly he holds the letter under the artist's nose.

Saw two patients since the beginning of the week. A neighbour's daughter chopped up badly by the abortionist from our quarter (netted me twenty francs), then a chance passer-by, some weird guy! Yesterday my doorbell rings; it's the butcher from the floor below who brings in this fellow with blood on his shirt. Deathly pale. Collapsed in front of my meat stall, the butcher says. I invite them in. Start to auscultate the guy.

Well, then, I'll be back to my shop, the fat butcher says and leaves me alone with the patient, who's tight-lipped. Seems afraid . . . At least he's dressed all right, but his neck is beyond filthy and he reeks of old sweat.

I question him, Let's hear what's happened to you, old chap. He hesitates, then tells me, It's the stomach. I have ulcer. His accent makes me think he's Russian or Polish. And I soon conclude there can be no doubt: he has an ulcer. Severe haematemesis, bright-red blood, without air bubbles and not foaming.

He is gradually stabilizing. So we talk. He says he's a painter, his name is Chaim (which he pronounces with a throaty 'ch') Soutine, has just returned from Amsterdam where he says he went to see Rembrandt's paintings; says he was strolling through the Batignolles Cemetery when he suddenly had to vomit and threw up blood . . .

He told me he's from Vilna, had a miserable childhood in a Jewish village in Lithuania, had dreamt of becoming a painter, which, he says, is an impossibility in that environment. The rabbis forbid it, though he doesn't give a hoot in hell about religion! . . .

Do I know Rembrandt's *Jewish Bride*? Sure I do, I say. And he gets going about the master's techniques: he painted parts of the sleeves with his fingers . . . Then he invokes the bride with a verse from the Song of Solomon: You, who sit in the gardens, the friends hearken to your voice; let me hear it . . .

And he continues, hits his stride. *The Anatomy Lesson*? Of course I do . . . And that hanging rooster . . . and *The Night Watch* . . . and *The Flayed Ox*? Of course! Of course! Of course!

For Hindus, dissolution means becoming, I tell him . . . He replies, Love is as strong as death.

Evening has come and we are still talking. Given his stomach, I can't advise he go for a meal. I give him some bismuth and pills to soothe his pain.

We discuss flesh . . . women . . . filthy stuff . . . he describes a flayed hare . . . I talk about African corpses . . . rotting flesh . . . women . . .

We can't just abruptly terminate the evening, so I take him along to the brothel . . .

Always yours, Louis

And why not? Chance is not rational, and for good reason. Nothing is really rational, though dreams may be. Destouches? Heard it before. In 1937, in La Coupole, when some friend shoves a photo in his face, he recognizes the doctor from Clichy instantly and takes fright. But a different name is printed underneath. Doctor Destouches, Doctor of Medicine, Faculty of Medicine in Paris, now uses his grandmother's given name as a gentle, female pseudonym: Céline. He has closed his moribund practice, bares his fangs and with a high arc catapults himself out of Clichy, and writes, still in mid-flight, a big novel, *Journey to the End of the Night*.

But the night is nowhere near its end. In 1936 Doctor Bardamu writes another one of those tranches from his toxic life: *Death on the Instalment Plan*. Indeed, death arrives in instalments and prefers diversions. The painter instantly recognizes Doctor Destouches, now a writer. It is the very same man, though under a different name. He has never been able to forget that face.

He often sees in his dreams that same Doctor Bardamu run after him in the streets of Clichy. He has changed into a venomous dwarf; in his hands rustle the corrosive sheets of paper on which he calls the bleeding patient, and others like him, vermin, scum, torturers of the West. They are his fulminating pamphlets: in his left hand, *Trifles for a Massacre*, and in his right, *The School of Corpses*. The doctor screams, his voice breaks, not for nothing is he a friend and admirer of that moustachioed grimacer: Exterminate, poison the plague of rats, down with the freaks! Let none remain, all right? None, you understand? screams the massacring doctor who had picked up and taken care of the painter that day in Clichy.

And Doctor Bardamu's wish is fulfilled: the Occupiers arrive in May of '40 and begin the cleansing job for which he has been beseeching them. They are stunned to find how avidly the poison has anticipated them. Bardamu is keen to outdo even the staunchest among them, puts to shame many of them whom he accuses of half-heartedness, and doesn't die in Sigmaringen but safe and sound in his bed in Meudon. If Doctor Bardamu had been dissected, pathologists would have marvelled at how much poison can gush from a corpse. No one has that much poison. And it doesn't stop. Later his admirers will greedily suck the corrosive juice from the holes left behind by the literary post-mortem, turn him into a loutish saint, and slur their words while gulping down the snot and hate of his smutty gospel. His logorrhoea of slaughter has found outstanding disciples.

The painter clearly hears Doctor Bardamu panting as he chases the black Corbillard; he runs as fast as he can behind the slowly advancing hearse. He has almost reached it, now bangs his fist against the rear window, presses a face against the glass that the painter recognizes with a shudder.

Vermin! Doctor Bardamu shouts. Scum! Rat!

And keeps banging his fist against the black metal. Does he belong to the Viking corps? To that scattered pack of black wolves that had charged the painter in his Corbillard? Through the rear door's two wings that have suddenly become transparent the patient distinctly sees the wolf-like doctor behind the car. The poisonous breath from the panting doctor's gorge seeps through and can be smelt inside.

Department of Health!

The painter is certain he has heard the words loud and clear from the other side of the door. He moves as if to rise from the metal gurney but immediately drops back, turns his gaze to the outside wall, curls up again, an embryo in pain. Outside, desolate potato fields visited by eager crows are passing by, when a hand touches his forehead.

THE CONSPIRACY OF THE PASTRY CHEFS

The painter in his white-as-light swaddling of sheets has noticed that the sounds from the hallway increase and decrease. In his room neither day nor night exists, nor does a window to the outside. His ear is attuned to the ebb and flow of sounds, registers them in a meaningless gratitude, and it is these ringing tides that lend a rhythm to his days, if one can call them that.

He has been healed, Doctor Bog himself has confirmed it for him. He is in a state of infinite freedom from pain. His ulcer has bid him farewell. Talk of bliss does not correspond to his state. But the pulse of life in him is gone; without his pain, he is no longer the man he was. He is the painter minus the pain. A heart without a pulse. He remembers two lines by a poet but cannot recall by whom.

With nothing around to care for, it's of no import if you are blitzed, encircled, reduced to nil.

And a feeling emerges that he does not want to call boredom, let alone weariness, because that it certainly is not. He does not miss the pain, and he lacks the discernment to consider pain precious. But he misses the bliss. There is nothing left to do in this white paradise of freedom from pain. He feels superfluous. Everything has been done, the operation has taken place or not, but either way he is the glorious outcome of a definite cure. He does not understand what French Triple means. He mutters to himself: It's all over.

And he is frightened by the sentence. If it's all over, something has to happen. The painter decides to wait for the sounds to completely disappear, but when in spite of their ebbing they do not stop altogether, he carefully folds back the glacier-white sheet and cautiously stands up. He had expected his legs to buckle but they do not. He has no idea how much time has passed and cannot remember when he last walked. His pain had always determined his pace; he had run from it, had driven himself to flee from it.

Now he puts one foot in front of the other and marvels at how easy it is, how little he senses his legs. Astounded, he takes two, three steps away from his bed, upright and not bent over, then determinedly walks to the door and quietly opens it. His head pokes through, turns left, then right. The sounds are still there. Instinctively he prepares an excuse, but he can offer it to no one in that entire long hallway. The sounds that simulate a babbling river do not come from any visible human source. They must be piped into the hallways through loudspeakers. But why? Hospital sounds, peaceful, without drama.

The painter is astonished, but the sounds from the tape recorder do not cause him alarm. His calm is imperturbable. Once more he turns his head to the left, and right, then starts walking to the left. Slowly, deliberately, he walks, watches himself walk, but there is no more pain to run from.

Without the scuffling or the shuffling of the sick and the weary, he reaches the end of the hallway. No one comes towards him; there are merely doors to his right and to his left that are slightly curved like the doors of portly, impassive refrigerators. Finally, at the end of the hallway, a window. He looks outside but does not dare to open it. And he realizes right then and there that it would be impossible. He does not need to reach out his hand and test it to be certain.

Apparently it is night outside, a white night. Searchlights that emit a glaring white light do not focus on anything. At least there is nothing he could identify as targets for the light. Indifferently, the beams of light criss-cross, disappear into a meaningless background black, not matt black but field grey, yes, field grey, at the restricted horizon.

One thing, though, bewilders him. A powdery, dense snow is falling; the white flakes gently tumble into the searchlights without really diminishing them; they simply tumble into them, then drift farther down where a thick blanket has formed.

For a while he stands at the window and watches the calm snowfall; he breathes the word 'Minsk' against the pane, tries to follow the flakes with his eyes. He rocks himself in their tranquillity, feeling an intimation of snowlike meaningless delight, gazes at the searchlights and remembers the headlights of the hearse that had stared late at night into the empty landscape.

Where had he left from that morning? Was it still the same day? He tries to remember the name of a particular place but it doesn't come back. *Chateau*, he mumbles, castle, and once more, castle. The name Jeanne d'Arc comes to mind. What business did he have there? The only thing he knows for sure is that it had been summer, August, most definitely August.

He gives up trying to come up with names, turns left and slowly climbs the staircase. The pain-free putting-one-foot-in-front-of-the-other has started to give him a little pleasure, a faint sense of wonder. Not even stair climbing causes problems. One floor up, he finds another endless hallway, one less illuminated, though, than the one he has just left. Again he walks to the window, tries to discern a horizon beyond the expanse, a row of houses, a residential tower, any feature that might indicate a town. But the bright curtain of snow and the beams from the searchlights block his view. And it had only just been August . . .

Suddenly a clicking sound behind him down the hall-way, way off in the distance. He ducks into the stairwell, where his white, slipperless socks shimmer. He pauses for a while, listens to the vanishing sound, returns to the floor below and tries to find his room. Only now does he realize that the doors are not numbered and is slightly alarmed and worried about not finding his room. His inner step-counter had roughly measured the distance to the window, so now he walks in the opposite direction and stops in front of a room. This could be it.

He opens the door, paying careful attention not to awaken another patient or alert any nursing staff to his unauthorized excursion. There is nothing in the room he can identify, no sounds of breathing, no quiet moans, no hospital snoring caused by tranquilizers administered post-operation. He is about to close the door when a small pinprick of curiosity gets the better of him.

He feels for a switch, turns on the light, is startled by the white flash but also by the sight. The room is empty. No bed, no commode, no towels or sheets. White, absolute emptiness. A cube of nothingness, within nothingness. He looks at the white floor with its mirror-like polish. There is something; something small is lying at the centre. It is a child's doll that he instantly recognizes and knows where it comes from. He looks down at it. And notices that the shoulder joints are dislocated, both of them. The arms are twisted outward completely. The hip joints appear to be solidly in their sockets, but one knee joint lies exposed.

Yes, those joints, the tender links of our vulnerability.

A lower leg has been severed, lies half a metre to the side. Who could have inflicted such injuries on the doll? It appears to have been tortured. Who would do such a thing in this clinic? In a completely empty white cube? He wants to withdraw quietly, and already his hand is on the door handle when the doll opens its eyes and looks at him with a gaze that is neither imploring nor questioning, but sternly scrutinizing. He notices its ancient face, lined and wrinkled. The painter cannot bear the doll's gaze, turns away and softly closes the door.

He walks backward. The room immediately adjacent must be his, so he reaches for the white door handle. He is wrong. This room, too, is empty and windowless. On the floor lies a well-thumbed, tattered book. He steps towards it and opens it at random, as if it were his oracle: Unworthy of good . . . incapable of gratitude . . . inept with love . . . wounded to the depth of my kidneys . . . broken palm tree . . . wine turned to vinegar . . . defiled image . . . singed garment . . . lost goblet . . . sunken ship . . . crushed pearl . . . gem flung into the floods . . . withered mandrake . . . oil poured on garbage . . . milk on ashes . . . I am sentenced to death . . . among the flock of the just . . .

What was that? The cover page is missing, has been ripped out hastily and roughly. It reminds him of something that one of the windbags circling Montparnasse like pesky satellites had once trumpeted in La Rotonde. It had sounded quite similar, was by some thousand-year-old

Armenian monk and was called *Book of Lamentations* or the like. But he can neither recall the monk's name nor that of the windbag. He can only remember an abbreviation: they called him MGM.

The next room is his. He finds his bed cover carefully turned back and his slippers tidily placed underneath the white metal at the foot of his bed. His excursion is enough for now; he sinks into his bed and falls asleep almost instantly.

How long he has slept he cannot tell. He had already noticed there were no clocks in the clinic, and he himself has never worn a watch. When you wrestle with the canvas, the wrist must be free, able to spring back, to vibrate, scrape or hatch. He lifts the sheet, touches his abdomen. Still no pain. It used to always return, could be relied on even if for a while it had kept capriciously silent: it always returned. Now its absence is almost roaring in his white belly.

He has decided to continue his forays, waits for the artificial sounds once again to die away in the hallway, leaves his room and creeps to the upper floor. He presses down on a door handle, softly eases one foot forward and stops short. In this room, he is expected.

A sort of committee or delegation—or so he thinks at first—sits on low chairs in a circle. Expectant faces immediately turn towards him and hold him in their gaze. This time he is unable to pull back; he feels caught out and forced to enter the room. There they all sit and he recognizes them immediately.

His little flock of people: those who are ignored, who serve, who have suffered indignities, who are startled by their own existence. He had painted them as if they were pharaohs, princes, dignitaries, albeit with eyes heavy with sadness, hands wrung in deep embarrassment. Weighed down, sorely tried, but upright.

The little pastry chef from Céret with the oversize right ear and the red handkerchief around his left hand that blazes like a blood-soaked flag. His cheeky-looking young colleague whose eyes are scales out of balance, the pageboy at Maxim's, the groom, the baker boy, the butcher boy, the communicant who looks like a little bride. The village idiot, the peasant girl, the boy in blue, the white choir boy, the red altar boy, the children with ancient faces, little girls holding crippled dolls like delicate little corpses. Little Charlot with his pointy nose; Marcel, the schoolboy in a blue tunic who looks at the world with such humility; the two children on public assistance with their shaved heads, hand in hand as always. He has never met other patients on his walks through the hallways, and now there is suddenly a whole room filled with a colourful crowd.

The communicant gathers her white, floor-length dress with her little gloved hands, stands up and addresses him in a thin but stern soprano: Please come in. We know you are in the clinic. You have been healed;

we know that, too. And Doctor Bog has forbidden you to paint; we learnt that as well. Come closer.

The painter hesitates. Children and adolescents make him uneasy because he fears they might recognize him as of one of them, or as the one he thinks he has long left behind: the child from Smilovichi. Children have this stern, probing gaze; it was difficult to have them sit for him for any length of time, so he had to be fast, catch their gaze, their oblique eyes, twisted hands, or the position of their shoulders, simultaneously awkward and confident.

How did they get here? Are they ill, have they had operation and are being nursed back to health and cared for? They look astonishingly unchanged, surprisingly well preserved, exactly the same as he had painted them in Céret, Civry or Champigny.

In front of him sits the serious-looking, stern committee intent on communicating something to him. Or is it a high court? Do they want to put him on trial for attempting to capture their injured dignity and their lives' truths? Did he make them sit for too long, until their young limbs hurt? Did he misrepresent them with his palette? The painter waits in silence. Time passes; they look at him with stern eyes as if to test him, and he says nothing.

A wooden doll falls to the floor. The group takes in the sound without looking at the lifeless doll; no one lowers their eyes.

We know Doctor Bog, the little pastry chef with the big ear and red handkerchief suddenly says. He switches his handkerchief from one hand to the other and flaps it as if to wave away his shyness.

Don't let him impress you. His commandments are not carved in stone. Do what you have to do when you feel you must.

The painter marvels because he remembers the terrifying determination in Doctor Bog's voice when he forbade him to paint in the clinic. It was not about dirt or paint stains, filthy brushes or oily streaks on white doors. It was not about hygiene and cleanliness. Only that he was never to touch another palette, never to hold another brush. Canvas was taboo.

Is this a conspiracy against Doctor Bog? Are the children trying to suggest that the painter Chaim Soutine ignore the prohibition against making images? He inwardly bursts out laughing, for he could never have imagined it. But they look at him sternly. Then the pageboy from the Maxim's gets up, takes his hand and leads him to the door. The little bright-red groom.

You must leave now. We must consult with one another. We'll get back to you if necessary.

So that was it? No accusations, no interrogation? Just this silent appearance in front of the commission, the inquisition of their eyes, the explicit invitation to ignore the prohibition?

The painter turns around one more time and lets his eyes take in the entire conspirators' committee or children's court. Then he softly closes the door behind him. But a mischievous curiosity gets hold of him. He wants to eavesdrop and find out what the assembly is about to debate. And he presses his ear against the curved white door.

The voices are difficult to distinguish, merging, on top of one another, speaking simultaneously, falling silent. Is it the pastry chef who speaks, the bellboy, one of the two children on public assistance, the communicant?

It was impossible to untangle anything coherent from the back-and-forth. At one point, there was talk about train tracks leading to places with Polish names. Then again they talk about the clinic, about certain procedures taking place inside it. He makes out questions followed by seconds of silence.

Does Doctor Bog know? What do you think?

Can he be trusted? We should be wary of him.

Why would he do that? Or does he actually do anything? I haven't seen him for weeks. He's hiding somewhere in here.

Then it is clearly Charlot's thin, quivering voice that now sounds decisive and reproachful, but whose first sentence the painter must have missed: With all the extremes . . . of unbearable pain and suffering? If he is omniscient, he must be aware of it, and aware of all who know pain and are silenced or made to scream by it. If he is omnipotent, he could have easily created a pain-free life. It would have been the better option. And it's what he would have done if he were good. But he plays into the hands of the torturers, has given them infinite opportunities to do their work. All those tender mucous membranes, eardrums, nail beds, nipples, silky testicles, the entire sensitive skin that encases human beings. Nothing but choice gateways for pain. Every day in the basements of the Rue Lauriston they celebrate his unwavering support. He has richly provided for the Gestapo. He has played the Beethoven records for Klaus Barbie.

One of the two blue children on public assistance could be heard now. He must have stood up; the scraping of his chair served as his little overture: The creator of everything surely has a patent for that, too. If he himself did not create pain, why does he tolerate it? And have you considered the suffering of animals, the slaughterhouses, the sudden suffocating confinement, the terrible fear of blade and stunbolt, the bursting bones, flayed skins, lacerated hides? He ought to be shocked by the endless scandal, ought to cry out, vomit with revulsion. Or at least fall silent from sheer horror. Which he has done for eternities. Maybe from shame.

The red altar boy clears his throat as if he were about to sing a Christmas carol: Some argue we need a certain amount of suffering in order to appreciate it when we are free of pain . . . or even happy . . .

Charlot interjects, But we don't need nearly as much as we have. We have more than enough to last us to the end of time.

One small conspirator bangs his fist on the table: Are the happiness sponges doing their rounds again? Moving from room to room? They give merciful injections to calm you, they put cotton balls into your ears and nose that they have dipped in some liquid, they plug your mouth with balmy arguments and soothing songs. They feed you the life you are supposed to have after the operation.

The baker boy stops him with a dismissive wave of the hand, a gesture the painter thinks he can see through the door: Much better to assume that there is no Doctor Bog. If there were, he'd be some neighing charlatan, some mindless butcher of a surgeon who has been botching things with his scalpel and is still at it. The operation of the universe: brutally botched; the sutures of stars, the abyss of black holes. Believe me, there's nothing more beautiful than to look up at the sky and die without consolation. You might as well be hanged for a sheep as for a lamb. Alone and unconsoled, lost and abandoned. To expect no mercy and no ever-after—that is the ultimate freedom. To recognize there is no hope of salvation—that is the only way to live. No pardon for you, Doctor Bog, and so be it. I love this white clinic; it is so much more beautiful than anything I could have dreamt up. A disconsolate paradise. Let's help the painter.

The groom in his red uniform suddenly speaks up: You don't think, do you, we'll ever get out of here? What sort of a hotel is this? Without lifts? There are only stairs.

But the painter has been healed, hasn't he? suggests the communicant, the gentle little barn owl.

The altar boy starts anew: Are you familiar with his series of the Man in Prayer? He painted it in Céret in the Pyrenees in 1920, the year Modigliani died. A Monsieur Racine sat for him. Some people call him a religious painter. The painter of crucified creation. And its salvation. Saved from what, though, and for what? There is no solution but colour. The stuff people come up with!

Hush! Someone's listening at the door. I'll check, says the pastry chef with the large red ear.

He gets up, tiptoes to the door and whips it open. There is no one outside. No one. The painter in his white slippers has slunk around the corner without a sound.

But now the altar boy stands before the conspirators' committee and insists that he saw the man in prayer in the clinic and instantly recognized him. And talked to him. And he tells how he approached the man with the oval face and bushy eyebrows: What are you doing here?

Can't you see? Pray.

Just pray? Nothing but pray?

For me, there's no better thing to do.

Because you love God? The Saviour who has been here, or the Messiah who will come?

The man in prayer looks sternly at the boy and calmly talks to him as if to someone long grown up: First, none has been here, and second, none will come.

No Saviour?

Neither now nor later, nor even much later. You want to be saved? What else do you want? Are you ever satisfied? You can manage without.

Aren't you looking forward to paradise? It will be glorious. We will sing and rejoice in the magnificent choir of the enraptured. It will be indescribable. Our bodies will radiate and bloom, and there will be infinite miracles. Everything will be bliss.

Bliss? Paradise? Are you kidding me? Why hasn't he managed to pull it off earlier? If it ever were to come, it would be way too late. Why this wretched waiting for salvation? The delay in itself is obscene. There will never be bliss magnificent and profound enough to compensate for all the suffering and hardship. Never enough bliss to heal all that has been torn and trodden down. There will be no reparations, you understand, how could there be, what could they possibly look like? They would be nothing but paltry alms for all the misery, for all the calamities that have occurred throughout the millennia. Some pathetic candy. He knows only too well that He will forever be in our debt, that He can't make any reparations. That's why He prefers not to come. No reparations for

God. Ever. And the Occupiers will mutilate the world as they see fit. All of Europe, you understand, and not only France. The whole world will dangle from the swastika, forever, you understand? Feet up, shoulder joints dislocated, nothing but inverted crucifixions.

God will not allow it, Monsieur.

God allows everything. That's precisely the problem. Everything and anything, every single filthy scandal. Why can't you get that into your rosy altar boy's brain? God has invented carte blanche for all of it.

Why then do you constantly pray?

Well, why not? That's why. God's son has died and is as dead as a doornail. And as is the son, so is the father. It is credible because there's neither rhyme nor reason to it. He who was buried has arisen, and He who has risen is forever dead. It is completely certain because it is impossible. *Credo quia absurdum.*

I can no longer follow you.

The altar boy tries to stop a conversation that has begun to make him uneasy.

But the man has one more thing to add: *In nomine patris et filii et spiritus sancti.*

Amen, slipped from the altar boy's lips.

And now leave me alone, I'm busy.

The man mumbles something incomprehensible, begins swaying his body back and forth and is no longer responsive.

The painter had quietly returned to his room and white sheets. He tries to forget that he cannot remember. He rides in the hearse towards his operation in Paris and remembers the white paradise. He lies in the white clinic and remembers a ride in a hearse from Chinon to the capital of pain. When does he dream of what? He shakes his head in his dream. So those little conspirators live in the same white clinic that he does? It seems unimaginable, so he rolls over and faces the snow-white wall.

Now he can see them in his mind's eye again, the mother and child he painted in '42, the year of the vast deportations. It is one of his last paintings; he painted it in Champigny-sur-Veude. The two heads could not be closer, they almost merge, yet this closeness harbours a tremendous tension that tears them apart. The mother gazes at the dirty brown floor. The rings around her eyes speak not of exhaustion but, rather, of a complete loss of hope. Her left eye in particular is darkly smeared with misery; it drowns in the colour of calamity.

The little girl's gaze, on the other hand, forms the centre, is full of life, slightly turned upward, cheekily escaping all that misery, and is probably directed towards the future, which, for the child, is of course not called that. Only the here and now exists and an almost palpable desire for life. Her eyes squiggle with joy; looking is pure pleasure. The girl won't stay long on her mother's knees. A leaden present, and only one of her mother's shoulders is visible, the other already sunk and erased by catastrophe. The girl's shoulders, however, billow with happiness, with the delight of rejoicing in her embrace of life on the rough canvas of misery.

One day the lively girl will adopt the careworn mother's posture. The two faces embody two stages of life, one of which is dead certain to change into the other. The mother's thick brown stockings prominently dominate the foreground. Have stockings ever expressed such misery as this double distress in peat brown? Life itself is a pair of constricting brown stockings. The chair leg to the left tilts so that at any moment the tenuously connected, dissimilar pair will tumble into the abyss for good. Why of all moments does the word *yama* come into his mind now? The deep-black shadow on the left could not be more infinite. Do any walls exist here anyway? Hardly. The space is the immense, empty preserve of misery.

But the blue of the two dresses! Two unmatched secret compartments with sky blue. On both their skins lies a shred of a promise of bright happiness. But for the mother, her gaze, posture and peat-brown stockings instantly deny it. The tiny bit of ruffled white underskirt reinforces the negation. For the little girl, the sky blue is the surface of the playfully skipping present. For exactly as long as she believes in it. A bit of the blue promise is tucked coquettishly around her eyes. Perhaps one day the little sky-blue girl will see more happiness. But nowhere is it written that she will.

The painter balks in his luminous white sheets. No, not happiness. Above all, not futile happiness. Happiness is beside the point. You'd be better to talk about milk. The colour of the future is the colour of milk.

MADEMOISELLE GARDE AND FUTILE HAPPINESS

He lies in his blinding-white bed and actually thinks about the word *happiness*, a word that seems entirely alien to his life. Really, this word? Does it have to be this one? A similar one, perhaps, but no similar one exists. Being perceived as Montparnasse's unhappiest painter was a suit of armour. An aura of unhappiness protects a man from an intrusive world. People are charitable and leave the unhappy man alone. He becomes untouchable, you understand? Fabulous prejudice protects him, just like overly strong body odour. Unhappy Soutine! sighs all of Montparnasse. Horrible childhood, appalling poverty, destructive loathing of his own works, debilitating ulcers, bred-in-the-bone shyness, utterly forlorn. And to top it all off, the Occupiers and their abetters hound him. Here he is, hidden in a hearse!

Or he was the second-to-last on the scale of misery, as always: the tenth of eleven. The painter of suffering humanity, they said; of the abased and humiliated, they said; of hunger, they said; of martyred animals. Crucified turkeys, hanging hares already flayed or about to be—they're all images of himself, they said. They probably thought he was the blood-drenched ox carcass, too.

Death, shimmering in all its colours, has appointed him an eyewitness. Death does not want to die unseen. Death means triumph, and it has magnificent plumage. The chicken with the blue neck, the dark scaly markings of the quail. Death was discerning, wanted to be painted in full colour. Unhappiness, undoubtedly, but in a dazzling, breathless exultation of the retina. Him, though, they have overlooked. He was invisible. And wanted to remain that way.

Andrée, a painter satellite of planet Montparnasse, once asked him directly in her bright voice, the only one who ever dared, Have you been very unhappy, Soutine?

He was baffled by the question, at first did not grasp it. Later in the hearse and between the sheets of the white paradise he remembers his answer: No! I have always been a happy man!

And, she claims, his face had beamed with pride and joy.

He rummages through his memories for the right kind of happiness. True or futile happiness—it's all the same. It had existed, had left a trace. That's what mattered most. The happiness of his escape from Smilovichi; of his arrival in Vilna, its night lit up by gas lamps; of his journey to the dazzling art capital of the world. Ten years of herrings, cabbage scraps and biting hunger. But then the entrance of Barnes, the pharmacist god, who could have dreamt that up; the deceptively persuasive simulation of prosperity; the exquisitely personal blend of pauper and prince, of Barclay hats and Chauffeur Daneyrolles. And of summer months in Le Blanc at Zborowski's and in Lèves at the Castaings', who feverishly waited for each of his paintings and paid for them royally after the 1929 crisis had ruined Zbo.

They were crazy about his paintings, welcomed them into their sumptuous home in Lèves, honoured them as their most important guests. The Castaings' mute, self-denying anticipation galvanized him. The whole world seemed to wait for a painting. For some futile happiness. And he pretended to doubt whether he would ever be able to paint another one. Each time he applied the absolutely last brush stroke for the very last time. He enjoyed the domestic comedy. During the summer months he lived a pampered life in the lap of the glorious French bourgeoisie whose quirks and rituals he watched curiously and found charming. The salon, Eric Satie's white music, the clinking of champagne flutes. An umbrella left behind by Satie in 1924 still hangs on the piano.

Dinner is served!

Could he have heard that sentence in the hearse? He is politely invited to the *dîner* and puts on a real suit, but even in his blue paint-stained overall he feels respected and welcomed. If only all of Smilovichi could see the spectacle! The servants are the only ones who eye him suspiciously when he wants to paint them. He does take a rather conspicuous interest in them. The cook, the butler. Nothing here resembles his childhood; the French summer has erased it.

Henry Miller writes: Soutine is less wild now, even paints animals that are still alive! No more blood, only sadness.

And women, reading, draped on lawns, captivated by books, staring at the pages with wide eyes. And the teetering Chartres Cathedral. At long last he has arrived. The landscape's light has taken him into its arms and gently tousled him. The landslide of Céret has been halted.

But not for a second does he forget where he is. He dives into the newspapers to learn which books are being burnt in a nearby country, which paintings are called degenerate, which war announces its imminent arrival. Colourful death is far from over. But now he even paints animals that are still alive. And Charlot, to whom he gives his palette as a present. Lost children in Civry and Champigny, small meteorites cast out by the universe.

And when the Occupiers come rolling in, it is his futile happiness that turns him invisible under his blue hat. That lets the stamp smudge his passport photograph. That leaves the star on the left side of his chest invisible. He did not fall into the trap of the Vél d'Hiv roundup.

They are looking for him; he has vanished. The futile happiness of vanishing. And the happiness of forged papers.

The stomach ulcer stayed; the pain silenced any happiness, which always arrived without warning. He was afraid of becoming a different person, of having become one. The old wound must remain open. If it disappears, his gift will suffocate. Poverty, hunger and ugliness are marvellous possibilities. Pure beauty rests in itself and takes the brush from his hand. Modigliani's beauties: he cannot see them. He made the bodies glow, a bit like paper lanterns. Beauty extinguishes them.

He becomes sad when someone speaks in his presence of a just world. The painter loves injustice, sees it as an opportunity. Justice strikes him as miserable goddess who strives to diminish people. To him, the slightest opportunity is vastly preferable. Everything has been distributed unjustly, you understand? Everything. Health, wealth, beauty, talent and fame. Inequality alone inspires and spurs us on. He'd rather see a game of catch than a better world. Barren longing, bitter desire, the hopeless wish.

He is afraid of turning into a different person. He burrows into the old sheets of his earliest injuries, of his worst grievances. That's where you come from. You come from your wound. It is your birth certificate, your passport to life. You must tend it and protect it and not squander it. With your paint-stained thumb keep your wound open. Do not make your scar look pretty. Do not disinfect anything. With the same thumb he once sprained while painting. That desperate thumb he recognizes even in Rembrandt's paintings. He, too, occasionally painted with his finger.

And then something happens he has not foreseen.

A hand alights on his forehead. He is astonished and first thinks of Marie-Berthe, but the hand is not hers. Each hand is different; each has its own weight, its distinct, pressing softness; each of its lines has its own temperature. He looks up in wonder. He instantly recognizes her.

Garde, what are you doing here, in the car?

The hand strokes his brow; one moment the fingertips, tender and cool; the next, the backs of her bent fingers, warmer and very light, back and forth. She lowers her smiling lips towards him.

Don't worry, my dear. Don't ask. Relax. You have to get there; they expect you; the doctors know.

But you are in Gurs, aren't you? How did you get away? And how did you get in here? Who called you? Who told you? Who allowed you in?

Don't ask. It's no longer relevant, I have come, that's all.

He barely hears her answer, sinks back into the cottony nest where he now lives, where his numbed pain lives.

He had met his guardian angel one evening in Le Dôme. She had not announced herself. It was October '37. With a hair-raising German accent she introduced herself: Gerda Groth-Michaelis. She simply sat there. Just as she now sits in the hearse that wends its way towards Paris, right next to him, quietly addressing the windscreen. But to whom is she speaking?

My name is Gerda Michaelis. I was born in Magdeburg, where my father, who was Jewish, traded in furs and leather goods. If you were a student in those years, you became a socialist in no time, just as easily as you became a Surrealist; it was similarly exciting. But we did notice there was another kind of youth besides us in Magdeburg. The brown shirts were marching in unemployed Germany. The seizure of power was quickly followed by the race laws. When my father's shop was confiscated and Aryanized, our family grew more fearful. I no longer felt safe and wanted to leave my country. I had a friend, Charlotte, who had already fled Germany and lived among farmers in a peaceful village in Normandy. I travelled with a small suitcase and almost no money. Over there, time stands still; every morning it exhales: I still am what I was yesterday. After three months, I was dispirited by a life that smelt of straw and milk, and decided to go to Paris. That's where there had to be a solution. One evening without telling anyone I caught the train. The very next day I sat in one of those cafes in Montparnasse that was frequented by many of the Germans who had been driven from their country.

Mademoiselle Garde had begun to speak in the hearse, but he soon realizes she is not talking to him. She had addressed him, caressed his forehead, certainly, but then she had turned towards the windscreen. Towards the future? It is deaf. Towards the drivers? Hardly. They were scanning the landscape, always ready to turn into some byway should any military vehicles appear, to hide behind a barn until the baggage train had passed. To dodge them and at all costs avoid getting stopped, to progress without taking risks. They figured nobody would ever stop a hearse in the countryside; one has to let it take its course: death does not like delays. The dying continued; there was nothing unusual about dying. People die in an occupied country as before, only in greater numbers. After the assassinations in the summer of '41, the executions of hostages had increased. Prison inmates were declared hostages and mass executions followed; on the place of the executions, blind-folded, they shouted, *Vive la France!* Guy Môquet was the youngest, a mere seventeen, after the assassination in Nantes on 22 October 1941.

The letters from Germany I received from my sister Alice did not bode well. Alice came to Paris with a few pieces of our mother's jewellery in her luggage that we were able to sell. We lived hand-to-mouth, but we lived. It was a daily struggle. But in 1935 we felt such an intense longing for our parents we went to Berlin, where by then they had ended up. I was shocked to see so many flags with their swastikas in Berlin. My father was old and sick, and he feared the future would be dark. He wondered whether he should seek refuge in Japan. My visit ended abruptly. Someone denounced me, and I was summoned by the Gestapo and ordered to immediately leave the territory. I got a big fright and boarded a train to Paris, alone. I never saw my parents or two sisters again.

Garde! It's me, Chaim. Talk to me. Who is it that you're talking to? Don't you hear me any more? I'm not dead yet! You've only just talked to me. When you went to the Vél d'Hiv and didn't come back, I was desperate, you understand? I wrote you a letter to the Gurs camp, wanted to send you money. I never heard back; you probably weren't allowed to write. I didn't want to give you up for lost, wore your clothes on the Villa Seurat to make you come back, sniffed your soap, found one of your hairs, followed your scent everywhere, looked for you in the closet, in the middle of summer wrapped your scarf around my neck. Sometimes I only said your name, called it out in the empty studio. It made me feel good just to shout your German name, although I had never liked the name. Gerda! It made me feel better. Suddenly your German name had become familiar, had become my hapless refugee.

I had received a parcel of almost new clothes from my mother. That day I looked quite well dressed. I walked up to the table where the Russians and Poles were sitting with Carlos, that fellow from Costa Rica. Everybody introduced themselves. I had never heard Soutine's name, but his companions at the table introduced him laughingly as a 'great painter'. He smiled and I immediately liked everything about him: his lips, the ironic smile that lit up his eyes behind the cigarette smoke. He spoke French with a Slavic accent; the *café crème* in front of him was noticeably light.

Garde, I went back later to the cafes in Montparnasse, asked around in Le Dôme and La Rotonde whether anybody knew anything about Gurs, about how the internees were kept, whether you got enough to eat. No one knew anything specific. Only that all Germans were being interned as enemy aliens. I went back to Civry, remembered our summer when I painted those children on the country road, tried to paint again, but nothing worked. My guardian angel had been swallowed up by the Vél d'Hiv, was now in the Pyrenees, and I remained without news.

Life in Paris became difficult again. I tried not to despair, but the Popular Front of 1936 brought no relief for us Israelite German refugees, either. If you wanted to exchange news, you went to the cafes in Montparnasse, where you'd always run into someone who knew what to do or could point you towards some small job. I did people's laundry and washed dishes, and, utterly exhausted after twelve hours of work, cried myself to sleep.

Garde! I didn't notice you right away. So many women passers-by came through the centre of the world. Le Dôme was buzzing with people speaking any number of languages, forever coming and going, meeting new people one minute and losing track of them the next. Passing migratory birds of chance.

We exchanged barely a dozen words. But in the following days I kept looking for him, ran into Carlos, told him I wanted to see that painter again, you know who, and Carlos took me to Soutine on the Villa Seurat. My goodness! Everything in his place struck me as filthy. The furniture was dusty and stained; countless cigarette butts littered the floor—the studio was one gigantic ashtray. The man who lived there seemed to live in a dream, oblivious to it all. He lived like an abandoned cat. Everything was decrepit, shabby, worn.

Garde! Rembrandt's Hendrickje, who steps into a stream, raising her underskirt, exposing her thighs . . . She gazes at the water. Modigliani has never painted anything as beautiful, Garde! It wasn't in the Louvre, but in London; I wanted to go there just to see this one painting, the woman stepping into the stream; I had a copy I took wherever I went, pinned up with drawing pins. Not a day passed without me casting my eyes on it. Garde! The woman who steps into the stream!

He apologized for not being able to offer us an aperitif. I have a stomach problem, he said; I'm not allowed to have alcohol. He had a gramophone and wanted to play a piece by Bach for us, praised its beauty. He opened his studio, but I could not see any paintings; it was empty yet still untidy. I didn't care; it was the man, not the painter, I had come to see. At the time I was living in a small room in the Hôtel de la Paix on the Boulevard Raspail; I invited him and some friends for tea two days later, bought cake and flowers. He didn't show up. He won't come, said one of the others that I had invited. Everyone knows Soutine has no watch. He forgets any get-together. Night was approaching, the tiny room floating in a cloud of cigarette smoke. Finally Soutine arrived, smiling. He had a splash of tea in a cup that he topped up with milk. He stayed on after everyone had left. Then he remembered that there was a bout of catch-wrestling that evening at the Vélodrome d'Hiver; we went there by taxi. Soutine picked the best seats for us, right by the ring. He was in a good mood and full of banter. I didn't really know what catch was. It's a very beautiful sport, Soutine said with a solemn smile. Kicks in the face are allowed and so is head-butting someone's belly. He laughed a quiet laugh and gently touched the corners of his mouth with the tips of his middle finger and thumb.

Garde! Our Sunday had a name. We often went to the Louvre. I had been convinced you can see well only if you are alone, had thought so for decades. Now each of us had four eyes and I saw everything anew. Garde! The soles of the feet of the angel as he leaves Tobias! The good Samaritan! How he turns back from the stairs to look at the man knocked down by the robbers. Bathsheba with David's letter! Bathsheba! The little altar boy with the holy-water vat and sprinkler in Courbet's Burial at Ornans! Do you remember that little altar boy? His gaze? And Chardin's Rayfish, don't forget the rayfish! For us, the Louvre was Sunday. Sundays were Bathsheba, a little altar boy, a ray.

Before the end of the last bout, he suddenly stood up and was not feeling well. An unbearable burning in his stomach. He wanted to go home right away and begged me to accompany him. All of a sudden he was plaintive and familiar, as if he'd known me a long time. I will help you, I'll look after you, I said. On the Villa Seurat I got him a hot-water bottle and a glass of lukewarm Vichy water. His pain calmed down. He lit himself a cigarette and began to chat, talked about his illness, which had tormented him for several years already. In his youth, he said, poor nutrition and alcohol had ruined his stomach. Every so often he would repeat in an anguished voice, But you aren't going to abandon me, are you?

Garde! There exists a belief among us according to which every human being has in his or her body a tiny bone called the almond. And do you know where it's tucked away, this tiny almond bone? Near the atlas vertebra. It is the seat of the human soul, a person's innermost core. Garde! This tiny bone is indestructible. Even if a person's whole body is torn to pieces, burnt, annihilated—that tiny almond bone is immortal. It holds the spark of each person's uniqueness. And according to the belief, people will be recreated at the resurrection out of this tiny bone. I have never believed in the resurrection, was not able to even way back in Smilovichi's sand. We can wait for all eternity—the Messiah will have forgotten us. But that tiny bone I do believe in, even today. When you were in Gurs, I kept telling it things in a whisper.

But the calm did not last long; the pain returned, more excruciating than before. I prepared another hot-water bottle; he fell asleep. Half the night I watched him sleep and he was beautiful as he lay there in his terrifying gauntness. At some point I sank down next to him, exhausted. At dawn I rose and was about to leave when he started from his sleep: Gerda, you aren't going to leave, are you? He clutched my arm: Gerda, last night you were my guardian, you held me with your hands, and now I hold you. He didn't like my German name, so he baptized me Garde, his nightwatch, his guardian. I began to forget my name was Gerda.

Garde! Again I travel to Paris, just as I did in 1913. Now I don't arrive from Vilna but from the Loire, not far from the demarcation line. There would be no point in crossing it today; I have waited too long. I have to get to my operation. I am travelling towards a white paradise. I am travelling towards the country of milk.

He was mysterious, lonely, full of suspicion. Everything about him was strange, and foreign. I lived with him without having a clue who he was as a painter. When he worked in his studio, he wouldn't tolerate disruptions. He used a whole lot of brushes and in the fever of composing would fling them one after the other over his shoulder onto the floor. Brushes were everywhere, as were paint tubes, squeezed and ripped open. Sometimes he applied the paint with his hands, spread it on with his fingertips, and the paint got stuck under his fingernails and couldn't be washed off. Once he finished his work, he turned the canvas to face the wall so no one would see it. I wasn't allowed to look at his paintings. He would lock them away in a closet. I wasn't welcome to view them. And I never demanded anything. For me it was enough to live with him. We were created to understand each other, I loved him. That's all.

Garde! No one has ever seen my paintings. They were invisible, like me. I was too scared to look at them again, scared to hear their voices tell me to destroy them, to slash the canvas with a knife, to burn them all. I never painted you so I would not have to burn you.

The two years before the war Soutine and I lived day to day, savouring each passing hour, the joy of being together, the modest sweetness of our endangered happiness. We chose to do away with our past and we closed our eyes to the future.

Garde! Who knows what the future holds. It will take us to Raspberrytown. It will be cold, and no one will love us the way we love each other now. It is a desert. Bitter Vermouth. Absence. There will be only strangers who shake their heads and close their eyes to avoid seeing us. Garde! In Minsk and Vilna I yearned to reach the future as quickly as possible; I was in a hurry and full of impatience. Paris lay in that future; that's where I wanted to go. But the future distracts us from the image that is born within us. To stop time, in those months in the Beehive, that's what I wanted then, and the rough canvas reluctantly obeyed.

In the Hôtel de la Paix on the Boulevard Raspail I met an Austrian couple who had fled, like me, from Hitler's terror. They were in Paris in transit, waiting to emigrate to America. I turned to Frau Tennenbaum and asked if her husband would examine Soutine. The doctor recommended an abdominal X-ray, and to please me, Chaim agreed. Soutine suffers from an invasive stomach ulcer, Tennenbaum told me. I am afraid it has progressed so far it has become incurable. His organism is weak and he's worn out. I don't think the man has more than five or six years to live. Is there no hope? I asked him. Let's hope for a miracle, Doctor Tennenbaum replied and wrote a prescription for bismuth, papaverine and histidine. At that time, we were all waiting for a miracle. You have the worst forebodings, war is looming, you hear the barking on the radio and you still hope for a miracle. Incredible, isn't it?

To have nothing but miracles on our minds was our error. Pain is an error that inhabits us. The white paradise is full of the milk that awaits me. I didn't want to drown in my own blood. Garde! Who never goes away never comes back, either.

Soutine threw away the medications, calling the doctor a charlatan. Madelaine Castaing knew a great specialist, Professor Gosset. His diagnosis was absolutely identical. By then Soutine was eager to recover, to eat well, to take whatever medications the doctors would prescribe. For years he had lived on boiled potatoes, bland noodles cooked in water, vegetable soups, milky coffee. He had lost so much weight you could see his raspberry-red ribs.

Now he took a new pleasure in eating; I bought ham for him, prepared beefsteaks, roasted chickens... He laughed when my plates arrived at the table, joked: Don't you touch the chicken, it's all mine! He thought it beautiful to be alive again.

The figures in the paintings were meant to tell time to stand still. Except the ulcer made itself known like an irregular pulse; an offbeat rhythm drove it on. Garde! You won't abandon me, will you, when I have to go to Paris for my operation? How often I have cried out for you lately! I seem to be travelling into the cold future. There exists a country of milk where everything is white, even the cows. I must pass through the white, and it will heal me, Garde!

With each passing month I noticed an improvement. His friends congratulated him. It made me happy; it was my accomplishment. Amazed, the lovers revel in their caresses. Sometimes he gazes attentively at my body. You are beautiful, he once told me with a laugh; you look like one of Modigliani's paintings. I know I sound ridiculous telling you that.

Garde! Talk to me, don't talk to the drivers or to the future, talk to me. Look at me! I am lying next to you on this metal gurney. You know my favourite colours: vermilion, silver-white, Veronese green. Talk to me!

In August '39 we left for Civry, a village near Auxerre. The Lithuanian painter Einsild had raved about it: delightful landscape, absolute peace and quiet, a world away from the Montparnasse fever. The bell towers of Auxerre came into view. Civry, with its lone grocery store, tobacco, milk, sausage and sewing thread. Coffee and aperitif in the same place. The room at Madame Galand's, simple and tidy; you had to fetch your water from the pump. The road to Isle-sur-Serein, all poplars and sunshine. Soutine has painted it several times. Dead hares, peasant children with smeared mouths. To make them sit still I handed out candy. It was our last, anxious summer; Soutine would lie nervously in wait for the daily paper, trying to grasp what was happening beyond the borders. 1 September 1939, Poland; two days later, France's declaration of war. Until then, we had been merely two oddballs from Montparnasse spending their summer in the village, but suddenly we came under suspicion as spies. Either way, we now were enemy aliens; whether or not we were perse-cuted was of no interest to anyone. A week earlier, Molotov and Ribbentrop had signed their non-aggression pact. And the mayor, Monsieur Sébillotte, puffed himself up with importance and banned the two conspicuous for-eigners with their suspicious German and Slavic accents from going anywhere 'until further notice'. We were stuck in Civry. The summer idyll had become shackles. After much back and forth Soutine was given permission to go to Paris to consult with his doctors. His pledges were intended to reassure me: You-are-my-wife, trust-me, I'll-never-leave-you, don't-lose-heart.

I desperately tried to get a travel permit for you. My ulcer was granted one but my angel was forced to stay behind.

In the cold autumn that followed I was left behind on my own. Everything that had been so luminous throughout the summer was now marked by a deadly sadness in this village of a hundred souls. Two months later Soutine came back with a valid travel permit for me. We cried tears of happiness when we saw each other again, and he was overcome with emotion when I gave him the blue jumper I had knitted for him with the initials C.S. The mayor puffed himself up even more and lectured us that in times of war the mayor and only the mayor has the right to strip us two suspicious aliens of their freedom of movement. I, Sébillotte, Mayor of Civry . . . At the end of April '40 we decided to ignore the ban, during the night packed our two suitcases with the bare essentials and walked all the way to Isle-sur-Serein. The village was fast asleep. The dark country road that Soutine had so often painted welcomed us; we were now the two schoolchildren who, hand-in-hand, tried to find their way home after the storm. At one in the morning we boarded the train to La Roche, changed trains and slowly approached Paris. At the Gare de Lyon Soutine put his arm around me and whispered into my ear: Garde, you have been saved . . .

The invasion began one week later; Europe was in turmoil. On 10 May 1940, Belgium and the Netherlands capitulated. As the German troops approached, the government ordered the internment of all German citizens as enemy aliens. It was a motley lot: Jewish refugees, communists, anti-fascists, artists and any other Germans who simply happened to be on French soil at that moment, all stirred into one mishmash of enemies and sent to the internment camps. On 15 May 1940, I was ordered to go to the Vél d'Hiv. We went across Paris in a taxi. We didn't speak. We got out, embraced for a long time. Then I stepped through a glass door and disappeared into the dark interior. I never saw him again.

When you walked away, I thought: this is the end. My guardian angel, my Garde, has abandoned me. Soon they will come for me, too, and off I go to we know where. When they scoop up the guardian angels, what's to become of the rest of us? They are the last ones that should be arrested. At night on the Villa Seurat I dreamt repeatedly of black, smouldering rubbish dumps where wounded angels lay scattered, their wings still twitching. It was night, their faces were smeared with coal and oil, and they whimpered in the dark. The rubbish crunched under my shoes like crushed glass, or piles of broken ceramic or porcelain. I was afraid I might step on the angels, and tried to wend my way between them. I had to search for my angel among them. Mademoiselle Garde! I opened my mouth wide and shouted but not a sound came out. I tried again, shouting even more loudly, as loudly as I could, but nothing happened. There was no reply, only this horrifying whimper as if from wounded rodents. And deafeningly loud, amplified by loudspeakers, I heard my own heartbeat. The dream gave me such a great fright I jumped up in my bed and shouted one last time: Mademoiselle Garde!

THE LOCKER

The painter looks at the blank, bright ceiling and waits for the sounds in the hallway to ebb away. It must be night-time or something akin to it in this land of snow and milk. He tries to remember but not much is left. The morning in Chinon, linden trees, the black Citroën, strange people talking to him in the hearse, the endlessly long ride to—where? Black wolves on motorcycles, belt buckles mocking arrogantly GOTT MIT UNS, sidecars, leather coats. He remembers Marie-Berthe putting a flimsy chain with a small cross around his neck and whispering that God had died for him. And he reaches for his neck but no longer finds anything there, neither chain nor cross.

The passage of time has been so slow, but it must arrive eventually: Come, night. Still it does not come. Only that white shimmer between the slats of the shutter. The flickering in front of his eyes, the snowfall that tries to nudge him to sleep. Who snows so much here to let him sleep? At the next ebb tide, when nothing but soft gurgles can be heard from inside invisible pipes, he leaves his room again, walks down the hallway towards the window. It is not the white night of the northern countries that he heard the Russians in the Beehive rave about. Not the midnight sun. Only the light of this strangely radiant white snow.

Still not a soul in the hallway. He steps up to the window, gently strokes the white paint on the windowsill with his left index finger, mindlessly traces with his other index finger the outlines of the clinic buildings opposite—and winces. As though his fingers had recalled Doctor Bog's words.

He has caught himself in the act; his index fingers have caught him. He was not allowed to paint in this place. He was healed. Has absolute freedom from pain. But not even a few lines, sketched by his index finger on a window pane? As in days gone bye, when he drew the wildest portraits with a pointy pine cone on the Baltic sand underneath the pine trees? Here was nothing but a pane of glass that wouldn't preserve the tiniest trace, given that it was not covered with any grime or dust.

He steps back from the window feeling guilty and disappointed and climbs up the narrow stairwell at the end of the hallway. The clinic's size is unfathomable, its layout obscure; countless arched doorways and lockers line the hallways. He is astounded that even when the sounds are ebbing he has yet to meet another patient or some stern orderly who would send him back to his room.

He is becoming bolder, enters several rooms on the upper floor where he had listened in on the room with the wooden doll and the conspirators' committee surrounding the little pastry chef. Not a soul, nothing but empty rooms. Glaring white light. He opens yet another one, expecting it also to be empty, and is taken aback. Inside the blindingly white cube both framed and unframed canvasses are vertically stacked on the floor in meticulous rows. Dozens upon dozens, the room is almost full, with only the narrowest of paths between the rows in which to move. They have been carefully stacked here—but by whom? In a clinic where painting was strictly prohibited?

With two fingers he timidly separates the canvasses from each other and looks at what they show. The shock is tremendous. It can't be true! He fears losing his mind when he recognizes his own paintings. But they are not the ones he sold to Guillaume or Barnes or the Castaings; these are without a doubt the ones he had destroyed with his own hands over the course of his life, had slashed in a rage at their inadequacy, burnt in an unbridled fury of erasure. Here they all are, diligently gathered up as if to to taunt him. He recognizes even those he burnt last, in Champigny just before his ride to the clinic in Chinon, burnt in the smoke-belching fireplace of the small house at the entrance to the Grand Parc on the road to Pouant.

How was it possible that they were all reunited here? What idiot had gathered up all the victims of his destructive fury? Can ashes and shreds of canvas ever become whole again? He did not believe in the resurrection, nor in the resurrection of destroyed paintings. Not even they could hope for the Messiah. Or did paintings, too, have an indestructible little almond bone? Here they were, neatly stacked as a comprehensive record of his destructive offences.

The entire hecatombs from his time in Céret, all preserved, all stored! What Zborowski and his chauffeur Daneyrolles had gathered up behind his back Jacques had restored with surgical precision, and what he had been able later to wrest back from their scheming: here it all was! Nothing had been lost, absolutely nothing. Preserved until when—the Day of Judgment? He slowly checks through his canvasses and remembers the boundless rage that had doomed them. Who would be interested in these shreds and accidents, for whom could they possess value when he had long ago disowned them? Who had stolen and safeguarded them so he would rediscover them here? What sort of celestial thieves of conservation, of integrity, were they?

Less and less does he understand this white place where he was promised and then granted a healing, where he was given freedom from pain but strictly prohibited from painting, yet where paintings were collected and stored that he had long ago consigned to annihilation.

He expects he'll fly into a monstrous rage and run to Doctor Bog, mad and furious, to complain about this sacrilegious restoration. To his amazement he remains calm and composed. Have they given him sedatives? Anyway, the god in white was nowhere to be found in these myriad hallways and had not put in an appearance since their conversation about blood being a special juice. He hadn't come back to his bedside conveying the hypocritical interest all doctors cultivate, or later with his chest all puffed up with pride at the fabulous healing. He no longer showed up.

Confused, the painter leaves and takes the stairs to the basement, by chance walks into a furnace room, marvels at the many bigger and smaller pipes, listens to their faint music, inhales the sweetish-dusty smell. Sounds travel to and from the rooms, pick up speed and slow down: a roaring and whistling, a creaking and cranking that abruptly calms itself again. Something squeaks and he jumps, feeling found out by the sound.

The painter is becoming lost in this white underground jungle of furnace pipes. Absentmindedly he opens several lockers, discovers them empty, opens one more—and recoils. Acrid-smelling rubbish has been dumped inside. To begin with, his eye can only make out glints of metal and compressed shapes, then he recognizes what he cannot avoid recognizing. They are paint tubes, twisted and squeezed, abused by an impatient painter's fist, gummed-up brushes and palette knives, wrecked canvasses. One enormous rubbish bin, carelessly emptied into the big locker, by who knows whom. At first he doesn't know whether to feel joy or pain, experiencing nothing but cottony, dreamy amazement.

However, almost like an automaton, he begins to retrieve the painting detritus from the locker one piece at a time, like treasures from the belly of a boat that has been rotting under water for decades, visited by uncomprehending fish, rays, grey subaqueous creatures. He lays out the gummed-up brushes, the metal paint tubes with their mangled bellies and colourful bellybands, the canvasses with their ulcers, the torn fabric with its wounds and weals. He spreads them on the furnace-room floor as if the whole pile had patiently waited for him to impose some order on it. A pointless performance in this dungeon, in this paradise where painting is prohibited, where painting means nothing but battered tools, nothing but trash that someone had grabbed and confiscated from someone else and had dumped somewhere, the acrid smells of turpentine and the jumble of mouldy, matted refuse and stinking wet linen.

When one of the pipes clanks particularly loudly, the painter is startled, hastily stuffs the painstakingly sorted painting waste back into the locker, straightens up and looks around. No one there. No one? He senses some kind of presence and pretends to slowly and casually saunter out of the furnace room. Back in the stairwell his steps quicken as he climbs and returns to his—the correct— hallway. He heads straight towards his room; his brain has measured the distance so he knows where to find his snow-white bed.

But something is resting on the floor in front of the door to his room: a white pot. He thinks of a chamber pot but on getting closer recognizes a white container on a short, slender stand. A thin line just below the top makes him think of a lid. Bemused, he lifts it up from where it sits directly in front of his room and slowly unscrews the top.

An urn! The word flashes through his mind.

Inside are snow-white ashes with a rippled surface.

Suddenly he hears from the far end of the hallway an old man's voice, high and slightly nasal. The painter screws the lid back on the urn and puts it back on the floor next to the door of his room.

Poor Doctor Livorno! the voice shouts from far away.

The painter can make out a white figure but no facial features; from so far away the face is a white oval. Perhaps a white coat, perhaps something shiny as well, perhaps glasses. When the painter glances at the container and then peers again down the hallway, the apparition has vanished.

Instead, he hears the same voice directly behind his back pronouncing each word with a whistling, susurrating sound with too many sibilants. The mouth hisses and whispers. The painter gets goosebumps. An elderly man is standing there, wearing not a doctor's coat but a white dressing gown that balloons over his portly belly, his feet stuck in fluffy white slippers. Somewhat stocky, he has the face of a little billy goat. After an unctuous sigh he turns to the painter with a jovial and sweetly poisonous smile and points at the urn: Oh dear, the good Doctor Livorno! He'd become sentimental in his old age. Told everyone here some weird story that no one wanted to hear. Something about camels and potsherds. He was obviously bored in this place, so ungrateful! At the same time he seemed overworked. Unfortunately, we caught him when he began to paint again, in one of the basement hallways. Which is of course, you understand, completely unacceptable. Flouting the prohibition and trying to start his old life all over again. And you know what? He painted nothing but naked women on beds and couches. So gross! We warned him, but when he didn't listen to reason, we had to liquidate him, you understand, Monsieur Soutinhaim?

The susurrating, venomous little billy goat in his white dressing gown bends down and fondles the white urn dreamily. He gives off a peculiar, stringent odour, a mixture of butterbur and urine.

Yes, yes indeed, liquidate. Oh, this little pile of ashes. And such a friendly man. It can't happen to you. You've been healed, after all. The poor Doctor Livorno! His whistling gave him away. We consider music nauseating if it doesn't come from us, especially whistling sounds. Don't talk to me about Bach! Livorno was simply careless. We like peace and quiet, the fine harmony of the graveyard, the serene tranquillity of the mountains. Also, children have become too much for us—so young and already so rebellious. Sadly, we had to remove them.

Who are you? the painter stammers in confusion.

Doctor Earman, at your service.

And the susurrating little billy goat hops and skips jauntily away in his somewhat greasy dressing gown and a cloud of sweet noxious gas. Bewildered, the painter follows him with his eyes. Then he carefully lifts the urn containing Livorno's ashes, carries it into his room, puts it on the floor some distance from his bed and gazes at it for a long time, deep in thought.

A short while later, during another expedition, the painter Chaim Soutine again steps to the window from where he first watched the tremendous snowfall and where he now is obliged to witness a gruesome scene. A man, completely naked, has been knocked down by faceless, blank-eyed guards wearing black peaked caps; they lunge at him and kick him in the gut with the tips of their boots until he vomits blood on the eerily white flagstones. Then they pound his head with weird, never-before-seen cudgels. Suddenly the battered man raises his swollen eyes to the window. The painter, who is still watching, cries out when he recognizes him: it is his brother Gershen. At that very moment, a woman is pushed from a black delivery van parked next to the scene. She throws herself on top of the bloodied man. Oh God, was that Tamara, Gershen's wife? She thinks she can halt the abuse, but instead she is now whipped with riding crops; her tormentors rip the clothes from her emaciated body and drag her to the other side of the van. What is done to her there is as visible to the painter as if he could see right through the black vehicle.

With both hands he bangs against the massive window, but it can't be opened; he shouts loudly, but the glass is too thick for sounds to penetrate. He suddenly remembers an encounter in a doctor's waiting room, possibly Gosset's, whom he went to see on one of his secret trips to Paris to get new medication for his ulcer. Someone waiting along with him addressed him out of the blue in an almost intimate tone. He had recognized the painter. Although they were suddenly alone in the empty waiting room, he spoke in a whisper about what had happened back home.

In July '41, his brother Gershen, Tamara and their daughter were murdered in Berezino by the Einsatzgruppen. The painter was shaking and wanted to learn more, but the strange patient he had never met did not know, or claimed he did not know, whether his parents and other siblings had escaped the massacre. Where are Sarah and Solomon, Yankl, Ertl, Nahuma and the others? It was so difficult to glean anything from the censored French papers. BBC Radio broadcast news about events in the east, but how could the painter obtain a clear picture from those snippets? His ear feverishly listened to the news for names he would recognize: Bobruisk, Borisov, Berezino, Baranovichi as well as Slonim and Slutsk. But these places were too small to attract attention among the major world events. The Wehrmacht, it turned out, entered Minsk after heavy bombardment on 28 June 1941. On 25 July, at noon, the Reichskommissariat Ostland is proclaimed. Death quickly divides Ostland up into large chunks, one of which, Generalbezirk Weißruthenien, includes a little place called Smilovichi. Where are Sarah and Solomon, Yankl, Ertl, Nahuma and the others? The Einsatzgruppen B are ambitious and voracious: by the end of the bloody year of '41, countless villages and shtetls have been razed to the ground.

Still speaking in a whisper, the man in the waiting room tells the painter Chaim Soutine about the Minsk ghetto, about the camps of Drozdy and Tuchinka and Maly Trostenets, about the horrific massacre on Yubileynaya Square in July '42. He can't believe his ears, and only slowly and incredulously shakes his head as the unfamiliar patient tells him of closed black vans driving into the ghetto. He refers to them by their Russian name: *dushegubki*. The foreigner explains what these gas vans, into which thousands of people were crammed, were used for. And what the *yama* was about, the large pit on the outskirts of town. Roaring and cursing, they drive them from their homes, order them to put their clothes on a pile, drive them with whips to the edge of the *yama* and then it's a bullet into the neck or chest; a commando unit carrying large shovels rushes in and hastily throws lime and dirt on top where screams and groans can still be heard from those who did not manage to die fast enough. How did that stranger get to know this? How did the news reach Paris? The painter wants to ask the strange patient many more questions, but the latter abruptly rises, disappears into the consulting room and leaves the painter behind in the waiting room, alone and shaking. Where are Sarah and Solomon, Yankl, Ertl, Nahuma and the others?

Suddenly, the painter recoils from the window and rushes to the upper floor where he had overheard the conspiracy of the pastry chefs; in a panic, he opens every door that might lead to them. All the rooms are empty. They are no longer there. He remembers one of his dangerous trips to Paris, remembers the sobbing woman who ran into the street, addressed him as Monsieur Epstein and begged: What are they doing with the children? Why are they deporting the children, too?

The painter is struck by a thought: Has Doctor Bog uncovered the conspiracy? Has he had the children deported? But that's not possible, they were sent after their parents as early as August '42. He knew the routes from the ever-present rumours: from Drancy and Compiègne, or from Pithiviers and Beaune-la-Rolande via Laon, Reims, and Neuburg to the east, to a place in Poland whose name will soon be appearing more frequently.

All the rooms are empty. He hurries back to the window where he had seen Gershen and Tamara. But that scene, too, has suddenly disappeared. All that exists outside are the indifferent searchlights and the never-ending snowfall. But, no, there is still the abandoned black van in the falling light. He did not dream the scene.

The painter wants to scream, open the window and roar like an animal, but the scream is stuffed back down his throat by this white wasteland, and no sound comes out; he swallows hard and staggers back from the window. The false white paradise is shattered, this silent happiness clinic with all of Doctor Bog's hot air, with the invisible Doctor Kno in the background, with the susurrating and whistling Doctor Earman, who liquidated Livorno. A clinic that only pretended to heal and that allowed the horrifying scene to unfold in its yard.

And in that same white-shimmering night the painter Chaim Soutine descends to the furnace room, retrieves the painting waste from the musty locker, once more lays out the squeezed paint tubes and checks how much paint is left and what it would be good for. He has to be frugal and avoid being caught. But his plan is clear: he wants to paint again, to disregard Doctor Bog's prohibition. He has seen enough of this snow-white prison whose sole, filthy refuge is the pile of rubbish at the back of the furnace pipes.

And now he understands. The scene with the tortured figures who looked like Gershen and Tamara, the stories of the foreign patient about the Minsk ghetto and the *dus-hegubki*, Livorno's urn with the white ashes, and the shocking emptiness of the room where the children and pastry chefs had gathered to conspire against Doctor Bog and had tried to instigate and encourage him, the painter Chaim Soutine, to paint again—all that has jolted him from this pain-free monotony. He now hates his shattered white paradise.

And down in the basement between the furnace pipes he resumes his old rituals. Initially hesitant and tentative, then agitated, and increasingly driven by the old painful obsession and frenzy. Yes, pain seemed to return, and he was willing to answer its call. It made him writhe, start, whimper under its fist. He was cured of his painlessness.

It is a new beginning. He does not paint the pageboys and baker boys, not Charlot and the communicant, not the lost children and mothers; he paints neither the teetering hills of Céret nor the climbing roads of Cagnes, nor the leaning cathedral of Chartres. He paints neither the god in white in front of a white canvas nor Doctor Kno hiding in the background, and not the billy goat Doctor Earman in his white dressing gown. A future viewer might say: There is nothing there, nothing to be seen. Nothing but white emptiness.

He is painting himself, lying between his light-white sheets, his legs covered and his hands clasped on top of the blanket, his fingers with their paint-rimmed nails tidily interlaced as if piously crossed. On his blanket lie gladioli. Those flaming-red gladioli whose haunted convulsions he had discovered in Céret in 1919. They resemble flaming flesh wounds, convulsing flower flesh. Bleeding flowers, like perforated stomach ulcers.

Several times he paints himself on his bed with the flowers. No, this is not supposed to be his deathbed but, rather, his bed in a white paradise to which the glowing-red gladioli are finally admitted. No longer the country of milk but the free country of colours. But he was depending on the small amounts of remaining paint he was able to wring from the squeezed tubes that had been left behind. It wasn't much. He works himself into a frenzy the way he used to, flinging the brushes over his shoulder after each application of paint and crawling around on hands and knees under the furnace pipes to gather them up again. Feverish, swearing, he curses the canvas—and at long last finds his way back into his true and proper life, back to colour, back to the task demanded by matter, back to the right wound, to the only faith still existing for him. Colour is implacable. Colour is the ultimate message of the total impossibility of salvation. It is the pure rebellion against Doctor Bog.

What was the point of prohibiting painting in this terrifying white wasteland, this pain-free clinic? What was Doctor Bog trying to achieve? He might as well have told him not to breathe. No, the painter no longer wants to lie healed and pacified in his hospital bed with his hands stroking the blanket. He wants to live again, and hence to paint—even if it has to be in the basement of life just like it used to be on the margin of the Montparnasse world. Lit by several bad, blinding light bulbs, eyes squinting, no proper daylight. It was painful to breathe again those turpentine smells. It is the last bit of triumph he has left.

Little by little, anguish and desire re-emerge; he searches and struggles to find red in the squeezed, crushed tubes. How fired up he is! He no longer wants a white paradise; it has to be scarlet red. The scarlet-red paradise. And when he runs out of scarlet, it is yellow gladioli that lie on the white sheet like slain, twisted souls.

Every night he descends into the room of sin where he does with banned paints that which has been forbidden. He does not make a sound, does not whistle like the hapless Livorno, whom Doctor Earman has had liquidated. He does not shuffle but slinks, does not trudge but glides through hallways and up and down stairwells. In the silence he has become lighter. During the day he obediently lies in the white hospital bed, waits for the tired Doctor Bog, who does not come, and listens to the ebb and flow of sounds from the always empty hallway. How much he would have liked to now listen to the cruel *Songs of Maldoror*, in the croaking, gurgling, screaming voice of Modigliani.

Then he quietly gets up and descends into his underworld of furnace pipes. And he paints and paints as if intoxicated. The pain has returned, as has the colour. *Les couleurs sont des douleurs*. Colours are pains. And he remembers the conversation he overheard in one of the Montparnasse cafes. Colours are scars and become wounds again, and in his first language *farbn* and *shtarbn*, colours and dying, still rhyme. Colours have long anticipated the dying. That should be enough, together with the residue from the tubes.

Then something occurs he hadn't anticipated. Hadn't he been careful enough? Had he let on how eager he was for these nights in the clinic's basement, for the white jungle of furnace pipes and the cherished bits of leftover painting waste that after each excursion he tidily put back in the locker along with the tattered, scraped and newly painted canvasses? Has someone secretly been following him? No, someone is ahead of him, lurking for him in the dark.

He has stormed into the furnace room, has fished his palette and brushes from the locker, all that wonderful, filthy stuff he needs. It is urgent: the white nights are short, and as long as the paint has not dried up in the crushed tubes, he wants to use every last bit.

He must have been furiously abusing the canvas for an hour when he suddenly feels watched. He hates being observed when he paints; painting demands the same modesty as dealing with his body's intimate business. Not even Mademoiselle Garde was permitted to see a painting in the process of creation, and as for the endless stream of passers-by in Céret, Cagnes and Champigny—cardinal-purple examiners who tried to approach the painter to demand accurate representations—he hated them like the bugs crawling on his canvas. The moment he spotted a gawker on the horizon, he would pack up his palette and easel and take off.

This time he hasn't even realized someone is watching him. He feels so safe and alone in the poorly lit basement floor, this furnace empire traversed by white pipes, so deeply locked away with the painting waste that he never even entertained the possibility. He spins his head around and suddenly sees her standing in a corner. In a white uniform, naturally, everything here is white, so why shouldn't a nurse wear white? It's her second skin. She doesn't say a word. Only scrutinizes him as he stands with his brushes in his fists, sweaty and hunched, panting with rage.

To begin with, he does not recognize her face. He wants to speak to her but her calm stare seems to rule it out. His memory is groping feverishly for faces; his dreaming fingertips would recognize hers instantly. He feels how those eyes, their shape, their darkness are slowly coming back to him. Minsk? Vilna? Montparnasse? Suddenly it dawns on him; he recognizes her even in her white nurse's uniform, her white shoes.

She has Deborah Melnik's eyes, the sad mouth he kissed furtively and fearfully one evening when he picked her up from the conservatory to walk her wordlessly home to her parents. They lived right next door to the art academy; she was sixteen, or perhaps only fourteen? She went to high school, wanted to become a singer, took courses at the conservatory. Her black eyes, her pallor, her throaty quick laughter. Sometimes they talked, self-consciously, at the entrance gate. He was as afraid of kisses as of bees.

Yes, she had the name of the prophet in the Book of Judges. Deborah, the bee who knows of the future. But he shoos the face away; his tattered backpack already sits packed in the corner, and Krem and Kiko have reached Paris and beckon him to join them. It's time for you to come to the world's capital.

She had popped up again in 1924 in Montparnasse— each road out of Vilna seemed to lead to Paris—still planning to become a singer, dreaming of honouring Paris with her voice. It happened in Le Dôme or La Rotonde, where everything in that city begins. They talked about the old days, for which he was not homesick at all; he was here, and only here, with no desire to ever leave again. A beguiling intimacy floated above their heads, a tender whisper, something they seemed to have in common, shared only between them, even if it was nothing but the memory of a few of Vilna's streets, of a long passageway into the courtyard where he had timidly kissed her.

But he waves her away as if having to chase off a dybbuk, or as if wiping spider web from his face. Why had she reappeared? She belongs in Vilna; it's an awful mistake for women from another time to show up and push themselves into one's life. Here I am, don't you remember—those days! He doesn't care for don't-you-remembers. Vilna was nothing but a running board to quickly jump on and leap off, a means to arrive in the future at long last. No path leads back there. Are you listening? None.

Afterwards, they went for a long walk through the night, wandered about, gingerly pursued strange paths through the quarter. She wasn't going to let herself be dismissed. They stayed in a tiny hotel on the Boulevard Raspail; his studio was too filthy. When they separated in the morning, he ran as if from an irksome shadow. On 10 June 1925, their daughter was born. Aimée, she named their daughter as if in mockery: Aimée. It was a clear demand: she was to be loved and her daughter along with her. He did not even want to see her, contested his paternity. Once in the thirties, one of his crowd in Montparnasse called her his spitting image.

Who're you talking about? I don't have a daughter, leave me alone!

He did not want to see her, but from that time on her face would be staring at him always and everywhere. As if to mock him, fate had stamped his daughter's face unmistakeably with his eyes, his nose, his lips, his mouth. He sent her away, along with the mother, right out of his life, any place where he was not. He was the one who decided which figures would be visible on his life's canvas and which would vanish. Fate would have no say; it was he who selected the colours. On every canvas he was his own tormented king.

It was the first year he truly felt he had finally arrived in Paris. After the sortie by the Philadelphia pharmacist, Zbo had sold a whole bunch of additional paintings, Americans were coming to Paris asking for a certain Soutine, his value rose rapidly, and Zbo added three, preferably four zeroes to the original purchase prices. For a while he lived in a state of grandiose, simulated affluence.

It is a time of triumph. Marcellin and Madeleine Castaing reappear on the horizon; having taken an instant dislike to him on their first encounter, they now woo him. In the early twenties they had met in a small cafe on the Rue Campagne Première; one of their painter friends had recommended they should buy one of Soutine's paintings as he had no bread and nothing whatsoever to live on. He showed up far too late, wanted to test whether they were serious, would wait for him. In each hand he carried a painting; he can't remember which, probably works from Céret or Cagnes. Marcellin Castaing is in a rush, impatient after all that waiting, pulls out a 100-franc note without looking at the paintings and offers it to the painter.

Here, take that, an advance; we'll look at your paintings another time.

The painter stands petrified, incredulous and incensed at the haughty impatience of the rich. He grabs the note and tosses it at Castaing's feet. The blind arrogance that makes them think they already own everything and only need to fish out a few measly banknotes. The hunger artist's stubborn pride. These were still his paintings to do with as he pleased. He resolutely grabs them and runs away.

Sometime after the mid-twenties they buy the great red *Choir Boy* from Zborowski for . . . 30,000 francs! The white surplice with its thousands of colourful streaks over the cassock. As if he had wanted to record the interplay of blood cells, both red and white, the great pairing of death and life in the human blood, according to Doctor Bog. The rich only stammered: *Magnifique!* Zbo told him about it. They had begged to get the painting, and he had ever so graciously relented.

The painter is half out of his mind, believes himself, finally, after all these years to have reached his goal, buys Barclay suits and hats, silk ties, elegant Hanan shoes and the polka-dot shirts he'd always fancied. His red-and-white choirboy has given him an entirely new wardrobe. He even delights in swinging a little cane. He has arrived in Paris, once again. After a dozen years, he had made it, and Zbo kept asking for more. Gone were the days when one could read in his eyes, You are no Modigliani!

He now dwelled in the bright future; after all, the American Barnes exclaimed, I'll buy the future!

What use did he have for a daughter and a woman from the past? He had long since departed from Le Havre and now resided in Merion near Philadelphia; a furious and filthy sleeve has wiped from his canvas all the shabby places, the Beehive and the Cité Falguière, the artists' hovels and bug bastions, the empty bottles of cheap red wine, the lousy canvasses. I dwell in the future, leave me alone! *Loz mich zu ru!*

She came from the world he had long left behind; what did the brick-coloured Vilna mean to him now? It's on a different planet, Lithuania's Jerusalem, the art school, who knows who is still there? One evening she shows up on the Avenue du Parc Montsouris, furiously bangs at the door he doesn't want to open, and screams:

Traitor! Traitor! I know you're home! She's yours!

They were living in two different dreams. Even now in the basement furnace room of the blinding-white paradise he hears a pair of fists banging at the door and a woman's loud voice screaming: Traitor! Traitor!

The nurse who calmly and sadly stares at him as he stands there with his paint-stained hands has Deborah's eyes, her pale skin, her mouth. She says nothing. It's her. It's not. Silently she scrutinizes him, and without a word she deepens his shame. He is not thinking of his disowned daughter Aimée but of Doctor Bog's commandments.

Under no circumstances are you allowed to paint again in this clinic. Do you understand? Under no circumstances. It would be disastrous for you.

And through his tiny spectacles the god in white had fixed his gaze on him as if nailing him to the bed. Now the painter Soutinchaim stands in the furnace room under the white pipes, and a silent scream rings out from the nurse's eyes: Traitor!

She says nothing, but something is suddenly blazing in her eyes that had not been there before. Deborah's eyes blaze with betrayal. At long last she is to get satisfaction for all the humiliations and the disavowal. Quietly she turns and moves slowly out of the furnace room as if out of his life, and he keeps hearing her steps growing fainter and fainter on the endless staircase leading upstairs.

Traitor!

The word echoes in his ears, but there is no negotiating with the past; he is here now with nothing but canvas and brush, the rest of the world gone. The nurse with the eyes of Deborah Melnik who caught him deep down in the furnace room in the forbidden act of painting does not remain idle and reports the incident to the clinic's administration. Every betrayal brings about another; every injury causes another. It keeps the earth turning.

Doctor Bog's face contorts into a bitter grimace, a disappointed smirk flickering behind it before he shouts, overwhelmed by rage: The ingrate! The traitor! Why did he have to start painting again? Why would he need to? He was healed! Healed! He could have stayed in the clinic for good. For good! But now, he can just get out!

With a flourish he signs Chaim Soutine's expulsion from the white paradise. Two humanoid hulks stomp into the room, barely able to keep themselves upright with their bulging leg muscles. They resemble the Michelin Man of the tyre advertisements, two *Bibendums* consisting of muscle tyres, dressed in white, two monstrously swollen bald heads with flashing eyes sternly fixed on him, who break into cheerful smiles at being finally allowed to swing into action.

They remind the painter of his Saturday excursions to the wrestling matches he used to enjoy at the Vél d'Hiv with Michonze, Benatov, Henry Miller and from time to time Mademoiselle Garde. How it excited him to gaze upon the mountains of muscle that grabbed and pinched and clamped, vice-like, onto reddened necks where sweat was painting mirrors. Soutine took his opera glasses to study the details of the interlocked muscle masses. The wrestlers made raw human flesh distinctly visible and the painter appreciated them for it. After the matches he was drained, dragged himself alongside Garde back to the Villa Seurat, unable to speak, and drank camomile tea.

So here they come storming in for the healed painter, rip the snow-white sheets from his legs, grab him under the arms, yank him unceremoniously into an upright position, drag him into the hallway and down the stairs. He barely needs to walk; they carry him off with giant steps, hands pressed into his armpits and tightened around his wrists like vices. They rush down the same staircase he took on his nightly excursions to the furnace room, that site of his sin where he had found, to his final happiness, those crushed paint tubes.

They whipped open the delivery van's back doors, on which the painter clearly saw 'Fruit and Vegetables' written in jaunty letters. It was Citroën's Corbillard model, and he had seen it before, but at the time it had been completely black. Now it had clearly received a fresh coat of paint.

Green! Finally some colour! he sighed, still in the grip of the robust Michelin men.

He was brusquely shoved inside, pushed onto the floor of the van, and strapped down with broad belts. The two bald wrestlers slammed the backdoor's two wings shut. A sharp click as if from a weapon, a dry snap from the waiting lock. The vehicle juddered, and startled, panicky pigeons took off for the blue beyond the roof of the white clinic. The white began to retreat as the blue took over on this ninth day of August. And already the driver had pulled out. The enraged Doctor Bog had called after the wrestlers: You know where!

They knew where. And so did the painter, who knew all the paths of this city where so often on sleepless nights after agonizing hours in front of the invincible canvas, alone with the pain in his upper abdomen, he had raced through the streets taking giant steps, avoiding the boulevards, hastening through dark alleyways, seeking the exhaustion that would rid his heart of painting. Only later to return home, breathing hard, and to fling himself onto the mattress, drained.

Marie-Berthe had kept vigil at his bedside after the operation. She was exhausted from the never-ending ride in the hearse. Had it been one full day, or two? Her head tilted sideways on Soutine's bed, resting on the sheet next to his feet. She was fast asleep. When she awakens with a start, the painter has died.

During the night he had his operation in the Lyautey clinic in the Sixteenth Arrondissement. No one remembers the arrival of the hearse. No written document provides evidence that the operation took place. No one knows whether it did take place. It would have been risky during the Occupation, and not only in medical terms. Secret operation on an invisible painter.

The two undertakers and drivers of the hearse have never been identified. They have suddenly vanished. The painter dies on 9 August 1943, at six in the morning, without having regained consciousness. The exitus is recorded on 11 August 1943, at 10 a.m. at the city hall in the Sixteenth Arrondissement by a Monsieur René Magin, forty years of age, clerk, 3 Rue Mesnil, Paris. Death certificate No. 1799. They avoided reporting it earlier in order to thwart an investigation. The Occupiers did not need to know that the invisible painter had slipped away from them after all. In any event, he was not taken to one of the stations from where the trains travelled to the east.

The Hungarian photographer Rogi André, aka Rosza Klein, who had taken portraits of many of the Montparnasse artists, was called to the clinic by Marie-Berthe. It's urgent; we have to move him quickly.

1. Photo in fine-striped pyjamas, face unshaven, hands folded, fingers crossed, a bouquet of gladioli on the sheet.
2. Photo in pyjamas, close-up of the unshaven face, hair uncombed.
3. Photo in black suit, with shoes, a bouquet of gladioli on his legs.
4. Photo in black suit, with tie, close-up of face, shaved, and hair combed.

The fingers could no longer be cleaned; they were indelibly ingrained. The paint around the rims of his fingernails had penetrated deeply under his skin and nail beds and had formed a crust. His hands will forever be stained. Colourful branding for the white beyond. No more purity, never again. May everyone recognize him for who he was, starting with the absent God. Let God look down his nose at the dirt. In 1936 Jerome Klein writes in the *New York Post*: Van Gogh bared his heart. Soutine bared his guts.

On his deathbed, the painter bared his forever-coloured fingers. A small addendum for Doctor Bog.

The burial takes place two days after the painter's demise. On Wednesday, 11 August 1943, at 2 p.m. Even the announcement of his death is an attempt at a cover-up. Marie-Berthe had it printed and at the very last moment crossed out 'Père Lachaise Cemetery' and written 'Montparnasse' above it. One more means of fooling the Occupiers and their informants, of covering his tracks, keeping the burial a secret. Attending were Pablo Picasso, Jean Cocteau, Max Jacob. And two women, Gerda Groth-Michaelis and Marie-Berthe Aurenche. Initially the grave was unmarked, as was befitting an invisible painter. His name is added only after the war, misspelt: Chaïme Soutine.

His painter's soul clearly recognized the northern entrance through the produce van's small windows. They were approaching from the Boulevard Edgar Quinet. As the red-and-white striped barrier was being raised, he realized they were entering the city of the dead, Montparnasse Cemetery. Then something happened he would have never dreamt of.

The green van's back doors gently opened, without a click, without a sound. His soul shyly glided out and flew up, relieved to leave behind the terrors of the Occupation, the hiding places and the bleeding stomach walls. One day a poet and compatriot will describe it this way: Tell me, Soul . . . tell me what life looked like . . . from a bird's eye view . . .

It soared high and delightedly made circles above the grand boulevards of the spacious cemetery. To fly! That's what his soul had longed for while it was locked in the tight prison of his gaunt body. To fly, always upward, riding the strong current that gives a soul a good airing. To the treetops and beyond, just as in the past in his forgotten childhood he had felt the sandy floor of the Baltic forest against his back as he intently gazed into the sky until hunger drove him home.

His soul could see the entire cemetery bend and twist just as he had painted the hills of Céret in a mighty uproar, an all-encompassing quake. It looked around and saw them all flying behind: the pastry chefs and butcher boys, the baker boys, bellboys and grooms, the choir boys and altar boys, the communicant, the peasant children. Little Charlot, too, had joined them. They paid his soul the rebellious last respects of conspirators.

Far, far below he saw Doctor Bog shake his fists and threaten him. His soul could hear him clearly. He screamed, almost roared up at the sky, The wicked strut about everywhere . . . when vileness is held in general esteem . . .

But Soutine's soul was carefree and would not be intimidated by threats and clenched fists. For his soul the prohibition against painting no longer existed, and neither did a prohibition against flying. Free at last, it appeared to be laughing. Soutine's soul was laughing in brilliant ecstasy. No one in Montparnasse can believe it. Everyone there thought he was, and always would be, the unhappiest of painters. The earth, however, was an immense ulcer he had left behind.

From far above his soul now recognized three men who were no doubt still alive. No Sacred Fellowship, no *Chevra Kadisha*. They had taken off their black hats and were gathered around Soutine's coffin. His soul slowed its flight, flew a beautiful curve, and paused a few metres directly above the coffin.

So there were these three men standing around him. Pablo Picasso, Jean Cocteau, Max Jacob. And Chaim Soutine's soul was thrilled, as if in a gentle transport of delight, though not an excessive one. Picasso stood there like a sun god, the brilliant star at the centre that made all others pale. Next to him a twin brother of Orpheus, Jean Cocteau, who had warmly welcomed Hitler's favourite sculptor—whose name Soutine's soul could not bring itself to utter—in May '42 in Paris when the Vichy government had given him an official ceremony. And now he stands there mourning at the grave of the painter Soutine? His conscience had become indignant at the lavish parties he had indulged in with the black-clad puppets. The Thracian singer had had his own dealings with death. Inscrutable Orpheus left behind his cloak on his way back from the underworld. He wanted to come into the light.

And who else is standing there, diagonally across from the grave of Baudelaire, who had been forced to live with his hated stepfather, General Aupick? The angelic Max Jacob, whom the Gestapo will arrest only a few months later on 24 February '44, in Saint-Benoît-sur-Loire, not far from Orléans, where he is hiding in a monastery among the monks. And who will die of pneumonia a mere two weeks later—the painter's soul, to its horror, foresaw it—in the camp at Drancy, north-east of Paris, while he waited to be deported to Auschwitz. Picasso thought it unnecessary to intercede on his behalf.

There's nothing to be done. Max is an angel. He doesn't need us to help him escape from prison.

In the early days, in the Bateau-Lavoir, Max had shared his room with and fed the new arrival from Malaga. Now the sun king was preoccupied with his own reputation. In Drancy, Max apologized to his fellow Jews for praying to a Christian god. He had himself baptized at age forty, with Picasso as his sponsor. Sorry, this is not a matter of confusion but, rather, a matter of one's life story. Then he died. But pneumonia—that much his absent sun king knows—was better than a ride in a crammed freight car to the ramp at the end of the line in Poland.

Circling above the Montparnasse Cemetery, Soutine's soul sees them standing side by side at the grave of the painter in whose body it had dwelled until recently. Pablo, Jean and Max: the fortunate sun king, the dazzling Orpheus, and the poor pulmonary Jacob, soon to expire.

And two women stand at the graveside, the second-to-last and the last. His guardian angel from Magdeburg, Gerda Groth-Michaelis, who taught him to eat again when he had long given up. Mademoiselle Garde! How pale she is now. She had managed to escape from the Gurs camp and was in hiding in Carcassonne. She had not seen the painter since her departure for the Vél d'Hiv on 15 May 1940. When she learns from Madeleine Castaing in Carcassonne that Soutine is living with another woman, she does not cry. You must be brave now, Gerda. She would live for another thirty years and never set foot on German soil again. And in the seventies she will—as Soutine's soul hears with amazement—dictate her memories to a journalist. Gerda! Mademoiselle Garde!

By then Marie-Berthe Aurenche won't have been among the living for thirteen years. The Surrealists' abandoned muse, Dadamax's ex-wife, Soutine's unfortunate companion, who was the one who searched out hiding places and decided on the endless transport to Paris. In 1960, seventeen years after that day in August, she will take her own life, though not in the famously beautiful manner of Modigliani's muse, the delicate Jeanne Hébuterne, who sailed from a window so as to never again crash on dark asphalt. Marie-Berthe will be put to rest in Chaim Soutine's grave, which was what she wanted. Just as they were together in the hearse on the accursed journey from Chinon to Paris.

How to forget Eleni's call in the middle of the night? She was furious about the opinion everyone had formed of Marie-Berthe. What if one day a note turned up written by the doctors in Chinon informing their colleagues in Paris they wouldn't risk operating because the operation would be too late and too dangerous? A referral note of sorts, passing the responsibility for operation on to their colleagues?

Let's assume they had simply given up on their patient. What option did Marie-Berthe have left but to risk the final, desperate transport to Paris? Eleni fumed on the phone: All that talk about the implacable angel of death, about the wavering woman, the bad decisions. Pure speculation! What was she supposed to do? Watch him die? So she used her contacts in Paris to phone a surgeon in the Lyautey clinic who promised to risk the operation in spite of its dangers. All she wanted was to give Soutine a last chance at life! And decided on the dangerous transport.

In a 1952 magazine article, Marie-Berthe writes about Soutine's last years and about the doctors in Chinon indeed refusing to operate. And so what if that was merely a weak attempt at self-justification by someone feeling guilty about making a decision that didn't have the desired outcome, did not save him? One is always wiser in hindsight.

No objections—that they could have been caught, that the painter's journey would have then led him to

Drancy and to the east—were accepted by Eleni. Without the gruelling, long odyssey the painter would have died in a hospital bed in Chinon; the poppy juice would have gently let him fade away. No torturous, frightening, excessively long journey . . .

Eleni remained adamant: You simply don't know what a woman in love is capable of! She saw only this one last chance.

Eleni hung up.

Marie-Berthe will experience the deliriousness of her city's liberation almost exactly one year after the funeral, on 25 August '44, another, happier August day. But her life will gradually go to pieces. The great painters were gone, and Dadamax had long been dead to her even if he was to survive her by sixteen years. Despite the liberation jubilation, Montparnasse had become a pale reflection of its earlier effervescence.

She wore a mad smile in the streets and bleached her hair. Thea says she looked like one of countless common hookers. She got accused of filching and flogging Soutine's paintings and not supporting his unfortunate little daughter. Towards any of her former acquaintances she harboured nothing but hatred. And woe to anyone who mentioned the name of Max Ernst. Everyone looked the other way when she showed up. When she entered a room, utter derangement would spread to all four corners.

Eventually she started to talk to herself and to address startled passers-by with bizarre pronouncements: It's my fault he's dead! If I hadn't fallen asleep, he wouldn't have died . . .

And she quizzed puzzled pedestrians: Is there an afterlife? A beyond?

No one would answer; they'd only glance at each other mockingly. And something else she told them: I want to enter a convent!

She grew lonely, became crotchety and nasty, would bicker and snarl. Her manic hands would rip things apart, no longer capable of keeping them whole. The only thing she was keeping was her way of fighting with each and every one of them, of destroying everything in her wake, of withdrawing with a twitch of her crazed lips and a brief, sharp laugh. One day she hanged herself from the ceiling in her room, from the light fixture hook. Two suitcase straps had been sufficient. And left behind no note about her reasons. None of your business. *Cela ne vous regarde pas.* Her life had ended long before.

The Allies launch Operation Overlord. The Battle of Normandy begins on 6 June '44, less than a year after Soutine's last journey to the white paradise and the Montparnasse Cemetery. The landings begin on the western beaches of Calvados, on the eastern ones of the Cotentin Peninsula. It is the longest day. There is a longest day in every life; for Soutine that day was 6 August

'43, when hidden in the hearse he was riding towards the capital of pain. On 19 August '44, the Parisian Committee of the Liberation called upon the people to rise up against the Occupiers, Paris was liberated on 25 August '44, and General de Gaulle makes his triumphant entry. General Leclerc enters the city with tanks from the south through the Porte d'Orléans, cheered by the crowds. He passes the hotel on the Avenue d'Orléans, where in Room No. 25 for days on end the invisible painter in his buttoned-up raincoat lay on his bed, sweating and staring at the ceiling, to escape the investigating officers who were looking for him on the Villa Seurat.

The Reichskommissariat Ostland falls apart as early as 1943 when the Baltic states are recaptured one by one by the Red Army. By that time the inhabitants of Smilovichi have long been massacred by the Einsatzgruppen B. The Minsk ghetto is liquidated on 21 October '43, by Hauptscharführer Rübe. Rübe? The monster Rübe? Him. Of the 75,000 inmates not a single one survived. Every last one exterminated. There is no one left he could send to the *yama* pit. And Doctor Knochen? Will soon become an insurance agent. Life insurance? With pleasure! You want to live your life in peace and quiet. No, Soutine's soul could not have foreseen it on its flight above the Montparnasse Cemetery. Where are Solomon and Sarah, Yankl, Ertl, Nahuma and the others?

Es wert mir finster in di oygen, everything is getting dark before my eyes, his soul whispers.

THE PAIN OF THE PERUVIAN

Life chooses the vehicle. Confusion is among its favourite manoeuvres. An ambulance, a haycart, a produce van, a hearse, or even the lowly wheelbarrow in which a delicate madonna, the little Jeannette, is pushed by a street cleaner to the Rue de la Grande Chaumière—they all carry life to its destination. Life is not picky. Movement is all it wants, and needs like a drug. It looks for a vehicle, any kind. With emergency lights flashing, or hay strewn in its wake.

The vehicle may be wrong, but the direction is always right. The journey may take terrible diversions, but the destination is known. As Doctor Bog said to those musclemen with their vice-like grip: You know where!

Every journey leads to the final operation, leads inexorably to the final stretch. Like homing pigeons returning to their dovecote, life moves towards its no-longer-secret destination in whatever vehicle happens to be on hand. Briskly off to the entrance gate, up with the red-and-white striped barrier and across the fatal line. Get on with it and get to it. It wants to end.

Take Chekhov. After he dies in Badenweiler on 22 July 1904, his extinguished life seeks a suitable vehicle. It allies itself with gourmet food and luxury goods as if to mock the man who loathed the pearly opulence of the rich. The green refrigerated wagon that took his body to Moscow carried seafood from France, the huge letters on the wagon reading 'For Oysters'. Because the coffin of a Manchurian general arrives in Moscow at the same time, military music rings out in the station. People are astounded. Military pomp for Chekhov? Life is a mis-understanding. It plays with confusion. Someone else was meant. Sometimes life picks the wrong vehicle, at other times the wrong music. Chekhov hated oysters.

Soutine's life picks a hearse for the journey to occu-pied Paris. Here, take the white sheet. Cover yourself. Play dead. As he himself had put it to Kiko in Vilna: If only you could paint it. It took him his whole life to learn to paint death. With the tyres of the wrong vehicle.

For a while the most absurd diversions are life's idle pleasures, distractions for a life that has had more than its fill and is too pampered to be bothered by anything. It lets them happen without paying much attention. In spite of all the diversions, the path is always straight. There is plenty of life on both the right and the left.

Chaim means life; in the language of the Bible the word exists only as plural. Only the plural of life? It has no sin-gular; it has to blend in with the whole—and vanish. A cemetery is called Beth-Chaim: the House of Life. Montparnasse is its name in a life that loves confusion, blithely and shamelessly. The home of the muses. A Greek mountain ridge that strayed into a French metropolis, a pagan site in the heart of Paris, full of demons lusting for life. A luxurious cemetery, filled with artists and admirals.

I used to live very close by, in a narrow alley only a few metres long that led into the Rue Daguerre and whose name was meant to honour the memory of some general or admiral, or other high-ranking military icon. Of one of the world's poor at any rate that are suited for the naming of short and narrow alleyways. And somewhere in that gigantic God's acre full of stone witnesses lies a black, anonymous gravestone with the inscription, *La vie ne meurt pas*. Life does not die. I have seen it a thousand times, this anonymous life in the singular, the short statement, the absence of biographical information, of year of birth and year of death. It was the time when the first AIDS dead moved into the Montparnasse Cemetery.

Chaim does not die. He is the plural. Every day I walked across the cemetery, knew its sleepy cats, went in and out of the House of Life where death gets lost. Chaim does not die. Chaim dies. Chaim.

Before the Revolution, the site belonged to the monastery of the Brothers of Charity. A windmill without wings still sits lonely among the dead, covered in ivy, appreciated by inventive birds. *Le Moulin de la Charité:* The mill of charity belongs to the dead. Here the aerial grain is ground, thousands and thousands of kernels, each a human life, the plural of life. A suddenly secular place from which the souls ascend in giddy rapture in their desire for air and space. In the century the painter was born, the 'turnip field' was located here—*le champ des navets*, in the language of penal colonies—a communal grave for paupers into which the bodies of people sentenced to death and executed were tossed. *La vie ne meurt pas.* Chaim does not die. Whether you believe it or not.

I have tried for years to figure out what it is about his paintings that overwhelms me. Ever since the moment in the Metro when Eleni saw the poster behind my back of the teetering Chartres Cathedral threatening to crash down upon me. It was 1989; shortly afterwards, we went to Chartres, barely a hundred kilometres west of Paris, and spent the night in a tiny hotel. Nearby we could hear trains rattle by while we made love, stammeringly, no longer knowing where we were. Only trembling fingertips remembered. As a poet put it: Human lips with nothing left to say keep the shape of the word last spoken. When we saw the exhibition in the bishop's former residence, we no longer needed to speak.

It is the fixation of the unique image, of the moment that determines everything. The unfathomable shame, the growing alienation, of being in the world. The desolation of all characters, the teetering of things in a world without salvation. Laconic lyricisms. Death at work, precisely recorded, shimmering in all colours. And unfailing vitality in that same moment.

It was shortly after the year 2000 when I went back to the Montparnasse Cemetery. I had long moved elsewhere, had left one day in a battered, dusty red Renault 5 with everything I was fond of. Years earlier I had written in a poem what it was that always came to my mind when I visited that cemetery: You head towards your happiness until it stabs you in the back.

And I kept going back to figure out why everything had turned out the way it had, and not otherwise. There was no other place that would let me see life's frightening singularity as clearly. And life's plural in the humble given name: Chaim.

I had visited the place almost daily in the '80s when I lived in the neighbourhood with Eleni, in that aforementioned narrow side alley of the Rue Daguerre. How often had I walked circles in the cemetery when things had reached an impasse or I needed fresh air. It was an oasis of stillness right in the midst of the metropolis I loved at that time. A ringing stillness, the cemetery is a choir of voices, and my antennae were attuned to listening mode. Now I went back to the grave with its misspelt first name and stood there for a long while. Division 1, almost at the end of the Avenue de l'Ouest, on the left-hand side. And sensed I was being watched.

An old gentleman with a black hat, scarf, and cane kept his eyes fixed on me from the distance of several rows of graves. And was in no mind to walk away. So I looked back at him, straight in the eye without turning away, in a way demanding an explanation. I figured that was the ultimate way to get rid of him.

That's when he finally approached, not in a hurry but with palpable relief and impatience, and asked without a greeting or other pleasantries: How did you discover him?

Why do you want to know?

I come here often. And I'll let you in on something else: I was already here for his burial.

By now I was becoming furious. I said nothing but let it show with a movement of my head. Was he one of those lunatics or braggarts who were on first-name terms with half the celebrities put to rest here? There are so many madmen in the world's cemeteries! The proximity of the dead enlightens and inspires them. Quickly I tried to estimate his age. 1943: unlikely. But not completely impossible. There are many people in their eighties or even nineties that are fit as fiddles and jauntily skip and hop through their days ... one shouldn't be too cocksure about one's estimates. So I said, But only Picasso, Cocteau and Max Jacob attended the funeral. And of course the two women, Gerda Groth and Marie-Berthe Aurenche.

No, I was there, too.

And you haven't left since, I remarked sarcastically to provoke him.

No, I have. But I do come here often. I sometimes watch who comes to see him. I have never seen you; you must be new.

You're wrong; I used to come here often enough when I lived nearby. You probably missed me many times. So why do you watch people? What's in it for you? Isn't it in extraordinarily poor taste to be watching people in a cemetery? You enjoy their misery and grief, don't you? Then off you stroll, pleased with yourself for still being alive, and have an aperitif on the Boulevard Raspail, right?

I was at the burial. Wednesday, 11 April 1943, 2 p.m.

How could you have possibly known? Marie-Berthe Aurenche had 'Père Lachaise Cemetery' printed in the death notice, most likely to mislead the Occupiers and their helpers, then at the last moment had crossed out 'Père Lachaise' and inserted 'Montparnasse' by hand.

Well, we do have our own information. Whether you choose to believe it or not—I was there. Not right next to the grave but very close by. I discreetly stood back next to that tree over there.

He sternly aimed his cane at the site.

And Picasso stood here, and Cocteau over there. The two women stood closest to the grave.

He pointed at the exact spots. He did not mention Max Jacob. Indeed, his attendance was doubtful. At the time he was hiding among the monks of Saint-Benoît-sur-Loire and at such short notice would not have managed to make it to Paris for the burial. The path from the Loire to Paris in occupied France was infinitely long for someone like him; Soutine had taken the almost identical path for his own last journey. But Picasso may have been right when he said Max is an angel. The business of flying would have been familiar to him, and so he might indeed have appeared on time on 11 August 1943 in the Montparnasse Cemetery.

What were you doing there? Why did you observe the scene if you didn't belong to the mourners?

In a certain way I did belong to them. But that is something I can't explain to you. Just let me repeat: I was here in 1943.

Don't you want to at least give me your name?

No need to. You can't know me.

Tell me anyway—names please one's memory.

Armand Merle.

The name meant nothing to me. But I was delighted to have met a blackbird. And why not? Bird names always have something airy; instantly song pops into your head.

Who are you? What policing unit did you belong to at that time?

The Merle guy continued with an unmistakably insolent undertone: Don't sneer at people who watch others.

They have their reasons for opening certain files, conducting investigations, gathering pieces into a mosaic, and gradually completing the picture. You on the other hand seem to be one of those dodgy writers who pick up a few facts and dubious anecdotes and invent the rest. And who then let loose upon the world their brazen fictions.

I was about to protest, but he was rattling on: Don't you kid yourself. Don't think you're above the hardworking agents of the world's secret police services. They are committed to the truth, and you are not. They move the general investigation forward, and you don't. The world is designed to end in a gigantic, universal trial. Not in a novel. Writers are nothing by liars.

I couldn't feel insulted because he may have well been right. And no objections would have stopped him anyway. He kept at it: We put ourselves into the mind frame of the subjects we investigate. We have to know everything about them. Even though I have to admit: Psychology doesn't exist. It's just a fantasy. No patterns exist in the minds of people. Every mind is different. Human beings are full of contradictions, never predictable. Every action is bizarre and inexplicable. I only realized it at the end of my career. Believe me: you have no right to get into someone else's head. It wasn't him. He is someone else. One day you might write a whole book about the painter's last days. I tried, too, but in the end stuck with my files. Time's too short.

You seem to have been a snitch who watched Soutine's burial from a safe distance, recorded whatever names you were able to identify. Maybe even took photos? Can I see them? The three men you would have recognized. But the two women? Or maybe you already had photos in your file to help identify them?

He did not respond at all to my questions but coldly continued, apparently a secret agent versed in literature: The interior monologue won't get you anywhere, as you will find out. You'll realize it's unacceptable. It gives the wrong perspective. And its invention has been the biggest lie in literature's kingdom of lies. You can't get into someone's head and talk on his behalf; that would be the biggest crime. And one more thing: he was a silent man. Don't make up words for a silent man. He does not want you to. If you can't do without poetry's flourishes, look for them elsewhere. You'll realize your failure and will have to rewrite the book. Beginning to end. Nowhere an I, only a he. Nowhere pure past, only impure present. You'll disregard all advice and then regret it bitterly because you'll have to start your investigation all over. It serves you right. You'll remember me and curse yourself for having ignored a pragmatist's advice. Let me reiterate: no interior monologue. It harms the investigation. No transfer of your voice into the mind of a silent man. Don't do it.

With this he turned, without a farewell, and, aggrieved, disappeared among the graves. Ten seconds later he could no longer be seen.

But one grave was always my favourite as I followed my familiar routes and approached the stations of the dead in their aerial topography. And this time, too, I did not want to leave the necropolis dearest to my heart in all of Paris without having paid it a visit. I had to do it, after that strange encounter with the old gentleman. It has the most beautiful epitaph the entire cemetery has been able to conceive. The grave belongs to César Vallejo, a Peruvian poet who came from a village in the Andes and in 1923 ended up in Paris. He dreamt of a brotherly republican Spain and died in 1938 of the long-term consequences of a malaria infection. No one has dreamt more poetry onto a stone: *J'ai tant neigé pour que tu dormes*. I snowed so much to let you sleep. To snow and to sleep . . . The I as a weather condition and a tenderly-cared-for you to be cradled into sleep. Because it is always sleepless.

But that day I did not find the grave right away, something that had never happened to me before. I was confused and annoyed with myself. Had so much time passed? Was I in the wrong cemetery? In the '80s, when I still lived here, I had an internal compass to point me towards the right spot in this sea of graves. Was the compass lost, its needle broken? I turned to one of the cemetery's uniformed employees who guard death in this place.

And what if pain does not end with death?

The poet, in anguish over his eternal Peru of worldwide injustice, wrote 'The Nine Monsters'. Now they are united in the syndicate of voices in the Montparnasse Cemetery, and the Peruvian of pain sings into the frightened, big red ear of the son of a clothes mender from the Belorussian Smilovichi:

And, unfortunately,
pain grows in the world every moment,
grows thirty minutes a second, step by step,
and the nature of the pain, is the pain twice
and the condition of the martyrdom, carnivorous,
                                    voracious,
is the pain, twice
and the function of the purest grass, the pain
twice
and the good of Being, to hurt us doubly.

Never, human men,
was there so much pain in the chest, in the lapel,
                                    in the wallet,
in the glass, in the butcher-shop, in arithmetic!
Never so much painful affection,
never did far away charge so close,
never did the fire ever
play better its role of dead cold!
Never, mister secretary of health, was health
more mortal,
and did the migraine extract so much forehead from
                                    the forehead!

And the cabinet have in its drawer, pain,
the heart, in its drawer, pain,
the wall lizard, in its drawer, pain.
. . .
The pain grabs us, brother men,
from behind, in profile,
and drives us wild in the movies,
nails us into the gramophones,
denails us in bed, falls perpendicularly
to our tickets, to our letters;
and it is very serious to suffer, one might pray . . .

By the time I reached the Peruvian's grave, I was scribbling with a pencil stub on the back of two coupons from the nearby Monoprix supermarket. I had nothing else on me, no matter how often I turned my trouser pockets inside out. Babel, the naked year, Sertürner's poppy juice. No one can be other than he is. There is in the sky above Montparnasse a star driven by its flagella: *Helicobacter pylori*. Whoever escapes childhood cannot expect to find paradise. *A mentsh on glick is a toyter mentsh*. An unlucky person is a dead person. The singular salvation does not exist. The only solution is colour. It is the last possible religion. No, it was rebellion I had meant to write. Its red saints are cinnabar, crimson, dragon's blood, red ochre, Indian red, Mars red, Pompeii red, purple, amaranth, cherry red, madder red, ruby, carnation. But who is Armand Merle?

THE 17 CHAPTERS OF
SOUTINE'S LAST JOURNEY